HERBS &
HERB GARDENS
OF BRITAIN

A quiet and restful herb garden at Lytes Cary Manor, stone-flagged paths and an
attractive sundial providing form and elegance.

A COMPREHENSIVE GUIDE

HERBS &
HERB GARDENS
OF BRITAIN

Published in association with
THE HERB SOCIETY

Elizabeth & Reginald Peplow

Webb & Bower
EXETER, ENGLAND

First published in Great Britain 1984 by
Webb & Bower (Publishers) Limited
9 Colleton Crescent, Exeter, Devon EX2 4BY

Designed by Malcolm Couch

British Library Cataloguing in Publication Data
Peplow, Elizabeth
    Herbs and herb gardens of Britain.
    1. Herb gardening—Great Britain
    I. Title   II. Peplow, Reginald
    635'.7'0941   SB351.H5

    ISBN 0-86350-018-8

Typeset in Great Britain by August Filmsetting, Haydock.

Colour reproduction by Peninsular Repro Ltd, Exeter.
Printed and bound in Great Britain
by Hazell Watson & Viney Limited,
Member of the BPCC Group,
Aylesbury, Bucks.

CONTENTS

Introduction 7

Contents

Times and dates of opening of gardens may vary from season to season and it is advisable to check before making a long journey.

INTRODUCTION

Visit a herb garden and you are immediately aware of three things—the shape of the garden, the colour and texture of the foliage and the scent of the herbs growing there.

Shape of the garden

Look first at the shape or form of the garden. Many are square or rectangular and divided into four sections by wide paths. This, indeed, was the basic pattern of the first formal gardens in Roman times where herbs were grown for decoration and ceremonial use. It is easy to picture Roman senators walking through their gardens discussing the politics of the day. The aroma of the plants would surely have uplifted their thoughts.

Another explanation for the formal shape of herb gardens was that the first garden—the Garden of Eden—was square, and through this garden ran four rivers crossing at the central point. Equally relevant to biblical students is the shape of the Christian Cross.

These early gardens would always have been enclosed by hedges and high walls. This was necessary for shelter and to protect the plants from roving vagabonds. The garden would have been a place of beauty and tranquillity to be enjoyed by those who worked there and took brief periods of relaxation among the herbs. These hedges and walls are still seen in traditional herb gardens though sometimes now they remain only as a small box edge or a row of parsley or chives grown beside a garden path.

Many herb gardens would contain a bird-bath, a fountain, a statue, a turf or chamomile seat or some other point of interest. These ornaments, known by the rather charming name of herbal 'conceits', would have acted as a focal point and drawn attention to the shape of the garden. Often a sundial was placed in the centre of a garden with a particularly apt quotation such as:

How could such sweet and wholesome hours
Be reckoned but with herbs and flowers.

Knot gardens became extremely fashionable at the end of the seventeenth century. They were one of the earliest types of pleasure garden and retain the traditional rectangular shape. Evergreen hedges of low-growing herbs such as thyme, hyssop and rosemary were planted to form interesting patterns. The completed knot garden might resemble a classical Roman tile with the different shades of foliage, ranging from silver grey to bronze green, outlining the shape. Sometimes the spaces between the herbs were filled with sand, coal dust or chalk to emphasize the design. A good example of this can be seen in a small herb garden recently planned at Abbey Dore in Herefordshire.

So whenever you see a formal garden divided into sections it is interesting to consider the origins of its present shape. There are, however, exceptions to the rule. At Hopetoun House, Linlithgow in Scotland, for example, there is a fascinating small garden of three intersecting 'O's outlined with red bricks. Intersecting spaces make a delightful place to plant different herbs. The letters are derived from the three 'O's in Hopetoun House. Other gardens are large and informal, used to grow herbs that attract bees and other useful insects, or are grown as back-to-nature gardens.

Of great interest today are groups of pots containing herbs placed on the patio. Many are planted as in Mediterranean countries with the pots on different levels. Some such as the sweetly scented lavender and useful rosemary and thyme can be grown in ornamental stone troughs. Herbs grown in this way particularly suit the contemporary scene and sprigs can be cut straight from the plant to flavour barbecues; their taste always seems more subtle at *al fresco* parties on midsummer evenings.

Colour in the herb garden

The colours in the herb garden are generally of a gentle hue. Lavender with its soft mauve flowers, marjoram with that lovely blush coloured flower, and lungwort with its pretty blue and pink spikes illustrate the sort of colouring you will find in the herb garden. There are many white flowering plants which add attraction to the garden; lily-of-the-valley, for example, with its gleaming white bell flowers that make such a vivid contrast to the green ovate leaves. Many of the white flowers, particularly lilies and roses, were grown to decorate churches at festival times, usually in part of the monastery garden known as a 'Paradise' which is, I think, a charming name for a garden with heavenly associations.

There are of course some vivid colours among the herbs to delight the eye. Pot marigolds add a vivid splash of gold wherever they are planted, nasturtiums bring gleaming orange right through the summer months. All these colours blend well with the quiet blues of hyssop, sage and borage.

The foliage of herbs also adds colour to herb gardens. Occasionally you see a very attractive bed laid out and clipped with foliage plants giving a charming 'fin de siècle' appearance. A favourite foliage plant is golden thyme which, appearing at its best in early spring, brings a true golden glow to the garden. The different variegated thymes, rue and mint all inject further diversity.

Silver leaved lavender, curry plant and cotton lavender are just some of the herb plants that stay ever-silver throughout the winter months, and are in great demand with those planting all-white gardens. This fashion, begun at Sissinghurst by Vita Sackville-West, has spread into gardens large and small and the popularity of the idea seems to grow each year.

Scent in the herb garden

A herb garden is full of pleasant scents from delicate old-fashioned shrub roses, orange blossom and lavender spikes. Many of the leaves are aromatic but the aroma is released only when the leaves are bruised. Next time you walk by a rosemary bush pinch a small sprig, rub your hands, and notice the overpowering scent.

Bees and other helpful insects that pollinate fruit are attracted by the scent of lemon thyme, lemon balm and of course the lovely bergamot which has the well-deserved country name, 'bee-balm'. Many medieval herb gardens contained beehives and in the newly recreated Tudor Garden at Southampton, bees automatically found their way to a hive placed in the garden wall.

The mixture of scents in a herb garden on a summer day when the sun shines after an unexpected rain shower is a veritable pot-pourri of sweetness. Resist if you can the urge to pick a small bunch of plants and bury your nose in their gentle fragrance.

The shape of the plants

What will surprise you as you walk through herb gardens are the different shapes and sizes of the plants growing there. Angelica growing 6ft (1.8m) tall in its second year with enormous palmate leaves and umbels of creamy white flowers the size of a dinner plate could fill a herb garden on its own. Then there is the tiny Corsican mint (*Mentha requienii*), which grows only about 1in (2.5cm) in height, and is so useful for cracks in rockeries and covering herb seats. One of the neatest and most attractive plants is wall germander with glossy dark green evergreen leaves. It never looks untidy. Chives with their straight spiky leaves make a good contrast to the fronds of curly parsley

A traditional herb garden.

and for this reason they are often grown together. Marjoram, pennyroyal and thymes all form colourful cushions and add interest to the herb garden.

Scented shrubs such as juniper, bay and rosemary earn a place in the herb garden where their architectural shape and height lend form to some of the more untidy members of the herb family. Such herbs as mint and lemon balm, for example, tend to sprawl and sometimes leap about in every direction but the one in which you want them to grow.

The definition of a herb is 'a plant useful to man either by its leaf, flower, stem or root' and to earn a place in a herb garden these are the conditions that the plant must fulfil. Herbs were grown in olden days for medicine, food, for making cosmetics and for decorations. So the silver-grey horehound you see in the physic garden would have been used for curing the coughs and sore throats of our ancestors. The sweet smelling violets were used for perfume, and, curiously, by the Greeks to cure a hangover. Herbs such as meadowsweet and mint were used as strewing herbs and very pleasant they must have been on the stone floors of baronial halls and in cold damp churches.

Until the discovery of chemical dyes, man was dependent on plants to dye his garments. Woad, of course, yielded the blue dye of policemen's uniforms, and the root of madder produced a dull red colour similar to that used in Oriental carpets. Claverton Manor, near Bath, is a haven of information if you are interested in home-dyeing. Not only can you see the plants growing but there are shade cards of the various colours they produce.

Herbs, fresh and dried, would have been needed by the cook to flavour her food and make her salads. Salads in centuries gone by were a carnival of colour with all kinds of herbs being arranged together and topped with marigold petals, nasturtiums and borage flowers.

So the herb garden you walk through, perhaps in a casual manner, holds a fascinating story for those who wish to delve a little deeper. Plant lovers will appreciate the growing conditions of the various plants and be amazed at how many of the familiar garden plants they already grow are classed as herbs. With the revival of interest in natural flavours and healthy living, herb gardens have much to teach the explorer of today.

I hope this book will give you the key to some of the attractions of herb gardens up and down the country. They all have a beauty of their own whether they are attached to a stately home like Hatfield House or consist of just a few pots of herbs on the porch of a country cottage.

How to make a scented corner

When visiting other people's gardens, a satisfying hobby for many of us, it is a delight to come across a corner where a welcoming seat and a sweet aroma offer a moment or two of peace.

The perfect place in which to create what might be termed a scented corner at home would have a south-westerly aspect, plenty of shelter from the wind and be in fact an oasis where you can pause and enjoy all the country garden perfumes on a warm July day.

Practically speaking, it is more likely to be made in a neglected corner where, say, the garage joins the house or even occasionally where the side of the house butts on to a neighbouring fence.

The plan illustrated stretches for about 6ft (1.8m) in either direction. It can easily be adapted to smaller or larger areas. The guiding rule for your own garden is to choose a place where you would like to sit and to build your ideas from there. It is usually possible with trelliswork or ornamental screening to improvise a corner.

The old-fashioned aromatic plants are enjoying well-earned popularity just now and should be easy to obtain from reputable nurseries. Beg cuttings from friends with established gardens.

To qualify for a place in a scented area, plants should appeal to all the senses. They should have a sweet or spicy fragrance, please the eye with foliage or flower, make you want to finger a leaf and pick a sprig, and encourage you to sit and relax for a few minutes or more.

The king pin is a Zéphirine Drouhin rose. This lovely Bourbon rose has medium-sized, bright pink blooms and will quickly climb to a height of 9ft (2.7m). It combines a sweet scent with flowers that bloom right through the summer months. As a welcome bonus, Zéphirine Drouhin has most attractive foliage and no thorns.

To balance the rose, plant on the other side of the corner that well-loved shrub philadelphus or mock orange. There are plenty of varieties to choose from, but 'Belle Etoile' seems to have the advantage, with its open white flowers and heavy fragrance.

This is the framework then for your garden seat. Either side of the seat, place large pots filled with lemon verbena and scented geraniums. Lemon verbena is that small delicate shrub with exquisite lemon scented leaves. It may need protection during the winter.

The most decorative of the scented geraniums is 'Lady Plymouth', with a rather creamy look and small pink flowers. The fragrance is in the leaves of these plants. They are all delightful but I think *Pelargonium tomentosum*, with its large downy leaves and rather pungent aroma, is my favourite. These plants must be taken in during the winter months.

As you will see, you have already created a fragrant place to enjoy a well-deserved rest. But press on.

To achieve elusive old-fashioned charm, next pave around and under the garden seat. Lay the slabs on a bed of sand with sufficient soil between the cracks to plant Corsican mint (*Mentha requenii*). This is the tiniest of mints with the strongest of fragrances. It spreads quite quickly between paving stones and thrives on being trodden on.

Around the paving stones plant a drift of lavender, maybe a Munstead. This neat growing variety has soft pinkish mauve flowers and a silver foliage which

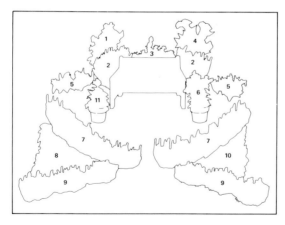

1 Philadelphus Belle Etoile

2 Rosemary

3 Purple Sage

4 Rose Zephirine Drouhin

5 Lily - of - the - Valley

6 Lemon Verbena

7 Lavender

8 Bergamot

9 Thyme

10 Pinks

11 Lemon - scented Geranium

blends well with the pinks growing nearby.

A border of mixed thymes adds interest. Thymes are good because they keep their colour right through the winter months.

Four rosemary bushes may seem a lot to include in this small area, but their good shape and perfume adds depth and symmetry.

Gaps can now be filled in with favourite flowers or aromatic herbs.

Herb Gardens

*Numbers referred to on map
denote page references within main text.*

.178

.184 ● Aberdeen

● Dundee

Stirling

180 182 . ● *Edinburgh*
● *Glasgow* 173

185 182

● *Londonderry* ● Dumfries   ● Newcastle
.171   186 *Carlisle*
.166   .151
Belfast
.167 .169
165 .

162 ● York
149 ● Leeds
.163
Liverpool *Manchester* .161
160 .153   ● *Sheffield*   .130
Chester   .117   ● Lincoln   .91
.156
.134   .122   ● Nottingham
.132   .121
Wolverhampton   *Leicester*   .89
● Birmingham   147   .139   .96
131   .128   100 .103   .98
Worcester   .142   *Cambridge*   .85   Norwich
.146   .83   .94
Gloucester   .128   .102
107 .138   .118 .126
.136   .115 .113
189 .109   52   60   *Reading*   45 30 ● *LONDON*
Bristol 48 .111   34 .37 .26
Bath 75   62   41 .42 .29
53   *Southampton* .64   .38
73 .76   56   50   58   24
.79 *Taunton*   *Brighton*
.67 *Exeter*

.71

.81

12

LONDON

CHELSEA PHYSIC GARDEN

66 Royal Hospital Road, London SW3

Telephone: 01-352 5646   **Owner:** The City Parochial Foundation and other trustees

Situation: 2m from Piccadilly Circus between Royal Hospital Road, Swan Walk and the Chelsea Embankment. **Open:** April–October, Wednesday and Sunday, 2–5pm.

Right in the heart of London there are nearly 4 acres (1.6 hectares) of intensively cultivated garden. Here the visitor will discover a wonderful assortment of foliage and flowering plants in one of the most peaceful plots in England.

The herb garden is in the north-eastern corner of the garden and here are grown all the familiar culinary and medicinal herbs and a great many others. Plants of particular homeopathic interest are grown together and there are also dye plants and sweetly scented plants needed for the perfumery industry. The focal point of this garden is a handsome clipped bay tree which, thanks to the mild climate of the area, has survived severe winters.

Herb lovers will find in carefully labelled family beds all the well-known useful plants. You will find the various mints and

A fascinating corner of Chelsea Physic Garden.

sages in the Labiatae section and tansy and wormwood in the Compositae beds. Although it is remarkably easy to find your way around it is perhaps a good idea to go armed with a book giving details of the botanical names of the plants.

The garden is laid out as a botanic garden to demonstrate plants from all over the world. There are wide gravel paths and at the centre is the famous marble statue of Sir Hans Sloane who gave financial support to the garden when it was so desperately needed. This fine statue which tends to dominate the garden has engraved on its base 'That their successors and posterity may never forget their common benefactor'.

Whatever time of the year you visit Chelsea you will be delighted by the fine trees which flourish here. An olive tree (*Olea europaea*) is 30ft (9m) high and when conditions are suitable fruit ripens in December. In 1976 for instance 7lb (3.2kg) were harvested.

Although the original library no longer exists there are many documents and botanical books stored here. Among the many valuable herbari and books are plant lists compiled by Philip Miller in the eighteenth century and a fine copy of John Parkinson's *Paradiso in Sole, Paradisus Terrestris*. Since Parkinson was known to love punning, it is always thought this is the reason for the first half of the title of the book 'park in sun'.

Research and investigation into the power of plants is just as important today as it was in the early days when plants were newly introduced into the garden. Research continues with the plant feverfew (*Tanacetum parthenium*) being investigated as a possible cure for the relief of migraine. Work is also being carried out in collaboration with the Imperial College of Science on a fungus called ergot (*Claviceps purpurea*) which grows on the rye plant.

Another important part of the work of the garden is the exchange of seed. In the eighteenth century that fine American botanist John Bartram would send seed over to be grown in the gardens at Chelsea. And, just as important, seeds were being distributed to various corners of the world; seeds of the cotton plant (*Gossypium herbaceum*) were sent out to Georgia to begin the cotton trade there.

At the present time thousands of packets of seeds carefully labelled are posted each year to different establishments for trial. And of course there are available in the garden about five thousand species of plants for scientific study.

The Company of London Apothecaries which started this garden has an interesting history. In the seventeenth century apothecaries cared for the sick and supplied the drugs needed for treatment. Many were keen gardeners and botanists who studied the habits of plants growing in their own gardens. Following the success of the recently established botanic gardens in Italy and at Oxford they realized there was a need for one of their own in London. So in 1673 they took over a patch of land in what was then the village of Chelsea with river frontage and a south-facing slope. The river frontage was important as the apothecaries already owned a barge and could travel along the River Thames and reach their own garden in ease and comfort. (It is worth recalling that the word 'physic' originally described things natural as distinct from the world of superstition and magic which surrounded medicine at that time.)

In the early days the apothecaries had great difficulty in finding enough money to maintain the garden, but somehow over three centuries it has been kept alive. Today it is beautifully cared for and continues with its programme of research. For the first time in the history of the garden, the general public are allowed in to enjoy this secret garden.

Some gardeners at Chelsea

John Watts—The first gardener, an apothecary who exchanged seeds with Leiden University. Was responsible for a stove which heated the conservatory. Lost interest in later years.

Hans Sloane—His interest in Chelsea Physic Garden came when he was eighty and had already had a long and distinguished career. He was able to spend the last fifteen years of his life working in the garden.

Philip Miller—A great horticulturist who did much to develop the garden and wrote the *Gardener's Dictionary*. The garden was visited by many important botanists during his time.

William Forsyth—In his time the earliest rock garden was built using many tons of stone from the Tower of London and lava from Iceland.

William Curtis—Joined Forsyth in the post of 'Praefector Horti' and demonstrator of plants. The founder of the *Botanical Magazine*.

William Anderson—Conservative Scotsman. Much respected but did not like change.

Robert Fortune—Dedicated plant hunter who loved to be out in foreign places collecting new specimens.

Thomas Moore—Remembered as editor

Hans Sloane, a benefactor of Chelsea Physic Garden.

of the *Gardener's Magazine* and for his work on holly, wild flowers and ferns.

William Hales—Responsible for much of the present layout. Worked here for thirty-eight years and was much respected.

Aphrodisiacs and all that . . .

The age-old belief in the power of herbs to promote thoughts of love and sweet contentment leading either to proposals of marriage or a rewarding romp behind the haystack is understandable. The very aroma, shape and manner of growth of some plants offer a promise, while the old herbalists catered for a population apparently obsessed with ways not just of initiating but of intensifying and prolonging the pleasures of the bed-chamber.

Continued overleaf

continued

Mandrake (*Atropa mandragora*) was at one time the cult herb for this purpose and of course the charlatans of the day were not slow to profit. They spread the belief that the herb was so potent and the harvesting of it so risky that much expenditure and trouble was required to avoid the terrible effects. In consequence, the price was enormous. Now a very rare herb, it may be seen in Chelsea Physic Garden and at Barnsley House.

An aphrodisiac garden—or perhaps a lover's patch—would contain most of the herbs known to man. But priority would have to be given to balm which according to a writer in the early eleventh century 'made the heart merry and strengtheneth the vitall spirits'. Kitty Campion, writing in *The Herbalist* (Jan/Feb 1983) records that Paracelsus mixed balm with potash and sold it for exorbitant sums to kings as an elixir of life, promising it would enhance their virility. A physician gave this mixture to an ailing chicken and within a few days it shed its tattered plumage, grew lustrous fresh feathers and started to lay again.

Peppermint—the Arabs swear by it—and rocket were used by the ancients and the Romans to increase lust in partners and the heady perfume of pennyroyal when introduced to a place of bathing is still said to help those whose mind is willing but whose flesh is weak.

A well-known contender for a place in the patch is southernwood, also known as Lad's Love or more descriptively as Old Man and Virgin's Ruin.

FULHAM PALACE

Hammersmith, London, SW6

Telephone: 01-736 7181   **Owner:** London Borough of Hammersmith

Situation: Bishop's Park, Fulham Palace Road, Fulham. **Open:** Botanic garden, 10am until one hour before closing time of parks ie between 3.30 and 8pm according to season.

Until quite recently the official residence of the Bishops of London, Fulham Palace is now used for offices but the magnificent walled kitchen garden has been retained as a place where budding botanists may nurture the roots of their future interest or profession. The council accepted the offer of the grounds in 1972 and although bestowing much care and attention on other areas it has clearly given a high degree of priority to what is now known as the Educational Botanic Garden.

The knot garden, for many years a straggling and unsightly mess, has been restored. Low clipped box hedges form an intricate pattern to encircle and embrace medicinal, culinary and scented herbs including lavender, tansy, rosemary, sorrel, tarragon, lemon balm, thyme and salad burnet. A lovely arch of wisteria separates this area from thirteen 'family' beds in which lie collections of plants brought on from seed sent from botanic gardens all over the world. These are arranged with two outer beds of monocotyledons (which have one seed leaf at germination) and eleven others of dicotyledons (those with two seed leaves at germination) in a radiating layout.

A medley of medicinal herbs at Chelsea Physic
Garden.

Bateman's, the much-loved home of Rudyard
Kipling, where a covered walkway offers a hint of
romance and peace.

The thirteen plant families were chosen primarily for their use and importance to man: woad, the dye-making herb, was chosen for historical reasons, and the grasses which include maize and rice were chosen because of their food value.

A family—or systematic—garden

A systematic garden is laid out to help in the study of plants and their relationships one with another. It usually takes the form of a series of 'family' beds, as at Fulham Palace. It would hardly be possible to have at home

something similar to this but collecting, growing and labelling perhaps a single or a couple of beds of families of herbs would be of great interest.

If for example you were to select the family Umbelliferae you would be planting many well-known herbs with a variety of characteristics. Angelica (*Angelica archangelica*), caraway (*Carum carvi*), coriander (*Coriandrum sativum*), fennel (*Foeniculum vulgare*) and dill (*Anethum graveolens*) are all members of this family and, as the excellent *Guide to the Glasgow Botanic Gardens* points out, are used both in medicine and in

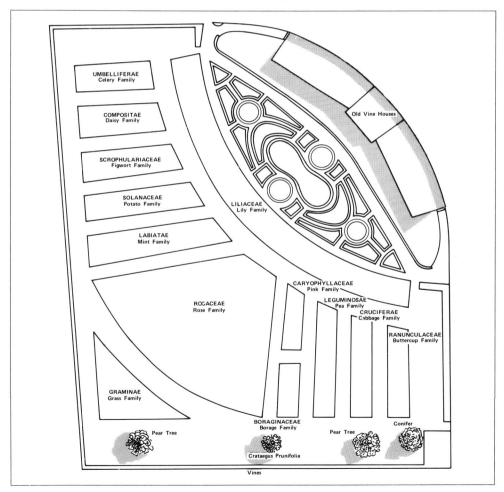

cooking. Parsley (*Petroselinum crispum*), perhaps the best-known culinary herb, is also an umbellifer.

Mint (*Mentha* spp.) is a problem for many people because there are so many kinds, and most grow so vigorously—but like parsley it is much used and often loved. It belongs to the important Labiatae family which also includes thyme (*Thymus vulgaris*), balm (*Melissa officinalis*), sage (*Salvia officinalis*), hyssop (*Hyssopus officinalis*) and rosemary (*Rosmarinus officinalis*). Other well-known family members are basil (*Ocimum basilicum*) and winter and summer savory (*Satureia montana* and *Satureia hortensis*).

The Cruciferae family gets its name from the arrangement of the four petals in the form of a Maltese Cross. Among the members of this group are cabbage, cauliflower, wallflower, honesty and candytuft. Pinks and carnations are members of the Caryophyllaceae family, while geraniums and the popular zonal pelargoniums belong to the Geraniaceae family.

Among important families is the pea family, Leguminosae; these have flowers formed in the shape of a butterfly. In this bed should be the garden pea (*Pisum sativum*) and bean (*Phaseolus* spp.), also clover (*Trifolium* spp.) and the common milk-vetch (*Astragalus glycyphyllos*).

Many well-known herbs such as borage (*Borago officinalis*) and comfrey (*Symphytum officinale*) are members of the family Boraginaceae (the inflorescence of most is shaped like the tail of the scorpion). A whole host of others come within the Compositae or daisy family, which contains over 13,000 species or more than one-tenth of the total number of flowering plants.

Another family to consider is the Solanaceae; this includes a wealth of medicinal and often dangerous herbs including woody nightshade or bitter-sweet (*Solanum dulcamara*). Friends might be astonished to find that you have also included, quite correctly, potato (*Solanum tuberosum*), tomato (*Lycopersicon esculentum*) and tobacco (*Nicotiana tabacum*). You might like to link such a family with the Ranunculaceae (or buttercup) family which covers most of the acrid plants, an example being the very poisonous monkshood (*Aconitum napellus*). If healing plants are more your cup of tea, think of the family Scrophulariaceae which has within it the most widely known medicinal plant, the common foxglove (*Digitalis purpurea*). As you may or may not have guessed, the family name is derived from scrofula, a disease which only a king could heal (hence the term 'King's evil').

THE MUSEUM OF GARDEN HISTORY

St Mary-at-Lambeth, London SE1

Telephone: 01-373 4030   **Owner:** The Tradescant Trust

Situation: Next to Lambeth Palace on the S side of Lambeth Bridge. **Open:** Monday–Friday 11am–3pm and Sunday 10.30–5pm. Closed second Sunday in December to first Sunday in March.

This sheltered retreat is a place where Londoners and visitors alike may pause and enjoy a half-hour of peace catching only a glimpse through the iron railings of a familiar red bus on the busy Lambeth Road.

Inside this beautiful redundant church the Trust has gathered an extraordinary collection of gardening memorabilia to form the

'T' for Tradescant at the Museum of Garden History, Lambeth.

A plant collecting kit

Some paper and plastic bags, a few elastic bands or pieces of string, a small container of water, a junior grow-bag, some sharp scissors, a packet of rooting powder, a small note-book, a permanent ink pen and some plastic labels are the bare essentials of the keen herb grower's plant hunting kit.

If you wish to increase your range and stock of herbs, carry the kit with you always. Even if you are not actually plant hunting, but spending a day or two away from home, don't forget the kit. You'll be sorry if a friendly gardener says 'Take a cutting or two' or 'Do help yourself to seedheads' and you've not an item of equipment with you. Opportunities like this, even if contrived by a conversation heavy with hints or even downright requests and offers of exchange, rarely occur twice.

Seedheads are best put into paper bags but cuttings and roots travel best in plastic bags which are dampened on the inside and then sealed with string or a band. For trips lasting more than a day, a few minutes in the evening actually striking the cuttings in a grow-bag are well spent.

Plants bought at garden centres and stalls often need a drink and will certainly require dampening if kept in a warm car. Every item should be labelled with name, date and place of acquisition and the same information with other facts should be recorded in the notebook.

Non-essential but useful additions to the kit are a sharp knife, paper clips, secateurs and what were once called visiting cards.

basis of a museum of garden history. Outside, the small churchyard is the last resting place of the Tradescants, father and son, the gardeners to whom many of us will mentally touch our caps. Their enterprise in collecting what were then termed 'outlandish' flowers, shrubs, trees and herbs from many lands, is an adventure story recorded here in a most dramatic way.

The southeast area has been landscaped in to a garden full of peace and beauty and includes a small knot garden designed by Lady Salisbury, whose family first employed John Tradescant the elder at Hatfield House. Box has been chosen to edge the garden and for the interlacing threads; on the Tradescant theme, four large 'T' shapes have been designed using sturdy cotton lavender. These two neat, slow growing herbs, form the bones of the garden.

Other herbs, useful and ornamental, have been donated by growers all over the country to ensure the success of the memorial. The aim of the Trust has been to use only plants known in Tradescant's day or discoveries which he brought back to this country.

The nearby Tradescant tomb has a long epitaph, ending with the lines:

These famous Antiquarians that had been
Both gardeners to the Rose and Lily Queen
Transplanted now themselves, sleep here,
and when
Angels shall with their trumpets waken men
And fire shall purge the world, these hence
shall rise
And change this garden then for Paradise.

Another monument in the churchyard recalls Admiral Bligh who died in 1817. His fame for his part in the mutiny on the *Bounty*, tends to obscure the object of the voyage—the collection of bread-fruit plants for cultivation in the West Indies.

WESTMINSTER ABBEY HERB GARDEN

Westminster Abbey, Westminster, London SW1

Telephone: 01-222 5152
Situation: In the centre of London and within easy walking distance of Westminster, Victoria and St James's Park underground stations. **Open:** Thursdays only. April–September, 10am–6pm; October–March, 10am–4pm.

Herbs used for many purposes in the fifteenth and sixteenth centuries are to be found in the abbey's compact herb garden, the gift of the British Herb Trade Association in 1980. The site chosen, is, appropriately, what could well have been the original infirmary plot where herbs would have been grown to make potions for the sick and low at heart.

The garden is approached through medieval vaulted stone passageways, sufficient in themselves to stimulate the imagination. Surprisingly small—just 23ft (7m) by 6ft (1.8m)—it would nonetheless have met the needs of the monastic community of the past. Here is thyme, which when mixed with honey was used for driving phlegm from the throat—much used by choristers?—and southernwood, the ashes of which were 'meddled' with oil to restore the growth of hair.

Rosemary was once burnt in the streets of London and in private courtyards in the hope of warding off disease. In times of

The rose of medicine

Of importance in the design and general scheme of a garden such as this at Westminster is the Apothecary's rose (*Rosa gallica* 'Officinalis'), which with its rounded crimson flowers is in its full glory in the summer when the garden parties are held. It is a good all-rounder, and an interesting addition to any garden where colour is important later in the year for the rose has rich red hips in the autumn. Golden marjoram, with soft gold leaves, is particularly striking in spring before the pretty pink flowers rush into bloom, and contrasts well with the rue, chosen for its finely cut steel-blue leaves.

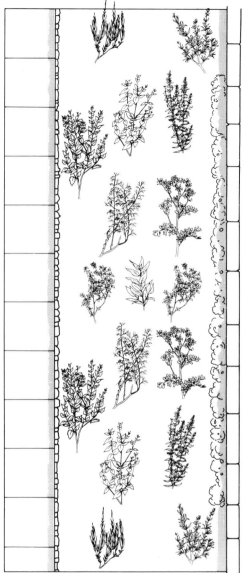

plague, the price shot up from a penny a bundle to nearly thirty pence. It might also have been used in the hope of lengthening as well as ensuring life, for the old herbals had it that frequent smelling of the wood of the herb preserved youth. Rue, the herb of repentance used by judges and others in nosegays as an antidote to pestilence and gaol fever, is also here as is hyssop.

Many years ago when it was the custom to wash only once or so a year, and even then with an undervest on, aromatic herbs had a major role to play in purifying the air around the person and removing unwanted small creatures from the unwashed and uncombed hair. If, as often happened, the hair fell out then herbs were used in an attempt to restore the thatch.

Marjoram was bound on the head to cure a cold, no doubt a frequent affliction in those fireless areas; and lavender was employed as being 'of especial good use for all griefes and paines of the head and brain'. Germander was planted for former residents of the abbey who fell sick of the palsy or suffered frequently from troubles of the skin, while bay was grown to commemorate the poets and the victorious who were once crowned with it.

Happily, the garden serves a different purpose now, providing not just a link with the past but an evergreen island throughout the year. The abbey has more than three million visitors each year and on Thursdays, when the garden may be seen, the planting is much admired.

THE SOUTH EAST

BATEMAN'S

Bateman's, Burwash, East Sussex

Telephone: Burwash (0435) 882302 **Owner:** The National Trust

Situation: ½m S of Burwash on the Lewes to Etchingham road (A265). **Open:** April–October, each day except Thursday and Friday, 11am–6pm (last admission 5.30pm); Good Friday, 11am–6pm.

Rudyard Kipling came to live here in 1902, and it was to be a much-loved home for the rest of his life. He writes of his first impressions on discovering the beauty of Bateman's in this vein: 'That's her the Only She! Make an honest woman of her—quick!'

From the windows of this sturdy Sussex house the garden appears to flow into the surrounding countryside. As a member of the family once aptly said, 'The house stands like a beautiful cup on a saucer to match.'

It is unlikely that herbs were grown by the Kiplings, for in the early part of the twentieth century, rose gardens, pools with fountains and velvet-smooth lawns for croquet were very much the order of the day.

There is no formally laid out herb garden, but a large collection of carefully tended plants fills a long wide border on the west side of the old kitchen garden. Well over a hundred different varieties indicate the revival of interest in the subject during recent years. Mr Woodbine Parish, the National Trust's first tenant at Bateman's, created this garden.

The plants have been chosen for their decorative value more than for culinary or medicinal use. Sage grows well in all its varieties including the red sage with soft plummy leaves and dark blue flowers. And in this sheltered border the tricolour variety (*Salvia officinalis tricolor*), its leaves splashed with pink, white and green, is a truly pleasant sight. Golden sage, with attractive green/gold variegated leaves, makes bright patches of sunshine during the early part of the summer.

Jerusalem sage (*Phlomis fruticosa*) is often included among the sages, though it is not a salvia. With scented grey foliage, this plant has unusual double-lipped yellow flowers in June and July, growing to about 3ft (1m) high. The leaves are not used for culinary purposes but do keep their fragrance when dried.

Look out too for the intriguing tree onion (*Allium cepa viviparum*). This plant grows from an onion-type bulb producing the usual cylindrical green leaves, but instead of flowers it produces clusters of small bulbils at the top of the stem. The weight of this causes the stalk to bend over, resulting in dramatic shapes among the more fussy-leaved thymes and pennyroyals.

Santolinas, blue and pink hyssops, woad, rosemary, lemon balm and several artemisias make up a mixed border which is loved by bees and visitors alike.

Reminiscent of the covered walkways of early herb gardens is the romantic cordoned pear archway planted in Kipling's time. Before walking through it pause for a few minutes and study the shadows of these trees through the fine wrought-iron gates which incorporate the initials R. K. The archway, perhaps some 40yd (36m) long with a wide brick path, leads to a sheltered seat and is a vision of loveliness in the spring. Borders,

about 4ft (1.2m) wide, run each side and are closely planted with spring flowers. Lily-of-the-valley, lungwort, *Viola labradorica*, comfrey and various hellebores complement the pear blossom and carry on giving pleasure throughout the summer.

Kipling's writings and life make this garden a very personal memorial. It is easy to picture happy days spent with the children and the excitement of building the pond with a concrete base to make it safe for boating and bathing. An entry in the visitor's book followed by the initials F.I.P. would mean the unfortunate person 'Fell in pond'.

A collection of sages

A collection of different varieties of one particular herb makes a good talking point in any garden. At Bateman's you can see several interesting sages growing happily together and this is an idea to try in your own garden. It is also a good opportunity to study the leaf shape and aroma of the different varieties of one particular species.

There are several hundred varieties of sages listed, but here are just a few to start your collection of this attractive foliage plant famed for its health-giving properties.

Common sage—Grows to about 3ft (90cm) high with greyish-green leaves and a rough texture.

Red sage—Soft plummy-red leaves with dark blue flowers.

Golden sage—Blending of yellow and green leaves gives a sun-dappled appearance.

Pineapple sage—Grows to a height of about 2ft (60cm) with soft, green, pointed leaves that have a pineapple scent when crushed. Attractive red flowers in the summer.

Sadly Kipling's last years were marked by increasing loneliness and it is hoped that the garden was a source of comfort. Many of his later books and poems were written in these beautiful surroundings. Just behind the house is the hill described in *Puck of Pook's Hill*, the name now used locally.

Kipling's well-known poem 'The Glory of the Garden' (written at Bateman's) gives a clue to how many years the beauty of Bateman's can survive:

Oh, Adam was a gardener, and God who
    made him sees
That half a proper gardener's work is done
    upon his knees
So when your work is finished, you can
    wash your hands and pray.
For the Glory of the Garden, that it may not
    pass away
And the Glory of the Garden it shall never
    pass away.

EYHORNE MANOR

Hollingbourne, Kent,

Telephone: Hollingbourne (062 780) 514   **Owner:** Mr and Mrs Derek Simmons

Situation: 5m E of Maidstone on the B2163, just 400yd N of the A20. **Open:** May, June, July and August, daily except for Monday and Friday, 2–6pm; bank holidays 2–6pm.

Built in the fifteenth century, Eyhorne Manor might then have been the only house to overlook this once quiet village green. Now it is only a short distance away from the busy A20 and the ceaseless flow of traffic passing through Kent. But Eyhorne Manor still manages to preserve the peaceful atmosphere of bygone times and this is due largely to the efforts of Mr and Mrs Simmons who have restored it most faithfully as a typical hall or yeoman's home.

The garden and house were in a sad state when the Simmons moved here in 1952 but over the years they have re-introduced many of the old-fashioned plants that originally grew here—violets, purple honesty, peonies, sweet rocket, lemon balm, feverfew, some old established shrub roses and a wide selection of sweetly scented herbs. Nothing seems too difficult for this hard working couple to tackle and the garden has responded marvellously to their tender loving care. It is, as one visitor put it, an 'exuberant' garden.

There are a number of small plots for herbs, one full of the golden varieties including marjoram and balm. Another positively overflows with sages. Elecampane, lungwort, rosemary, many different mints and thymes are all here looking very much as one imagines they would have done in the seventeenth century.

Sweet rocket (*Hesperis matronalis*), the uncommon herb with long white, mauve or purple spiky flowers, grows wild in the garden. A perennial that self-seeds vigorously, it has become one of Mrs Simmon's favourite flowers and she takes credit for keeping this cottage garden plant in circulation by distributing the seed to visitors.

All plants are friends, and it is the sort of garden where weeds are just considered to be plants in the wrong place. The owner clearly loves her fascinating jumble of herbs, scented plants and shrubs and says, 'I'm a sucker for scent, and when I'm out in the garden its like being in another world.' But even she admits, rather ruefully, about this

little paradise on earth that she is 'never in control'.

This gentle energetic lady actually finds time to use herbs as the lady of the manor would have done in medieval days. Angelica is crystallized and caraway seeds are dried to flavour and decorate the home-made cakes visitors are encouraged to taste. An especially sweet pot-pourri made to a secret recipe is left in open baskets in the rooms. Hanging over the fire in the great hall are bunches of sweet smelling melilot (*Melilotus officinalis*) which would previously have been used to absorb the multitudinous aromas of communal living. Nothing at all is wasted and seeds from the plants growing in the garden are dried in paper bags hanging from the ceiling. Sometimes these are sold but often they are given to visitors.

One great speciality of the garden is the Roman chamomile (*Anthemis nobilis* syn.

Chamaemelum nobile). With double creamy-white flowers resembling daisies and growing to about 6in (15cm) high, this is a particularly sweet smelling variety. The legend that chamomile is known as the 'plant's physician' and if grown near roses will result in more vigorous growth and bigger and better blooms appears to hold good at Eyhorne.

Inside the house, one of the most interesting of the unusual rooms is the laundry. Here herbs are very much in evidence. When recalling pictures of all those ruffs and frills of past generations, it is fascinating to observe how herbs were used in this domestic area.

Wild arum, sometimes called cuckoo pint or lords and ladies (*Arum maculatum*), also has the name starchwort. Starch was made from the root but Gerard, the sixteenth-century herbalist, says that although it made the most 'pure and white starch' it was 'hurtful for the hands of the laundresse'.

Another starch was made from bluebell bulbs, which contain a gummy juice.

Lavender and rosemary were at hand to 'sweeten clothes', and many a lady of the manor and her lord—and perhaps the lower orders too—would have lain between clean crisply starched lavender-scented sheets at Eyhorne. Cotton lavender and feverfew acted as deterrents against moths and other harmful creepy-crawlies. Fascinating as it is to discover these nuggets of knowledge, the pleasure is in seeing the plants growing outside and actually in use in a laundry.

Mr and Mrs Simmons have devoted a lifetime to restoring this sturdy yeoman's dwelling. Every inch of house and garden has been transformed into an authentic slice of history. As Mrs Simmons says of her garden, 'It appears artless, perhaps rather wild, but it is loved, cherished and allowed to wield its own magic.'

A sucker for scent

Scented plants are a pleasure to grow and however small the area you can have a fragrant garden to enjoy. Choose a border that has the advantage of full sun and build your design around a beautiful fragrant rose such as 'Zéphirine Drouhin'. It has bright pink flowers that bloom for much of the summer and have a heady fragrance. Underneath this climbing rose, popular with gardeners because it has no thorns, plant sweet smelling lavender and a cushion of fragrant creeping thyme. In this way you will begin to create the same effect that Mr and Mrs Simmons have achieved in their exuberant garden.

Fragrant plants can be enjoyed for their scent which wafts in the surrounding air. Aromatic plants have a powerful scent which can only be appreciated when the leaves are pinched or rubbed together.

Washday blues

To appreciate the freshness of herbs in newly laundered clothes try planting a row of lavender underneath your washing line. The fragrance of the flowers will drift on to shirts, sheets and nightclothes as they blow in the breeze. Smaller items such as socks and underwear can be stretched over the lavender hedge and will be impregnated with a sweet lavender scent when dry.

IDEN CROFT HERBS

Iden Croft Nurseries and Herb Farm, Frittenden Road, Staplehurst, Kent

Telephone: Staplehurst (0580) 891432   **Owner:** Mr and Mrs D. Titterington

Situation: South of Staplehurst just off the A229. **Open:** Throughout the year, Monday–Saturday, 9am–4pm. Other times by appointment.

To see herbs grown commercially, spend a few hours at Iden Croft. The stately angelica normally occupying a favourite corner of the domestic garden is here in row after row and is specially cultivated for confectionery manufacturers. Thyme, dill, tarragon and other great culinary herbs are brought on specifically for the hotel trade. There is a splendid array of other herbs in these $4\frac{1}{2}$ acres (1.8 hectares) of intensively cultivated land.

The enterprise began in the early 1970s and is owned by Rosemary Titterington in partnership with her husband. Ask her 'Why herbs?' and she will explain that she 'grew up' on comfrey for bruises and peppermint tea for colds and that her grandmother was a practising herbalist.

In the small display herb garden, set apart from the commercial area, all sorts of scented and useful plants clamber over each other to attract the attention of butterflies and bees. The unusual pathway that runs through the garden is made from local Bethesden marble, scattered with fossils. This makes a perfect framework for the many different thymes that grow up the walkway and in summer it resembles a Persian carpet with the different pink, mauve and deep crimson flowers.

Rosemary Titterington has this sound advice to offer beginners and enthusiasts alike. 'Gardening should not be too strict. The whole essence of a successful herb garden is to blend the different patterns.' And to emphasize her love of this particular garden she adds a personal detail. 'This is the place where I like to come to drink my early morning cup of tea before work gets too hectic.'

Visitors are free to wander about the garden and the thriving commercial area, where new growing and marketing ideas are continually being put into practice. During our visit five tons of angelica stalks had been ordered by a well-known confectioner for crystallizing, a bit of sweet success for a British herb grower as until now angelica has been imported from the Continent. It is hoped that the angelica grown on this good Kentish soil will give a sweeter flavour to chocolates and such delicacies as tutti-frutti ice cream.

There are twelve propagating houses, some greenhouses and others the fashionable 'plastic' tunnels. French tarragon, chives, thyme and dill are just a few of the herbs that are grown for the hotel trade. It is good news for growers that each year more and more chefs are asking for British herbs.

To provide the fresh green foliage so much in demand, cuts are made as frequently as possible. This helps to prevent the plant rushing into flower; once this happens the flavour disappears from the leaves.

At Iden Croft research is being carried out on garlic growing under different conditions. French tarragon grows vigorously in tunnels; rows of good Kent raspberries ripen in a sunny corner; and trials are under way to develop the perfect thyme and sage for the catering trade. Organizing the national collection of marjoram, that confusing species, is a job that would daunt many herb growers but to Rosemary Titterington it is one more challenge.

29

Commercial growers of culinary herbs have to obey the regulations for cleanliness where food is concerned. Cutting is quite a specialized affair and different methods are continually being assessed to discover the most economic approach. Chives, it seems, are one of the more difficult crops to harvest quickly.

Borage flowers are much in demand and these pretty blue star-shaped flowers find their way into wine cups at race meetings, garden parties, anniversary dinners, and even royal receptions. To keep their colour and freshness, they are picked in the early morning and packed in special bags with a tight seal.

The plants on sale in the nursery are all grown in a special mix of soil and compost blended for Iden Croft. This keeps them healthy during the time they stay in containers and ensures quick growth when they are planted out.

A good collection of culinary, medicinal and aromatic plants are attractively displayed and visitors will find buying herbs a most pleasurable experience here.

A scented walkway

A scented walkway such as the one at Iden Croft could be made across a corner of lawn or as a path through a formal herb garden. It is one of those interesting herbal trimmings that can be just a mere 2ft (60cm) or stretch the length of your garden. Start by laying paving stones or crazy paving to form a walkway leaving generous gaps between the stones. Fill these spaces with a mixture of sand and soil and plant the following:

Thymus serphyllum Makes a tidy mat formation with bright green leaves.
Thymus lanuginosus Cushions of woolly grey foliage that spread quickly.
Thymus serphyllum Albus White flowering with pale green leaves.
Thymus coccineus Bronze green foliage and rich red flowers.

Thymes planted in this way have a softening effect on paving stones and seem to do well in any small pocket of soil between the cracks. Not until you walk on the plants do you get the full value of their delicious warm aroma.

KEW GARDENS

Royal Botanic Gardens, Kew, Richmond, Surrey

Telephone: 01-940 1171   **Owner:** The Ministry of Agriculture, Fisheries and Food

Situation: Kew, S bank of the Thames, a mile from Richmond. **Open:** Kew Gardens, all the year except Christmas Day and New Year's Day, 10am. Closing times vary according to season, summer 8pm and winter 4pm. Kew Palace, April–September, 11am–5.30pm.

At Kew, less than ten miles from the centre of London, there are three hundred acres of delightful garden. Go to Kew say all the guidebooks and indeed it has become one of the leading tourist attractions for foreign visitors, rivalled only by Buckingham Palace and the Tower of London.

Kew is a gardener's dream as well as a fine memorial to the devoted work of botanists, gardeners, and the intrepid explorers who risked their lives to collect rare specimens. It has many royal associations; George III lived at Kew in what at that time was called the White House.

The parterre with a fine Venetian wellhead; note the
rotunda on the mount to the right.

The recently created Queen's Garden is of great interest to herb lovers, the basis being a parterre with central fountain and a sunken nosegay garden encompassed by a raised walkway underneath a laburnum arch. Other attractions include an alley of pleached hornbeams and a mount from which can be seen the Thames, the garden and the house.

There is no evidence of a previous formal garden on the present site, possibly because of the risk of flooding before the river embankment was made up. So in the 1950s the area had become an eyesore when Sir George Taylor, Director of the Royal Botanic Garden, had the idea of constructing a garden here to fit the style of the building.

The plan was not to create an exact replica of the garden that a house like Kew Palace would have had adjoining it, but to incorporate all the different garden features most popular at that time. The basic design was inspired by a drawing of a French garden at Verneuil illustrated in *L'Art des Jardins* by Georges Gromort (1934).

The parterre boasts a fine Venetian wellhead and a statue taken from Verrocchio's Boy with a Dolphin in Florence. Some of the beds are filled with cotton lavender (*Santolina neapolitana*), a plant which the herbalist Parkinson said was used 'to border knots with, for which it will abide to be cut into what form you think best, for it groweth thick and bushy very fit for such works, beside the comely show the plant itself thus wrought doth yield being always green and of a sweet scent'. The silvery foliage makes a good contrast with the greenish bronze of box edging also used in the parterre.

Nearby is a replica of the Tudor-style 'mount' erected in the enclosed gardens of monasteries or castles to provide some means of looking over the wall to the world outside. By a stroke of good fortune, there

The Rotunda

The Gazebo

Stone Seat

Boy with Dolphin

Satyr with Flute

Venetian Well-head

A plan of the recently completed Queen's Garden at Kew Palace.

was already here a pile of ashes from the glasshouse furnace and this was converted into the mount seen today. The climb is approached by a spiral box-edged path. On one side is a view over the river and on the other the house and garden.

In contrast to the formal parterre, the sunken garden contains about two hundred different species of plants likely to have been grown in an early seventeenth-century garden. All are carefully labelled and grown 'to please the outward senses'—as Gerard said in his famous herbal—and where possible the labels include the botanical name, country name of that period and the reason (according to Gerard) for growing the plant. Many happy hours can be spent here studying herbs that in earlier times would have been used by apothecaries to treat suffering and illness wherever it existed.

Of the statuesque globe artichoke (*Cynara scolymus*) we are told that 'if the young buds of Artichokes be first steeped in wine and eaten, it provoketh urine, and stirreth up the lust of the bodie.' Of the Christmas rose (*Helleborus niger*) it is said that 'A purgation of blacke hellebor is good for mad and furious men, for melancholike, dull and heavie persons, for those that are troubled with the falling sicknesse and for lepers.'

The sunken garden is also referred to as the nosegay garden because in the past sweet smelling herbs were used in this way to dispel the foul smells caused by the lack of drainage in city streets. Marjoram would have been grown because, as herbalist Parkinson recounts, 'The Sweete Marjeromes are much used to please the outward senses in nosegayes and in the windowes of houses.'

A striking sweet smelling herb is angelica and this would have been used among others as a strewing herb to protect against the plague. Gerard writes: 'The roote of garden Angelica is a singular remedie against poison, and against the plague, and all infections taken by evil and corrupt aire,

A chamomile seat

A chamomile seat of Tudor design can be constructed by cutting the shape from a mound or steep bank of earth and covering the sitting area with thin strips of wood, planting chamomile in between. Another way is to select a sunny corner of the garden or, more traditionally, an alcove in a hedge and lay a low wall of bricks. Edge the top with bricks to produce a container and fill this with garden soil or compost in which you then plant the herb. The best variety to choose is the double or Roman chamomile, a tough growing perennial with a pleasant appley aroma.

if you do but take a peece of the roote and holde it in your mouth, or chew the same between your teeth, it doth most certainly drive away the pestilentiall aire.'

At the northern end of the sunken garden is another traditional herbal feature of that time, a chamomile turfed seat. Surrounded by box edging, it is raised to a height of about 2ft (60cm) and is both comfortable and fragrant. The scent of the herb is released by bruising the leaves. It is most pleasant and could even be beneficial, for Gerard declared that 'oile of Cammomill is exceeding good against all manner of ache and pain, bruisings, shrinking of sinewes, hardnesse and cold swellings'.

Roses earn their place in this garden with the sweetness of their scent and their appeal as traditional English flowers. The fine selection includes the white rose of York (*Rosa Alba* 'Semi-plena') and the red rose of Lancaster (*Rosa gallica* 'Officinalis'), together with the rose combining both houses in one flower—the York and Lancaster rose (*Rosa damascena* '*versicolor*').

Shaded alleys, an important feature of Tudor herb gardens, are represented by the magnificent laburnum walkway that surrounds this garden and produces cascades of golden flowers in the early summer.

Named after the present queen and opened by her on 14 May 1969, this lovely garden at Kew is encouraging many thousands of visitors from all over the world to learn a little more about the history of their native plants and perhaps to create a garden of similar style, though on a smaller scale, on their return home.

KNOLE

Knole, Sevenoaks, Kent

Telephone: Sevenoaks (0732) 53006 **Owner:** The National Trust and The Lord Sackville

Situation: S end of Sevenoaks on the A225. **Open:** Garden, the first Wednesday of the month, May–September, 2–5pm. House, varies (check by telephone).

We know that herbs have been grown for a long time at Knole for in 1692 it was reported that a gardener, Mr Olloynes, was paid ten pounds a year for his work and that he also ran up a bill for seeds of 'sweet yerbs, sorril, spinnig etc'.

Little remains of his garden now but a fairly new one has been constructed. It came about following one of the frequent visits to the house by Margaret Brownlow, who kept the famous Herb Farm at Seal. She was either collecting wild herbs or riding through the park for pleasure when she was asked by Lady Sackville to bring a bunch of rosemary to the kitchen. Spurred on by this simple request Margaret Brownlow suggested planning a herb garden at Knole. After all there was plenty of room.

The idea was approved and on a cold windswept day she studied the site and, in the words of a former garden designer, considered the capabilities. A sheltered spot just outside the orangery and backed by a high wall proved to be ideal and planting was completed in 1963.

The attractive square garden is surrounded by yew trees and measures 30ft (9m) on all sides. This is a plan that could easily be modified for smaller gardens. In the small central wheel-shaped garden a statue of a boy, looking particularly appealing, provides a focal point. The spokes of the wheel are made from the neat growing silvery leaved cotton lavender, and to form the rim, golden thyme grows in a complete circle. Opposite sections of the wheel contain red sage, rue and an attractive dwarf form of hyssop (*Hyssopus aristatus*).

Wide grass paths separate this circular garden from the triangular beds in each corner of the square. These triangles are edged with thyme and are filled with herbs

The sunken garden, also called the nosegay garden, at
Kew is a treasure trove of early seventeenth-century
plants.

A section of the attractive herbal rockery at Marle
Place.

useful for the pot or decoration. As for rosemary, the original raison d'être of the garden, this aromatic shrub is well represented both in the entrance and behind the seat.

Originally lavender was planted to surround the garden with its sweetness but this did not do well. Lord Sackville thinks it may be something to do with the surrounding yew hedge, which has now grown tall and thick.

An ornate seventeenth-century lead tank filled with scented pelargoniums is a feature of this enclosed garden, which must be a pleasant and secluded place of retreat in an area as vast—and as lovely—as that at Knole.

A small square garden—child's play

A small square garden such as the one at Knole set at one side of a large lawn has a special appeal. Perhaps it is because it looks like a doll's house garden with trim edges and miniature paths. All in all a wonderful garden for a child to watch his first plants growing in—and of course the plants would be useful in the kitchen. Mint grows quickly enough to please an impatient child and can be enjoyed with new potatoes. Parsley, with its green curled foliage, looks as pretty as a picture and is always in demand, and so are chives with their spiky leaves and strong onion flavour. Cheerful golden marigolds and nasturtiums can quickly be grown from seed and will add a splash of colour bright enough to please a youthful gardener.

MARLE PLACE

Marle Place Plants, Brenchley, Nr Tonbridge, Kent

Telephone: Brenchley (089) 272 2304. **Owner:** Mr and Mrs Williams

Situation: Just off the B2162 between Horsmonden and Lamberhurst. **Open:** For the National Gardens Scheme and by appointment.

Marle Place is an extremely elegant house surrounded by a large garden which fades unobtrusively into the wooded Kent countryside. The garden is run as a small nursery and Mrs Williams, a keen gardener and, as she says, a compulsive propagator of plants, sells mainly to local garden centres and to visitors. She is also an established artist who enjoys painting plants in the garden and in the surrounding countryside.

Herbs have pride of place in a large rockery, much in keeping with the period of the house. Large stones give the plants good protection and form pockets of soil where the plants can grow happily. Crazy paving steps lead up to the top of the rockery and smaller thymes, marjoram and pennyroyal spill over the edges making a scented walkway. It is an unusual experience to see so many herbs at different angles.

Some plants are grown for their flowers, but mainly it is decorative foliage that appeals to the owner. There are golden thymes, golden marjoram and the variegated balms and sages which contrast so well with the grey stone of the rocks.

37

Large terracotta pots full of quite ordinary herbs add extra charm and are at every corner of the upward climb or returning descent. Placed so that one can brush the foliage and enjoy the aroma, they are just one more indication of Mrs William's artistic eye.

A herbal rockery

Since so many herbs are of Mediterranean origin, it is strange that a herbal rockery is so unusual, but take a tip from Mrs Williams and plan your herbs to grow in this way and then you can enjoy seeing them from different angles. Vary the foliage type so that feathery leaved plants grow next door to ones with bolder leaves.

A few large stones attractively placed against a garden fence or even to cover a tree stump provide the basis for a herbal rockery. Fill the spaces between the stones with a mixture of sand and soil and select your plants. Suitable choices for a rockery herb garden include the following:

Fennel, bronze or green. Strikingly attractive plant with feathery leaves reaching a height of approximately 5ft (1.5m).

Germander. Attractive shiny leaved evergreen plant with reddish green stems, and small pink flowers.

Golden thyme. Lovely golden leaves in the spring when there are few flowers.

Pennyroyal. Low growing with small dark green leaves and pale mauve flowers.

Pot marjoram. This variety is chosen for the small heart-shaped leaves and pale pink flowers.

Lavender (*Lavandula stoechas*). Low growing with bright mauve bracts forming neat cushions.

Sage. Broad greyish-green leaves with a rough texture. Restful plant to include in a rockery.

MICHELHAM PRIORY

Upper Dicker, Hailsham, East Sussex.

Telephone: Hailsham (0323) 844224   **Owner:** Sussex Archaeological Society

Situation: Just off the A22 on the road to Upper Dicker near Hailsham. **Open:** Easter until the middle of October daily, 11am–5.30pm. House closed 1–2pm.

Surrounded by a medieval moat and 7 acres (2.8 hectares) of beautiful lawns and gardens, Michelham Priory dates back to 1129 when the Augustinian canons established a religious house here. At the Dissolution of the monasteries in 1536, part of the priory buildings including the church were destroyed, but the remaining buildings became the basis for a Tudor house.

The Physic Garden is on one of the surrounding lawns and is planned with the idea of creating an old monastic garden. The garden is designed to show a selection of plants which might have been used in the

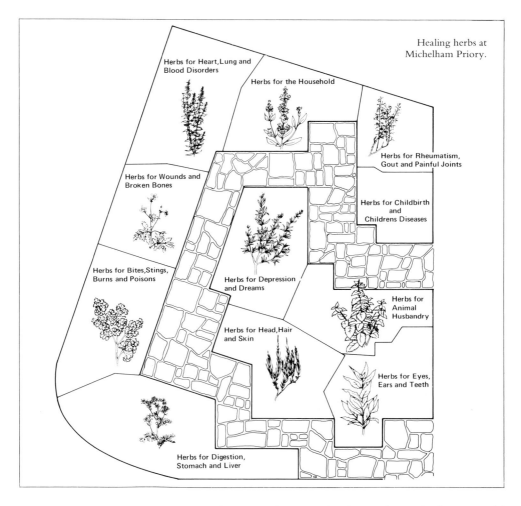

Healing herbs at Michelham Priory.

Herbs for Heart, Lung and Blood Disorders

Herbs for the Household

Herbs for Rheumatism, Gout and Painful Joints

Herbs for Wounds and Broken Bones

Herbs for Childbirth and Childrens Diseases

Herbs for Bites, Stings, Burns and Poisons

Herbs for Depression and Dreams

Herbs for Animal Husbandry

Herbs for Head, Hair and Skin

Herbs for Eyes, Ears and Teeth

Herbs for Digestion, Stomach and Liver

practical application of 'physic' or medicine, rather than for a study of the subject.

Virginia Hinzer, a landscape gardening expert, advised on the plan and the choice of plants and became so fascinated with monastery gardens that she has created a work of art here that can vie in importance with many of the paintings of contemporary artists.

She consulted many references including Gerard's herbal, which was used as a source of plants. All the plants grown here would have been known in England during the sixteenth century, and many of them can be recognized today as plants which grow wild in hedgerows and fields.

The layout of the garden is modern, forming a rough square shape enclosed with hurdles. These it is thought will be taken down when the surrounding yew hedge has grown high enough to shelter the plants. To construct the garden additional labour was recruited from the Manpower Services Commission. Six boys with a leader managed to level the sloping lawn with little mechanical equipment. Great credit is given to this team who worked extremely hard and appeared to enjoy the exciting project.

Soil preparations and design work were completed by April 1981, and planting started that year. Within eighteen months all ninety-two varieties of the chosen herbs had been obtained. Half of them were grown from seed at the nearby agricultural college and the rest were obtained as plants from various herb nurseries, local gardens, allotments and WI markets.

Plants are arranged in groups according to their medicinal uses. Those described here would have been cultivated in an infirmarer's garden and used for administering doses of purgatives, skin and eye ointments, cordials, cough medicines and other remedies.

Groups of plants

Rheumatism, gout and painful joints —mugwort, mustard and lily-of-the-valley.

Use in the household—sage, soapwort and tansy.

Childbirth and children's diseases —stitchworth, horehound and violet.

Heart, lung and blood disorders —plantain, mullein and coltsfoot.

Wounds and broken bones—self heal, comfrey and salad burnet.

Bites, stings, burns and poisons—orris, mallow and calamint.

Digestion, stomach and liver—sorrel, chicory and rue.

Depression and dreams—poppy, feverfew and borage.

Head, hair and skin—fumitory, love-in-a-mist and pennyroyal.

Animal husbandry—balm, sweet cicely and chickweed.

Eyes, ears and teeth—marigold, wall germander and bistort.

The amusing descriptive labels are engraved on blue enamel and show monks preparing various herbs. They add great

One of the 'collector's item' labels.

style and beauty to the garden and each one is a collector's item designed by an American art student, Patricia Musick. To avoid the chance of them being 'lifted' they have been put on cast-iron stakes and inserted at least 3ft (90cm) into the ground.

One of the two seats in the garden is made from Chilham stone, and by chance a visitor recognized it as being the work of his grandfather. Perhaps for this reason he immediately bought £20 worth of herb plants at the priory shop.

When the garden was opened in July 1981 it was blessed by the Bishop of Lewes. In his opening speech he confessed that his track record was not good for he had blessed a piggery and shortly afterwards the pigs died. The same thing often happened when he was asked to plant a tree. But fortunately the herb garden at Michelham Priory has prospered. Perhaps it is because the bishop is a monk.

Killing a cold

If you wake up one morning with a nasty tickle in your throat and the depressing knowledge that a cold is on the way, reach for your herbal remedies.

Onions and their first cousin, garlic, are good for colds and can be eaten raw or made into nourishing soups. Indeed, when you have the snuffles a baked onion straight from the oven is very comforting. If the taste lies heavy on the breath, chew a few sprigs of parsley.

Herbs do undoubtedly provide useful remedies for respiratory disorders and an inhalation of sage, peppermint and thyme leaves will help your breathing and surround you with a healing aroma. A tea made with peppermint, yarrow and elderflowers will also help to rid the body of a fever. Home-made herbal wines such as cowslip or coltsfoot are very soothing.

SCOTNEY CASTLE

Scotney Castle Garden, Lamberhurst, Kent

Telephone: Lamberhurst (0892) 890651

Owner: The National Trust

Situation: S of Lamberhurst on the A21. **Open:** Garden only, April–October, Wednesday–Sunday and Bank Holiday Monday, 2–6pm. During the summer an exhibition is held in the old castle.

Photographers and artists alike are inspired to try and capture the beauty of old Scotney Castle and its romantic gardens. And in the foreground of many pictures of this medieval tower and Tudor building set inside a moat is the circular herb garden designed by Lanning Roper.

Despite its name, Scotney Castle was built about 1378–80 as a fortified house rather than a castle and with various additions and modifications remained a home for many years until the nineteenth century. Then it was that Edward Hussey, a talented and artistic young man, inherited the place and decided he would prefer a new house on the estate. He studied carefully the influence of landscape designers such as Humphry Repton, who were designing gardens which although works of art appeared to have been carved from nature. And in this quiet

Herbal follies

Jokes or follies can be discovered in many gardens so why not have one of your own? Here are three suggestions. 1. Acquire a wagon wheel, lay it flat and plant a selection of herbs between the spokes. If possible, paint the names of the herbs along the rim. 2. Obtain a large heavy ladder of the type used in barns, lay it flat and plant culinary herbs between the rungs. If you put this near the kitchen door you can carry the whimsy a stage further by painting on it 'Every step a cook's friend'. 3. Search about for an old metal pig-trough, paint it white and plant it with herbs for the kitchen. Sign-writing should not be needed here.

Kentish corner Edward Hussey realized he could achieve a similar result.

Mr Hussey selected a site overlooking the old Scotney Castle and quarried stone from the land in between. This created a gorge of sorts, offering dramatic views from every aspect and none more magnificent than that of the old castle on the other side of the newly dug valley. Ancient grey stone walls, water and fine trees created a mixture of textures that could hardly fail to enchant.

In this century the late Christopher Hussey spent much of his life improving the garden at Scotney. Vantage points were added in the quarry along a winding pathway down the valley until the garden of the old castle is approached. They remain as places from which to admire the romantic landscape at all seasons of the year.

The herb garden is in the grounds of the castle. Set within a circular grass path with an ancient wellhead as a central feature, it gives the appearance of having been there since time began. The quiet colours of the herb foliage—golden marjoram, lady's mantle, purple fennel, sage and cotton lavender—planted in large clumps around the centrepiece succeed where brightly coloured flowers would have only distracted. The dream-like quality of this garden imitates nature until nature herself never looked more fair.

Each summer a Shakespearian play is performed. The ruined castle, moat and herb garden make a setting where Shakespeare would surely have felt quite at home with his travelling company of troupers. Here, in *A Midsummer Night's Dream*, King Oberon would find yet another

. . . bank where the wild thyme blows,
Where oxlips and the nodding violet
grows
Quite over-canopied with luscious
woodbine,
With sweet musk-roses and with eglantine.

SISSINGHURST

Sissinghurst, Nr Cranbrook, Kent

Telephone: Cranbrook (0580) 712850   **Owner:** The National Trust

Situation: 2m NE of Cranbrook and 1m E of Sissinghurst village on the A262. **Open:** April–15 October, Tuesday–Friday 1–6.30pm, Saturday, Sunday and Good Friday 10am–6.30pm.

Vita Sackville-West, the poet, writer and knowledgeable gardener, fell in love with Sissinghurst Castle when she was house-hunting in 1930. She wrote, 'I fell in love; love at first sight. I saw what might be made of it. It was Sleeping Beauty's garden; but a castle running away to sordidness and squalor; a garden crying out for rescue. It was easy to forsee, even then, what a struggle we should have to redeem it.'

Today, some fifty years later, we can marvel at the splendour of this garden divided into separate compartments like so many outdoor rooms. The struggle was well worth the effort and the gardens, now owned by the National Trust, are a fitting memorial to the many happy hours Vita and Harold Nicolson must have spent planning and planting.

Walking from garden to garden one follows in the footsteps of these two fine gardeners, who set the fashion for this

An informal garden (*above*) and fine rosemary (*left*) on the steps at Sissinghurst.

informal style of gardening. Now, town and country gardens are all filled with herbs, shrub roses, sweet williams, pansies and other forgotten cottage garden plants.

The herb garden at Sissinghurst was the last of the separate gardens to be planted, and work did not begin until 1938. Then it was quite a small affair with only about a dozen different herbs growing. During the war Vita managed to keep, as she said so aptly, 'a table-cloth sized' herb garden going. When the war ended the garden was overgrown and was first replanted with potatoes before being replanned. It was then considerably enlarged with twenty small beds containing a variety of plants cultivated for use in the kitchen and for their decorative foliage.

The herb garden is traditionally designed in the shape of a cross and surrounded by a high yew hedge. A large marble bowl resting on three lions, brought back by the Nicolsons from their travels, makes a fitting centrepiece.

At about this time too, the famous stone seat was built by the chauffeur. Human touches like this appeal to all herb lovers and bring this garden to life. Perhaps it was not quite the seat Vita had imagined, but it became an integral part of the garden being referred to as 'Edward the Confessor's chair'.

Many of Vita's favourite herbs can be seen at Sissinghurst and are associated with her writings. Sweet woodruff was grown because it was so good natured and would grow in shady corners under trees. Other cherished plants were rosemary and lavender; these she referred to as 'grandmotherly'. It was Vita who had the idea of growing rosemary near doorways so she could pinch a sprig and appreciate the aroma as she passed by.

Dill (*Anethum graveolens*), an annual herb with bright green feathery leaves and yellow umbels of flowers, is recommended as being decorative and useful and good to grow anywhere in the garden. This may be the reason Vita wrote, 'I like muddling things up, and if a herb looks nice in a border then why not grow it there.'

The thyme lawn is just beyond the herb garden. Different varieties used include creeping thyme (*Thymus serpyllum*) and *Thymus coccineus* with low-growing grey leaves and rich pink flowers. This type of herb lawn makes a dense covering and is easier to maintain than the more traditional chamomile lawn which needs constant weeding.

The garden was to Vita Sackville-West and Harold Nicolson both an extravagance and a hobby. It provided a meeting place for two very different characters and may well have helped them survive a stormy marriage.

Because of Vita's articles and books one feels on familiar ground at Sissinghurst and admirers will be keen to discover every nugget of information. Today the National Trust is fully aware that Sissinghurst has become a place of pilgrimage. With the constant flow of visitors increasing each year it is hoped to maintain it at the high standard it enjoyed during its heyday.

Muddling things up

If muddling things up produces the exciting effect that Vita Sackville-West achieved at Sissinghurst, perhaps we should study the art of mixed borders more carefully. For herbs such as golden marjoram, mint, sage and thymes add restful pools of colour with their diverse foliage in a mixed border. The spiky leaves of chives with their attractive globe flowerheads makes it a good edging plant. And to add height at the back of the border the choice is endless. Angelica, growing to a height of 8ft (2.4m), lovage, just a little less, and the beautiful tansy, with yellow button flowers and finely edged leaves, all add interest—and most of them are useful too.

Study the borders carefully in the different gardens at Sissinghurst and you will be surprised how widely herbs are distributed throughout them. You will come home full of new ideas for 'muddling things up' in your own garden.

WISLEY

Wisley Garden, Wisley, Nr Ripley, Surrey

Telephone: Guildford (0483) 224234   **Owner:** The Royal Horticultural Society

Situation: In Wisley just off the Portsmouth Road (A3). 22m from London. **Open:** All the year. Weekdays 10am–7pm (or sunset if earlier); Sunday 2–7pm (or sunset if earlier).

The recently designed herb garden at Wisley covers an area of 30yd (27.5m) square and is to be found among the model gardens. It is easily identifiable by a fine hedge of rosemary, known here as 'Jessop's Upright'. A vigorous grower, this variety makes an aromatic and evergreen hedge very appropriate for a herbary. A hornbeam hedge encloses two of the other sides and on the north side a pyracantha makes a good dense boundary marker.

The geographical outline of the garden is the design of David Palmer, a former Wisley student, at that time technical assistant to the director. Two wide pathways, suitable for wheelchairs, run diagonally across the garden forming a rondel in the centre where a sundial acts as the focal point. Around these main pathways are sections of square and triangular shapes. The triangular beds are preferred here as plants can then be seen from all directions and labels are easily studied.

Altogether there are thirty-one beds containing more than two hundred herbs to illustrate culinary, medicinal, dye and economic uses. A touch of fantasy is not forgotten, for the gardens also cover the important part played by herbs in folklore.

Plain-leaved parsley (a form of *Petroselinum crispum*), which has plain fern-like leaves as against the more usual curly-leaved varieties is prominent here but is uncommon in many other gardens. The flavour is stronger and for this reason it is becoming increasingly popular in the world's kitchens.

Another less common herb is sweet or Florence fennel (*Foeniculum vulgare var. azoricum*). This thick-set plant resembles green fennel, but is smaller in shape and cultivated as an annual. The base of the plant develops to form a white bulbous sweet vegetable which is delicious raw or cooked.

Among the dye-plants false indigo (*Baptisia tinctoria*) catches the eye as does woad (*Isatis tinctoria*) with its yellow wash of flowers, bright enough to cheer up any garden. As any school-child might tell you, ancient Britons used to paint their bodies with a paste made from wound-healing woad leaves before entering battle with the Romans who, incidentally, brought to these shores many of the healing herbs used by our forefathers.

There is much else to be learned at Wisley and the atmosphere is conducive to study. For example, one learns that hog's bean (*Hyoscyamus niger*), sometimes known as henbane, was used to make love potions and as a magical herb was an important ingredient in a witch's brew.

The humble violet (*Viola odorata*) with rosettes of evergreen leaves and sweetly scented flowers was much loved by the Greeks and became the symbol of Athens. Romans too appreciated the merits of the sweet violet and would make garlands of the flowers for their foreheads to cure hangovers. So perhaps it is not surprising that violets have a reputation for easing headaches and giddiness.

Another of the folklore herbs is vervain (*Verbena officinalis*). Growing to about 3ft (90cm) with toothed lobed leaves and pale

mauve flowers, vervain is one of the sacred herbs and was formerly used in religious ceremonies to protect the participants from the wiles of the devil. But all is not folklore at Wisley, not by any means. The many types of gardens, famous throughout the world, attract and stimulate visitors from every country who seek and gain knowledge here.

The herb garden area can be enjoyed by everybody and comfortable seats at strategic places ensure that a quiet half-hour can be spent in study and contemplation.

Nearby in one of the model gardens is a herb wheel particularly suitable for a small area. This wheel shape has various culinary herbs planted between the spokes so that vigorous herbs such as mint can be effectively confined to a small area. This design coule easily be adapted as a raised bed for the enjoyment of handicapped gardeners.

A day, at least, can be spent enjoying the

rest of this 300 acre (120 hectare) botanical treasure trove. Enthusiasts will find much of interest, including the skilled training of fruit trees, and vegetable cultivation.

If you are a member of the Royal Horticultural Society, take your herbal queries to Wisley. The highly competent staff will be happy to help you. A shop provides a comprehensive selection of books that will appeal to beginner and expert alike. And among all sorts of herbal frills and fancies and souvenirs difficult to resist, are more serious items including the society's own manual on culinary herbs. Outside there is a well-stocked sales area where herb seed and herb plants, often unusual ones, can be purchased.

A wagon wheel garden

Where space is limited, build a similar garden to the one designed at Wisley. A circle of bricks 3ft (90cm) in diameter is raised to a height of approximately 2ft (60cm) and divided into ten sections, each devoted to a favourite culinary herb. A good selection would be rosemary, lemon thyme, tarragon, sage, rue, chives, marjoram, bay, garden thyme, parsley and lemon balm. A raised garden such as this would look very attractive on the patio from which herbs can be picked quickly for the kitchen or for barbecues. It would also be a pleasant garden for a person confined to a wheelchair to maintain successfully.

THE SOUTH

THE DOWER HOUSE

Badminton, Avon

Telephone: Badminton (045421) 346   **Owner:** Mr David and the Lady Caroline Somerset

Situation: At the gates of Badminton House, 5m E of Chipping Sodbury. **Open:** Occasionally for the National Gardens Scheme and other charities, or by appointment.

Rich green pastures fringed with cow parsley and narrow winding lanes are the rural background for this country house set right by the gates to Badminton House. The present owners have lived here since 1964 and have developed a garden of charm which is full of original ideas, reflecting their personal tastes.

The west side of the house, painted a soft apricot colour, has white valerian, lady's mantle and different thymes to add fragrance and interest. And in the cracks and crevices of the stone paving, little alpine strawberries thrive and ripen quickly in a minimum of soil. To make it a truly herbal terrace two fine lemon-scented verbena plants grow in square white wooden tubs.

A small gate on the left of this terrace leads to the delightful herb garden. Situated in a corner by the kitchen door, it is small enough and neat enough to be a garden for a doll's house with brick paths focussing on a

An extra-special container

Outside the library door leading to the terrace at the Dower House, Badminton, are two deliciously scented lemon verbena shrubs growing in wooden tubs. As you pass it is a joy to stretch out to pick a leaf and revel in the warm lemon fragrance.

The type of square wooden container here is of particular elegance and known as the Versailles 'Caisse'. Each one is constructed with four panels, one of which can be removed so that extra compost can be added or the roots of the plant given attention. This also makes it very easy for half-hardy plants—such as lemon verbena—to be brought under cover during the winter months.

If you can find a place in your own garden for these square wooden containers, which add style wherever they are placed, look around garden centres in your own area or try specialized garden shops and you may be lucky enough to find a reproduction.

Lemon verbena in a sawn beer-barrel.

bay tree in the centre. The designer, Russell Page, who is a friend of the family, advised on the design and planting.

Lady Caroline has a particular affection for this garden and says, 'The herb garden is of immense use for cooking. It is very small and I grow nothing rare but I dearly love it.' Traditional culinary herbs such as chives, parsley, fennel, sorrel, thyme, mints and lovage all do well in separate compartments and yield good crops of green leaves, except for parsley which has always been a problem herb here.

Leading from the herb garden is a pleached lime walkway culminating in a lofty tunnel walkway of more limes trained to resemble cathedral arches. Mr Somerset has worked on these and has planted many broad-leaved trees on the estate to form the basis of an arboretum.

The planting in the large walled kitchen

garden is bold and dramatic. Lady Caroline says, 'I love straight lines'; and here there are no gentle curves or muted outlines. She preserved box hedges when all around were discarding theirs.

Pathways lead to an elegant wooden framework in the centre of the garden. Formerly this was covered with cascades of shrub roses and known affectionately as Queen Mary's toque. Sadly the hard winter of 1981/82 put an end to these roses. Experiments are now under way to see what can be put in their place. It is rather like playing musical chairs with plants and all gardeners will appreciate Lady Caroline's comment: 'Failure does not exist—only solutions.'

BEAULIEU
Hampshire

Telephone: Beaulieu (0590) 612345   **Owner:** Lord Montagu of Beaulieu

Situation: In Beaulieu 5m SE of Lyndhurst and 14m S of Southampton. **Open:** Easter–September, every day, 10am–6pm; October–Easter, every day, 10am–5pm.

The estate is right in the middle of the historic New Forest country and in the valley of the Beaulieu river. The Cistercian abbey here was founded in 1204 and there is a tale that the abbot was accused of poaching in the New Forest but because of the

Paving stones reminiscent of monastic days are a special feature of the borders.

celebrations when the abbey was dedicated in 1246 the case was dismissed and the abbot forgiven his lapse.

To find the herb garden, go through the extensive grounds until you reach the splendid ruins of the abbey. The mellow grey stone walls make a good background for the different foliage herb plants growing in small beds approximately 5 × 10ft (1.5 × 3m). These borders, planted around the sides of the cloisters, are set against most attractive paving stones placed diagonally. The stones look quite in character, for this is no cottage-style herb garden growing haphazardly, but a carefully planned architectural feature which is both uplifting and appropriate. In bygone days this cloister garden would have been known as a 'garth'.

It must have been quite a problem to select the herbs but the choice for the shady corners is particularly appropriate. Lady's mantle (*Alchemilla mollis*) with its lovely cloak-shaped leaves, lily-of-the-valley (*Convallaria majalis*) with beautiful white bell-shaped flowers always referred to as 'Our Lady's tears', and sweet cicely (*Myrrhis odorata*) are just three that grow happily here. And since most gardens have a shady corner we can take a leaf out of Gerard's herbal and plan the same effect in our own plot.

Authentically detailed, an exhibition entitled The Monastic Life at Beaulieu is on display in one of the original abbey buildings. This gives an insight into the story of the development of our abbeys and monasteries and a glimpse of the day-to-day life of the Cistercian community.

A shady set up

Most of us have a corner or border in the garden that gets no sun at all. Either we prefer to forget about its existence altogether or we just shake our heads in disbelief when plants fail to produce an abundance of leaves and flowers. But, as was recognized in the cloister garden at Beaulieu, there is a good selection of plants that actually thrive in a shady situation.

Hostas all do well if there is plenty of moisture, and with their large ovate leaves make a useful background. Lungwort (*Pulmonaria officinalis*), an attractive old medicinal herb with white spotted leaves and blue and pink flowers in the spring, also needs little sun. Lily-of-the-valley (*Convallaria majalis*) is another shade lover of herbal origin, with sweetly scented white bell flowers to delight us throughout May. Consider also the hellebores and their relatives. These all grow well in a sunless position and will flower

from Christmas until Easter.

Among the tall-growing herbs, sweet cicely (*Myrrhis odorata*), angelica (*Angelica archangelica*) and lovage (*Levisticum officinale*) form a good background against a boundary fence or wall.

THE OLD RECTORY

Burghfield, Nr Reading, Berkshire

Telephone: Burghfield Common (073529) 2206   **Owner:** Mr and Mrs Ralph Merton

Situation: Just off the A4 W of Reading to Burghfield village. Turn right after the Hatch Gate Inn and the entrance is on the right. **Open:** Occasionally for the National Gardens Scheme and on the last Wednesday in the month from February to October (not August). Also by appointment.

The gardens at Burghfield, overlooked by a Georgian house of warm red brick with extensive views over the Berkshire countryside, have become well known to countless visitors who come to enjoy the peace and quiet of this large rambling garden and to buy some of the rare and unusual plants propagated by Mrs Merton after having been collected on her botanizing expeditions to the Far East.

Mrs Merton is both a keen gardener and a good cook, and herbs are needed to flavour and garnish the dishes she prepares for her friends. The sorrel growing here is the 'true' French sorrel (*Rumex scutatus*) with light green oval succulent leaves. As distinct from the more usual garden sorrel (*Rumex acetosa*), this plant rarely runs to seed and the leaves have that sharp lemon taste which adds 'bite' to early salads. It is also the basis of the famous French sauce—'sauce verte'.

Here too can be found the Welsh onion (*Allium fistulosum*). Resembling coarse chives the leaves remain green all year round and can be used to give a mild onion flavour. It is a mystery why it is known as Welsh onion because this particular variety is grown extensively in China and Japan, the word 'fistulosum' meaning foreign.

As is fitting for a good cook, Mrs Merton is very proud of her large and well-flavoured garlic. Her advice is to plant the cloves during October for harvesting the following year. Although a slightly off-beat procedure, the results speak for themselves.

Mediterranean plants, herbs, shrub roses and rare treasures grow together in happy

Sink gardens

At the Old Rectory, Burghfield, a collection of sinks have been arranged together to form the basis of a herb garden. Since most herbs will grow well in sinks, provided there is adequate drainage, this is an idea that can be adapted for use in your own garden.

For herbs with low-growing roots choose the shallow stone variety. These will look extremely decorative when arranged on a base of bricks to reach a height of about 1ft (30cm). Just as eye-catching if you treat the outside with a mixture of peat, sand and cement are the deep white porcelain sinks which are more readily available.

To prepare the sink for planting put a layer of gravel or broken pots in the base and then build up with a good potting compost. Water well before planting. Perennial herbs do well in sinks and only need an occasional boost of liquid fertilizer or an extra layer of compost to grow well throughout the year.

Culinary herbs to plant in a sink garden include balm, chives, hyssop, marjoram, mint, parsley, sage, savory and thyme.

Ornamental herbs suitable for planting in a sink garden are bergamot, chamomile, geranium, hyssop, juniper, lavender, lemon verbena, marigold and nasturtium.

profusion in this much-loved garden which occupies much of Mrs Merton's time.

In one corner a collection of sinks looking like a series of miniature gardens are filled with mints, thymes, marjoram, heartsease pansies and other herbal delights.

In complete contrast a large lake boasts a magnificent statue purchased from the famous sale at Wilton. Dramatic tales are told of the problems of siting this very heavy statue in the centre of the lake. Another story is the excitement of discovering that it was a true Roman statue having at one time been the property of Cardinal Mazarin.

CLAVERTON MANOR

The American Museum in Britain, Claverton Manor, Bath, Somerset

Telephone: Bath (0225) 60503   **Owner:** The American Museum in Britain

Situation: 3–4m SE of Bath via Warminster road (A36) and Claverton village, 2½m from Bath station, via Bathwick Hill. **Open:** March–October, 2–5pm daily except Mondays, also bank holidays. During winter, on application only.

A gift of the Southampton (New York) Garden Club, the herb garden at Claverton Manor is square in shape and quite small, which would have suited the early pioneers' wives. It shows that a wide variety of sweet smelling and useful plants can be grown tidily and make an attractive feature in an area approximately 12ft (3.6m) square.

With a backdrop of an impressive stone house built in the early part of the nineteenth century, the garden has paving-stone slabs as a surround and these make an interesting contrast to the edging of a double row of cobble stones. In the centre is a traditional beehive set among sweetly scented herbs and a circle of paving stones. To reach this central path there are two more paths so it really is possible to touch and study all the lovely aromatic plants that grow so well here.

First on the list of herbs must be lemon thyme (*Thymus × citriodorus*) with glossy green leaves and a rich heavy scent. Beekeepers will appreciate that with lemon thyme growing, bees do not stray far from the hive. Another delicious scented plant is lemon balm (*Melissa officinalis*). The name 'Melissa' is derived from the Greek word meaning honey, and it is one of the many herbs with attractive foliage.

It is worth pausing to study the large ornamental display board outlining the herbs used for dyeing; the herbs mentioned grow nearby. When this display was being planned in 1964, many of these plants had been neglected or forgotten in England. Even Margaret Brownlow, the director of the famous herb farm at Seal and author of *Herbs and the Fragrant Garden*, was surprised to learn about the American custom of growing dye-plants in a herb garden—or more appropriately, herb yard.

Dawn Macleod worked with the American Museum during 1964 helping them with the design of the herb garden and advising generally on the sale of herbs. She found as a point of interest when working on the display board that many herbs, for instance tansy (*Tanacetum vulgare*), had been used at different times for medicinal and culinary purposes, as a fragrant herb and as a dyestuff.

Among the colouring herbs at Claverton is woad (*Isatis tinctoria*), formerly used to

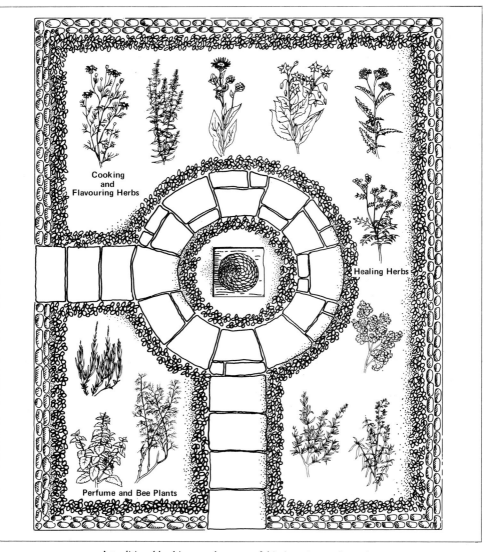

A traditional beehive sets the scene of this American-style garden
at Claverton Manor.

dye homespun clothing a rich blue. Another herb yielding blue is indigo (*Indigofera tinctoria*) which is not so smelly as woad and easier to cultivate. Alkanet (*Anchusa tinctoria*) grows to a height of about 4ft (1.2m) with bright blue flowers; the root of this herb was used for production of maroon red dyes. Weld (*Reseda luteola*) provides a yellow dye when the whole of the plant is simmered in a dye-pot.

Take time to visit the Mount Vernon garden, just a short walk away from the herb garden. Here you become aware once again of the importance of the exchange of plant materials and ideas. In 1785, the Fairfax family sent a variety of plants and

54

seeds (and a farmer) over to Virginia to assist George Washington, the first President of the United States, to enlarge his garden. Here you see a replica of this same garden, with roses and other colourful flowers growing in beds neatly edged with box. It is fascinating and somewhat awe inspiring to see the very same species of plants that a busy man would have cared for in his garden. This garden was a gift of the Colonial Dames of America.

On the fine wide terrace running round the house are some mophead bay trees of about 7ft (2.1m) in height and 4ft (1.2m) across the top. Their setting against this magnificent stone house is in perfect proportion.

The herb shop, a very busy emporium, presents a display of home-dyed yarn from local plants; and the colours are soft and subtle. Here you may find a 'tussie mussie', a small nosegay of fresh herbs and flowers arranged artistically for colour, shape and fragrance. The history of the tussie mussie goes back to the days when ladies of noble birth would not venture out without their delicately perfumed nosegay of flowers to insulate them from disease and the less than pleasant smells of the streets of our cities.

The type of herbs you will find in this lovely garden at Claverton Manor would have been needed for survival by those brave pilgrims who crossed the Atlantic in the seventeenth century. As Ann Leighton tells us in her *Early English Gardens in New England*, herbs were needed for 'meate and medicine'. Next to a roof, a garden was a necessity of life. Medicine and cookery went hand in hand and were the responsibility of the housewife.

Cathleen Maxwell, in *The Claverton Herbal*, points out that when America was colonized, in the early sixteenth century, it was still the custom in Europe for the good housewife to have a working knowledge of the growing, drying, distilling, and use of herbs for simple medicinal remedies, as well

as for flavourings, perfumes and dyes.

An assortment of useful seeds and plants therefore formed part of the very restricted luggage of the early settlers. One of these, according to early American accounts, was spearmint, a herb supposed to have been brought to England by the Romans, who regarded it as an excellent appetizer, as well as an aid to failing memory. Pennyroyal was another herb that crossed the Atlantic early; it was probably used to purify the water on many emigrant ships. Plantain, one of our commonest weeds, probably reached North America inadvertently in sacks of seedcorn. The Indians observed it growing around the white men's settlements and called it 'White Men's Footsteps', attributing to it strong magic, especially in curing the effects of snakebite.

Besides seeds and plants, the more educated and prosperous settler might own a 'herball'—a list of plants with a full description of their appearance, cultivation and use. The most famous of these, published in the late sixteenth and early seventeenth centuries were Turner's, Gerard's and Parkinson's. Then, in 1657, came one written by a physician named Nicholas Culpeper, an exponent of astrological botany. This became so popular, particularly in America, that no crop was planted or harvested without consulting one of the many almanacs of the day, to make sure that the stars were in their right conjunctions.

Settlers who made contact with the Indian tribes found that they were another useful source of information. The beautiful bergamot (*Monarda didyma*), whose lovely red flowers and subtle scent give so much pleasure during August, was a herb much used by native tribes. Bergamot tea has a pleasant refreshing taste and was appreciated all the more by the colonists after they had tipped the imported tea into Boston harbour to avoid paying heavy taxes. The Boston Tea Party, one of the incidents that heralded the American War of Independence, was yet one more occasion that gave herbs a role to play in the making of our history.

The many rooms of Claverton Manor are furnished to illustrate significant episodes in the development of American civilization. Herb enthusiasts will find the Shaker room with its simple but beautiful high slat-back chairs hanging from the walls of special interest. The Shakers were a religious group living in small communities and cultivating herbs commercially for medicinal purposes. They hoped to make enough money to support themselves, though their needs were few. After their evening meal, they would hang their high slat-backed chairs from a beam and dance away. This was their only form of amusement, as their lives were guided by the principles of order, utility and harmony.

Attracting bees

The beehive in the middle of the garden at Claverton Manor is symbolic of the association herbs and bees have always enjoyed.

Watching the bees at work on apple or plum blossoms makes you realize how important they are for the pollination of our fruit. It may be a surprise to learn that it is colour rather than scent that first attracts bees, and they find their way to yellow, blue, mauve and purple flowers.

Since there are so many different kinds of gardens why not include a 'Bee Garden' in your plans. Plants to include are thyme, sage, rosemary, lavender, catmint, bergamot, mint and in fact most of the sweetly scented single flowers in the colour range described above.

Should you have the misfortune to be stung by a bee, try the soothing effect of rubbing a comfrey leaf on the affected part.

CRANBORNE MANOR

Cranborne Manor Gardens, Cranborne, Wimborne, Dorset

Telephone: Cranborne (07254) 248   **Owner:** The Marquess of Salisbury

Situation: 18m N of Bournemouth. **Open:** April–October, the first Saturday and Sunday of each month, and bank holidays.

Constructed in 1956, the herb garden at Cranborne has eight beds enclosed by a tall limestone wall and yew hedges, one with 'windows' providing a glimpse of the fine trees in the surrounding pastures. Designed by Lady Salisbury on the site of an ancient burial ground, this is very much a secret garden, for until a narrow entrance cut into the yew hedge is passed the visitor cannot tell what he or she will see. As such, it reflects the style of earlier gardens—the need for enclosure against bands of vagabonds and animals and the practice of dividing the beds with wide grassy paths along which to stroll and appreciate the aromas and subtle tones of the herbs.

The paths in Cranborne's herb garden lead to a wide circular grass path with a stone sundial in the centre. The eight beds are arranged symmetrically and are all

A glimpse of the secret garden at Cranborne.

edged with cotton lavender (*Santolina incana*). The visitor thus views the garden not as a number of separate plots but as a well-constructed picture, the silver edging unifying them in a most pleasing fashion. Eight honeysuckles trained into standards with mopheads of flowers stand at the edges of the beds, accentuating the circular grass walkway.

Although created comparatively recently, the Cranborne herb garden serves to recall that a herb garden such as this had a special function—to provide aromatic, culinary and medicinal plants for house, kitchen and still-room.

There are many varieties of thyme growing well in the chalky soil and between the foliage herbs are groups of colourful and sweet smelling flowers. Scented tulips, a Salisbury 'speciality' introduced during the early part of the eighteenth century, are a spring-time feature. In the early summer a long border of lily-of-the-valley edged with chives and backed by a rose hedge has great appeal, running as it does along the length of the garden.

Old-fashioned roses are a favourite with Lady Salisbury and their heady perfume drifts right through the garden. They are carefully labelled and you will find the bourbon 'Honorine de Brabant' with pale lilac flowers, the gallica 'Tricolore de Flandre' with double striped flowers and 'Maiden's Blush' which has pearly-pink flowers.

Another aromatic touch is a seat with lemon verbena (*Lippia citriodora*) on either side and groups of sweetly scented shrubs within easy reach.

The knot garden

The knot garden planted as recently as 1971 is a particularly fine example of the art. It has four sections, each edged with dwarf box to give a sense of unity and a twisted spiral box bush as contrast. Being an open knot, the garden may be entered rather than just looked at from outside. Depending on the

Underneath the arches

Apart from the herb garden and the broadwalk, Cranborne has so much to offer the visitor—and not least is the apple arch. The trees have been trained to make a fruitful fence along each side of the path and to form loops overhead, the apples hanging down all ready to drop, it would seem, into welcoming hands.

Although something of a major project, testing patience and endurance, such an arch can be constructed today and will bring both hard work and rewards for many years.

You will need a number of lengths of iron to form the framework, each bent to a curve so that they allow a pathway of 6ft 8in (2m) and give head clearance of 7ft 6in (2.3m); they should be spaced 6ft 9in (2m) apart and embedded firmly into the ground. Run three lengths of stout wire along each side of the walkway to link the arches; the first 12in (30cm) from the ground, the second 24in (60cm) and the third 36in (90cm).

This somewhat shaky structure is enough to support young trees which will eventually be the stronger element.

---

time of year, it is filled with crocus, narcissi, iris, scented tulips, gold-laced polyanthus and varieties of violas and pinks which so amazed the gardeners and flower-lovers of days gone by. A fine statue and a garden seat surrounded by scented plants complete a romantic scene.

Cranborne has much else to offer, not least being a mount covered by shrub roses and 'made to be clambered up to view a fair prospect.'

Lady Salisbury first saw Cranborne when she was fourteen years old. But the original vision stayed with her and, as stated in the book *The Englishwoman's Garden*, she married into the garden here. She was influenced by the work of John Tradescant, the seventeenth-century gardener who travelled widely in Europe and America for the Salisbury family, collecting rare plants for the gardens at Cranborne and Hatfield. It was George Eliot who observed that a garden should be 'pleasant to the eye and good for food'. As the visitors might agree, George Eliot would find little to complain about at Cranborne.

THE ROMAN PALACE AND MUSEUM

Salthill Road, Fishbourne, Chichester, Sussex

Telephone: Chichester (0243) 785859   **Owner:** The Sussex Archaeological Society

Situation: 1½m W of Chichester. Turn off the A27 into Salthill Road. **Open:** Every day March–November. During March, April and October, 10am–5pm; May–September, 10am–6pm; November, 10am–4pm. December–February, Sundays only, 10am–4pm.

Excavations carried out at the Roman palace of Fishbourne have revealed traces of a garden built in the first century at the time of the Roman occupation. Part of this has now been replanted and visitors can enjoy the unusual experience of walking along neatly clipped box-hedged pathways, recalling the fine style the Romans introduced with their architecture and gardening skills.

Herbs, it is believed, came to this country with the Romans who used them for flavouring their highly seasoned sauces and other haute cuisine dishes. Bay, basil, fennel, hyssop, rue, parsley, pennyroyal, thyme and dill are all mentioned in the writings of Pliny and other poets of the day. Herbs were also needed for garlands and decorations for festivals. Rose petals were showered on important guests and the perfume was much appreciated by Roman matrons.

Students of history and herb enthusiasts can learn much from the museum which relates the history of Fishbourne from the days of the initial military base until its destruction by fire in about AD 270.

Details are given of some of the beautiful and useful aromatic plants that it is thought would have decorated this garden. These include rosemary, rue, madonna lily and roses. Another important Roman herb, acanthus (*Acanthus mollis*), is featured in the museum. The glossy leaves with wavy outlines were used as a model for the decorative element on the famous Corinthian pillars, which gave the plant a place in posterity.

Today the northern half of the original plan of Fishbourne has been reconstructed. This consists of a lawn enclosed by a box hedge planted in double, and sometimes triple, layers. Alcoves have been built into the hedge where statues or seats would originally have been sited. Along one avenue, fruit trees have been planted to reproduce part of the original design.

A sales area has been started by the enterprising gardener working here, and visitors have a chance to start their own collection of herbs grown in Roman days. The plants, neatly labelled, are set out on three-tier stands. Behind are large display

---

Roman elegance

A small town garden enclosed by walls would make the perfect situation for recreating a Roman peristyle or courtyard garden. Remembering that garden ornaments were the great love of Roman senators, you would need to include a statue, a stone seat and a fountain to complete the image.

Having set the scene in this way add a low hedge of box (*Buxus sempervirens*) and other plants as needed. Myrtle (*Myrtus communis*) could find a home here with its deep-green glossy leaves and fragrant white flowers. Other favourites of Roman days would include violets, roses and lilies. And find a place for bear's breeches (*Acanthus mollis*), that noble plant with purple or white spiky flowers that looks so dramatic in July and August growing to a height of about 3ft (90cm).

A Roman garden such as this was considered to be an outside room. It was embellished with garden ornaments and shady evergreen plants as a place where conversation on literary, artistic and political affairs could be carried on.

---

boards giving details of herbs grown during the Roman occupation (AD 70–270) and the uses of the plants.

HOLLINGTON NURSERIES

Woolton Hill, Newbury, Berkshire

Telephone: Highclere (0635) 253908   **Owner:** Simon and Judith Hopkinson

Situation: 3½m S of Newbury and signposted to Woolton Hill from the A343. **Open:** April–September, Tuesday–Saturday, 10am–1pm, 2–5.30pm; Sunday, 11am–1pm, 2–4pm. October–March, Tuesday, Wednesday and Thursday, 10am–1pm; Friday and Saturday 10am–1pm, 2–4.30pm.

The old walled garden of Hollington House makes an ideal setting for this herb nursery which specializes in selling container-grown plants and herb garden design.

It is difficult to realize that when Simon and Judith Hopkinson bought the garden in 1976 it was, to use their own words, 'chin high in weeds and rusting bedsteads'. Now every inch of the garden is under cultivation. About three hundred different herbs are cultivated for sale and many of these can be seen growing in the attractive display garden which gives customers the chance of assessing how the mature plant will look.

Attractive borders of mixed planting line a wide grass path which leads into a traditional square garden enclosed with wooden palings and a sweetbriar hedge.

Sages, thymes, parsley and mint all grow here, but there are also some unusual herbs to tempt the connoisseur. For instance arnica (*Arnica montana*) which is also suitable for rockeries and has golden yellow flowers growing from a rosette of downy green leaves. A tincture made from the whole plant is useful for relieving sprains and bruises. Another of the herbal plants quite at home in the rock garden is the popular houseleek (*Sempervivum tectorum*). Reaching a height of only 6in (15cm) the leaves are pinkish–green, succulent and used for soothing insect bites. A popular plant for growing in sinks and ornamental containers, the houseleek spreads rapidly. In olden days it grew on house roofs and was reputed to have powers of safeguarding buildings against fire and lightning.

A pot of thyme at Hollington.

Wide paths lead from the display garden through beds of stock plants. Cuttings are taken from these to be potted on in the many plastic tunnels occupying one side of the nursery. The rows of neatly labelled plants are for visiting customers to buy and for dispatch to local garden centres.

The Hopkinsons run their herb enterprise as a partnership. Judith chooses which plants to grow and looks after the propagating side. She considers tarragon and basil to be two of the best sellers. At least eight different

An impression of Hollington Nursery's award-winning garden at Chelsea

varieties of basil are grown. Bush basil (*Ocimum minimum*) has the traditional warm aroma and a mass of tiny leaves. Then there is the lovely dark purple leaved basil (*Ocimum purpurea*), an unusual variety with large soft lettuce-like leaves (*Ocimum crispum*) and the holy basil (*Ocimum sanctum*).

The one they recommend for providing the best flavour with tomatoes and other Italian cookery is sweet basil (*Ocimum basilicum*).

It is rather confusing to learn that a plant resembling basil and in fact known as wild basil (*Clinopodium vulgare*) is not a true basil at all. As Judith explains, 'This is just one of the snags herb growers have with country names and shows the need for using botanical names.'

Hollington Nurseries have several rare trees and shrubs for sale to discerning customers and specialize in providing olive trees (*Olea europaea*). This small tree with dark green oblong leaves can grow outside but needs a sunny sheltered spot to encourage flowering and the fruit to ripen.

Simon Hopkinson concentrates on the marketing side. His exhibits at the Chelsea Flower Show have delighted visitors for the last few years, winning many compliments. In 1983 their show garden was awarded the highest accolade of all—A Gold Medal.

Burying the sage

If your favourite sage plant is developing middle-age spread and your thymes have a bald patch near the centre, take a tip from the experts.

Taking care to leave soil around the roots, dig the plant out and then with sharp scissors or pruning clippers give the foliage a good trim, back and sides, getting rid of dead and dying material and any flowering heads.

Next, dig a large hole and bury the plant so that only 1in (2.5cm) or so is above the surface. Water well and label.

Within a few weeks, or in the spring if you do the work in the autumn, the stems should be a mass of roots, enabling you to exhume the plant, cut off and set out individual pieces and discard (or, if you wish, replant) the mother herb.

This technique may be employed with many plants, including pineapple sage and hyssop. Lavender and other shrublike plants are also suitable candidates for this seemingly barbaric but highly effective treatment.

SUTTON MANOR

Sutton Scotney (Nr Winchester), Hampshire

Telephone: Winchester (0962) 760586   **Owner:** The Sutman Trust

Situation: Just off the A34 N of Winchester. **Open:** April–October, Wednesday–Sunday, 10am–6pm (7pm June–August); bank or public holidays during the season 10am–7pm.

A herb garden featuring many rare and exotic species, a sculpture park presenting twentieth-century works of art in an open air setting and the staging of musical concerts and theatrical events are just some of the delights in store at Sutton Manor.

Based on a house once owned by Lord Rank, the property was acquired by the Sutman Trust in 1981 and extensive restoration is under way. It is hoped that with the leadership of the energetic and enthusiastic director, Alex Herbage, Sutton Manor will play a leading role in the life of the community.

The first glimpse through wrought-iron gates is of roses and herbs growing amicably together. A splendid brick wall with ridge-tiled coping encloses the herb garden which has the advantage of a south-west facing slope, and each of the square 'plats' or herb beds is divided into triangles and planted with four different varieties. (Occasionally if the herb grows vigorously this is restricted to two.)

There is no evidence of herbs being chosen for their culinary, medicinal or historic interest and it is rather a puzzle at first to know how the planting has been organized. However, Mr Fred Broomham, the head gardener here for twenty years and responsible for the garden, explained that he had tried to ensure that herbs with foliage appeal should be planted with herbs with colourful flowers. As he said, 'I split the colours'; and so nasturtiums, cornflowers, marigolds, borage and bergamots are planted with mints, sages, marjorams, lovage and pennyroyal. Throughout the garden there is always some herb in flower to attract attention and provide a useful source of nectar for the bees.

Mr Broomham has become completely fascinated with growing herbs and is a fund of useful information. 'Herb growing', he explains, 'takes up the whole year. First there is the seed to sow, then it is cuttings and harvesting. After that since we save our

A splendid brick wall makes an attractive backdrop for herbs at Sutton Manor.

own seed there is that to do, and then it is time to divide plants.'

In this garden can be seen the largest herb, elecampane (*Inula helenium*), which grows to a height of over 6ft (1.8m) with

Lemon verbena—an unforgettable fragrance

Like many beautiful people, lemon verbena (*Lippia citriodora*) will not thrive in a windy spot and insists on a well-drained location. It is best suited to large pots or wooden tubs and makes an ideal greenhouse plant. It can easily be moved into its growing area when the frost has gone.

There are many ways in which you can use this herb. Try blending one or two leaves with tea and enjoy an aromatic 'brew'. The leaves add a lemon flavour to a sponge cake. Just add one or two leaves to the tin after you have

greased the base. Another good idea is to brighten up the flavour of stewed apple by adding a leaf or two while it is cooking.

The dried leaves are useful in pot-pourri and herbal bags, either to scent your clothes or pop under your pillow to help you sleep. They offer an unforgettable fragrance and blend well with rose petals, lavender and other scented herbs to provide a long lasting reminder of hazy, summer days.

enormous ovate leaves. The smallest is the tiny Corsican mint (*Mentha requienii*) which reaches only about $\frac{1}{2}$in (1cm). With minute leaves and a strong peppermint scent, this tiny plant is perfect for growing between paving stones or for cushions in a herb seat.

All the herbs growing here are on sale as container-grown plants. And the thriving garden centre also sells chrysanthemums, carnations and many other home-grown specialities.

Other exciting enterprises to make Sutton Manor an important herbal centre are under way. New laboratories are to be built for full-scale herbal research. As well as investigating the properties of native plants such as feverfew and digitalis, Alex Herbage hopes to build up interest and knowledge in the use of herbs in the undeveloped and developing countries. When thoroughly researched, these may prove a great asset in providing remedies in countries where the cost of western drugs is prohibitive.

In conjunction with this project, over a thousand different tropical plants, many with reputed medical properties, are being planted in the glasshouses. An expedition to Kashmir to collect plants is being sponsored by the trust and all herb seed collected is to be grown at Sutton Manor under controlled conditions.

Many herb gardens are recreations of past glories, but the one at Sutton Manor is taking a gigantic leap into the future. A new form of gardening is taking shape where it is hoped the power of plants will have an important role to play in helping to create a better world.

TUDOR MUSEUM, SOUTHAMPTON

The Tudor Garden Museum, St Michael's Square, Southampton

Telephone: Southampton (0703) 24216   **Owner:** Southampton Corporation

Situation: In Southampton. **Open:** Tuesday–Friday, 10am–5pm; Saturday, 10am–4pm and 2–5pm.

The Tudor House Museum, overlooking Southampton Water and within a stone's throw of the city's West Gate, can now include among its treasures an authentic sixteenth-century-style garden.

The entire garden is approximately 30yd (27.5m) square and is typical of a small town or 'privvy' garden which would have acted as a model for latter-day herb gardens. It follows the instructions of the sixteenth-century writer William Lawson who says of his ideal garden in *The Countrie Huswife's Garden* that it should be 'square and encompassed on all the four sides with a stately arched hedge'. There is a fine selection of Tudor features to be discovered in this enclosed yard.

A seat, hidden by honeysuckle and sweetbriar along one side of the garden is typical of the arbour or 'herber'. Here lovers could (and perhaps still do today) meet and whisper sweet nothings to each other far from prying eyes.

The knot garden has been based on a pattern taken from *The Gardener's Labyrinth* by Didymus Montaine (this being the pen-name of the sixteenth-century writer Thomas Hyll). A similar design was found on one of the carved panels of the Tudor House Museum, illustrating the use of the same pattern books by gardeners and woodworkers.

This central knot is slightly raised and wooden palings run along the sides to support the earth. Edged with cotton lavender, dwarf box criss-crosses the gardens and spaces in between are filled with coloured earth. Originally, gravel, coal dust, sand and chalk were used to create interesting textures in such a garden. Following the expeditions of Tradescant and other intrepid collectors, new discoveries found their way into knot gardens and the fashion for using coloured earth declined.

Perhaps most intriguing of all is the private or wild garden. This contains a collection of Tudor gardening parapher-nalia and a few treasured plants that can just be seen through a gap in the wall.

A straw bee skep in the seventeenth-century wall enclosing this garden has become a home for a swarm of present day bees. This is just one of the many things that delights Mrs Sylvia Landsberg, the designer of the garden. A dedicated historian and gardener, she has studied the herbals of Gerard and Parkinson and the gardening books of Thomas Hyll and Thomas Tusser. She also consulted experts on the subject for detailed information, attended every exhibition she could, and steeped herself completely in Tudor-style gardening before beginning work here.

The result is a garden that brings history

A herber of sweet scents

A herber, similar to the one planted in the Tudor Museum at Southampton with scented climbers growing up to enclose the seat, can make a pleasant place to spend a sunny afternoon in a twentieth-century garden. To construct a similar model, choose a place where you can enjoy the late sunshine but where the sun is not shining directly into your eyes.

You will need eight rustic poles of about 8ft (2.4m) in length, which can be obtained at your local garden centre. Insert four of these firmly into the ground to a depth of 2ft (60cm) and cut the remaining poles into lengths suffi-ciently long to make a framework around the upright poles. This will add the necessary strength. Once completed, sweetly scented ramblers can be planted around the base and will soon turn your garden seat into a fragrant leafy boudoir.

Make your choice from among the following plants:

Honeysuckle (*Lonicera periclymenum*) This deciduous climber soon attains a height of 15ft (4.5m) and has fragrant yellow flowers streaked with pinkish-red during the summer.

Mock Orange (*Philadelphus* 'Belle Etoile')
This sweetly scented shrub grows to about 10ft (3m) with single white flowers.

Jasmine (*Jasminum officinale*)
A vigorous climber that can reach 30ft (9m) high with white flowers all the summer.

And if you want to include a fragrant rose try one of the following:

Rosa 'Albertine'
With richly scented pink flowers this climber will soon reach 20ft (6m).

Rosa 'Mermaid'
Single yellow flowers and attractive leaves that are almost evergreen. This rose is popular because it will grow in a north-facing situation and soon reaches 30ft (9m).

to life. The many Tudor features, the king's and queen's beasts, painted railings and terracotta pots are all present. Just as fascinating is the lack of different varieties of growing plants—for at this time the great adventure of plant hunting in far flung countries had hardly begun. Mrs Landsberg, claiming complete accuracy for her garden, says, 'If Queen Elizabeth the First were to visit this garden, she would recognize every plant growing.'

The knot garden at the Tudor Garden Museum was based on a pattern taken from *The Gardener's Labyrinth*; its completion is a dream come true for designer Sylvia Landsberg, who consulted many herbals and gardening books to complete the work.

THE SOUTH WEST

CASTLE DROGO

Nr Chagford, Devon

Telephone: Chagford (06473) 3306　　　　　　　**Owner:** The National Trust

Situation: 4m NE of Chagford. **Open:** April–October, every day, 11am–6pm.

Herbs are not a major feature at Castle Drogo and anyone who has travelled many miles just to visit the herb garden here is bound to be disappointed. But there is more to the place than herbs and what is known as the 'Castle Drogo experience' can turn even the shyest hedge-trimming recluse into a person of vision, at least for an hour or two.

In an area of 12 acres (4.8 hectares) which is at an altitude of 1,000ft and receives rainfall of 45in (1.1m) a year, merchant adventurer Julius Drewe and architect Edwin Lutyens began work in 1910 on designs for a house on a vast scale. They had visions of a medieval fortress on the tip of a granite spur. Only a third of what was intended eventually came to pass but the house is there, perched high like an eagle overlooking a valley planted with rhododendrons, tree magnolias, camellias, cherries and maples.

There is only one garden near the house itself and here there is a huge fig tree, which in most years bears masses of fruit, a camellia

67

A hillside setting for herbs at Castle Drogo.

and a splendid *Garrya elliptica* with its tassel-like flowers during winter and early spring.

Via a flight of granite steps you enter the main garden consisting of, perhaps surprisingly, a series of formal terraces and borders. The first terrace has a number of rectangular rose beds forming a parterre and borders devoted to white flowers on either side of the entrance. The roses are all modern cultivars and have been chosen for disease resistance and their ability to withstand wind and rain. At each corner of this terrace, arbours of yew hedges each contain four beds of shade-loving plants and four weeping trees. Originally these trees were weeping elms, but they had to be replaced in 1980 by specimens of the 'iron tree' (*Parrotia persica*) after succumbing to Dutch Elm disease. The bold geometric form of Lutyens' original concept has been interpreted in the design of the new supporting frames for these trees. The arbours are linked on either side at a high level by a serpentine path of Indian pattern and herbaceous borders full of old varieties of traditional plants.

At the head of the steps to the second terrace are groups of yuccas and wisterias growing over the retaining wall. The herb borders are edged with lavender, and prominent among the plantings are sage, rue, angelica, purple fennel and rosemary.

A double flight of steps leads up to the shrub borders designed in 1927. The sloping path leads to a huge circular lawn with a diameter of 180ft (54.9m) surrounded by a tall yew hedge. Originally the lawn was laid out for tennis, but it is now used for croquet. This vast green circle is all part of the Drogo experience in taming nature and turning it into simple architectural forms.

Sissinghurst—'divided into separate compartments
like so many outdoor rooms . . .'

The mellow grey stone walls of Beaulieu make an
excellent background for herbs.

A peaceful corner of the much-loved garden at The
Old Rectory, Burghfield.

True blue

For anyone having lost a near relative in conflict, a tiny room at Castle Drogo provides a crumb of comfort and sharing. It is a memorial to the elder son of the family; there are the familiar school and class portraits, the rowing colours, the jolly caps, the medals and, sadly, the official notification of a gallant young man lost in action.

It was such a room that made us and probably many others think of cornflowers. On regatta days the boys always used to sport a bright blue cornflower as a buttonhole, which looked most attractive on their dark navy blazers. We grew them then and a few years later a daughter at a cathedral school asked for them for the girls to wear in their blazers to celebrate St Etheldreda's Festival (25 June). It was, she disclosed somewhat shyly, a symbol of purity.

The cornflower (*Centaurea cyanus*) deserves its return to popularity and will give a lovely splash of colour to delight the eye. It is a hardy annual and grows up to 3ft (90cm). There are many varieties but as a true blue, 'Blue Diadem' would be a good choice.

Centaurea moschata or sweet sultan came originally from Persia and has white, yellow, pink or purple flowers. This grows to 18in (46cm) and is excellent for cut flowers.

Compact varieties which do not grow more than 12in (30cm) high make welcome additions to borders and are good for growing in pots. Here you might like to consider 'Dwarf Rose Gem'—as the name implies this is a real rose red; 'Jubilee Gem', vivid blue; and the 'Polka Dot' mixture in a range of colours. There are several ideas here for a silver display.

There is a tall perennial variety called *Centaurea macrocephala*, with huge yellow blooms. This is a joy to flower arrangers.

DARTINGTON HALL

Totnes, Devon

Telephone: Garden Centre—Totnes (0803) 863291   **Owner:** Dartington Hall Trust

Situation: NW of Totnes on the A384. **Open:** Except for bank holidays, all the year round; organized parties require the garden superintendent's permission. Dartington Hall Garden Centre (old walled garden and nursery area) is open 9am–1pm, 2–5pm every day including Sundays.

Herb gardens take so many forms and come in so many shapes and sizes and are used for so many purposes by so many people that an all-embracing definition could prove tedious. By the same token, it is difficult to describe a garden. This problem clearly faced Terry Underhill when he came to revise Dorothy Elmhirst's original draft of the booklet *The Gardens of Dartington Hall*, for he suggests that if the word garden implies a wealth of flowers then for Dartington it is a misnomer. Rather, as he says, this is a garden where form has dominated design and where compositions have been attempted 'using the contours of the land to intensify the natural effects of height and depth and distance'. Trees and shrubs are used to give structure to the composition and lawns to emphasize space.

This is a gentle warning that there is no

herb garden at Dartington—but herbs there are in abundance and a sense of history to go with them. Immediately on entering the great gate that leads through an archway into the enclosed and quiet fourteenth-century courtyard, the eye falls almost greedily on the rosemary and lavender growing in great bushes against the soft grey stone of the ancient buildings, so lovingly and well restored.

Roses there are in profusion, including the double yellow Banksian rose among a feast of climbers from many countries; the potato vine from South America and a winter-flowering jasmine from China are well to the fore as are Mexican orange blossom and honeysuckles, seemingly by the multitude.

A sunny border and restored tiltyard lie beyond, as does an ancient bowling green with its terraces unaltered since Elizabethan times. And among other treasures are four myrtles (*Myrtus luma*) set against the ruined arches of a medieval courtyard. This is the herb which over centuries has been carried by royal and other brides and then hurried back to the bride's new home by the bridesmaids in the hope of it rooting and bringing love and happiness to the union forever.

The sunny border, a blend of biennials, perennials and shrubs has been designed to blend with the buildings and the colour combinations here are pale yellow, purple and blue, and silver and grey. Rue has an important place as have catmint, cotton lavender and a sea of artemisia.

Dartington Hall gardens have so much else to offer—a heath bank, rose border, valley, field and Eldorado (which you must discover for yourself), upper terrace, high meadow, woodland, glade and even a bronze donkey made for its site in 1938 and beloved by generations of children.

Like so many other gardens, these at Dartington were the result of a partnership, for both Dorothy and Leonard Elmhirst were intimately concerned with their creation. Since their deaths many people have carried on this work of art which tempts one back to experience new wonders, new hope and, above all, peace, beautiful peace.

A rosemary hedge

When given a sheltered position, rosemary makes an excellent hedge and if planted with lavender there will be flowers on the hedge from the end of April until August. This type of planting can be seen at Dartington Hall in Devon where the effect of the silvery and green foliage against the stone is very restful. Treat your rosemary with respect. Do not clip it back too hard—and resist the temptation to snip little pieces off before it is properly established. Then you can follow the example of Sir Thomas More who wrote: 'As for rosemary, I let it run all over my garden walls, not only because my bees love it, but because it is the herb sacred to friendship.'

GAULDEN MANOR

Tolland, Nr Taunton, Somerset

Telephone: Lydeard St Lawrence (09847) 213   **Owner:** Mr and Mrs James Starkie

Situation: 9m NW of Taunton, signposted from the A358 N of Bishop's Lydeard, and from the B3188. **Open:** 1 May–11 September, Sunday and Thursday, 2–6pm; also on bank holidays during this period.

Herbs have played a big part in the life of Gaulden Manor for at least seven hundred years and continue to do so. At one time, when in the ownership of the priory at Taunton, it would have provided fish from its pond and herbs from its gardens for the monks and could well have been the source of certain aromatic and medicinal plants for the New World. In 1628 Henry Wolcott left his family home here to embark with the early settlers for America and many members of the Wolcott family now living overseas return to visit what they regard as their ancestral home.

Gaulden Manor is now owned by Mr and Mrs Starkie who look on it very much as a home to be lived in and enjoyed, but also as part of a continuing historical trust. Both keen gardeners, they have created from a paddock the series of different gardens which surrounds the house. As Mrs Starkie says, 'It has become known as the Little Gardens of Gaulden.'

One of these was the herb garden planted in 1974 with the Brendon Hills in the background. It is truly a little garden with such a character of its own that it is not difficult to imagine monks of the past returning to plant once again herbs for flavouring their food and for healing potions to treat the sick and aged in their care.

In the traditional shape of a cross, the garden is divided into four separate beds. Ancient apple trees and an elder hedge interspersed with hawthorn form green and leafy boundaries.

Inside the garden the brick paths lead to a sundial which tells all who care to pause the time,

> Shadow round about my face
> The sunny hours of day will trace.

The whole aspect is one of peace and beauty enriched by the many shrub roses dropping their scented petals. As Mrs Starkie explains, 'Perhaps it is not over-neat, but it is full of interest.' It is indeed, and no one will find it surprising that visitors return

A secret garden

In truth a secret garden should not be seen at all, or only discovered with the utmost difficulty, and so it is at Gaulden Manor. Here the secret garden is reached only after surmounting the obstacles of a lake and the woods.

A secret garden is a place of retreat from the ever demanding telephone and the persistent whirring of the lawn-mower. Not much space is needed but there should be room for a seat, preferably one painted white, and perhaps a willow-leaved pear (*Pyrus salcifolia* 'Pendula') like the one at Gaulden Manor.

As ground cover grow sweetly scented silver-leaved lavender, set a gleaming curry plant or two and have several carefully chosen members of the artemisia family. A clump of white foxgloves would add a special sense of woodland mystery to the scene.

Neat, and compact—the herb garden at Gaulden Manor.

year after year to enjoy a magic afternoon in this sweetly scented garden.

The back of the herb garden contains a touching memorial to a pet dog, Carlo, killed in 1974. Behind this an impressive comfrey hedge (*Symphytum officinale*) grows to a height of about 5ft (1.5m) with a mixture of pink, white and purple flowers. How practical, we thought, upon first seeing the hedge. Comfrey contains a rich source of protein, minerals and vitamins. Its root contains a jelly-like substance which was used in country medicines to help heal fractured bones, hence the old names knit-bone and bone set. Although a rampant grower, the plant can be put to good use today. The leaves, and indeed the whole plant, will soon mulch down if cut and left in a pile to rot. This makes an extremely useful compost, rich in potash and beneficial for tomatoes and soft fruit.

The herb garden is just one of the many 'little gardens' created by the Starkie family. The view garden, surrounded by more shrub roses, is a restful place in which to spend half an hour gazing over the distant hills. The bog garden has a fine planting of lilies and beyond is a secret garden planted with white and silver shrubs and roses. A silver-leaved pear has pride of place here.

The return walk takes the visitor through a bank overflowing with sweet-smelling shrub roses into a small terrace garden known as the Bishop's Garden. This has more formal planting with tubs of agapanthus and geraniums.

Book lovers will enjoy browsing in the small shop overlooking the herb garden. There are books on gardening, herbs, history and the local countryside which reflect Mrs Starkie's own tastes. As she confesses—'These are all the books I would like to own.'

LACKHAM COLLEGE OF AGRICULTURE

Lacock, Chippenham, Wiltshire

Telephone: Chippenham (0249) 656111   **Owner:** Wiltshire County Council

Situation: On the A350 Chippenham to Melksham road. **Open:** Several times a year for the National Gardens Scheme and other charities, also college open day. Parties may visit any afternoon or evening by prior arrangement.

Lackham College, established by the Wiltshire County Council, offers courses in agricultural, horticultural and rural home economic subjects. The students have the run of a farm attached to the college grounds and maintain the gardens to a high standard under the watchful eyes of their tutors.

In a splendid walled garden, the large herb garden is laid out in chequerboard style. Concrete paving slabs 2ft (60cm) square alternate with squares of individually planted herbs. Altogether there are seventy-two paving slabs and over eighty different herbs.

This design works well, particularly when the purpose of the garden is to study single species. A smaller garden planned on these lines would be very sensible for the housewife wanting to use herbs for culinary purposes. It makes it so easy to pick a bunch of herbs without getting muddy feet.

All the cookery herbs, mints in flower-pots sunk in the ground to restrict growth, marjoram, chervil, coriander, lemon balm, dill and basil, to name just a few, are here. But there are also ornamental and unusual ones such as Jerusalem sage, jumbo garlic, vervain, camphor and mace.

Surprises may be in store too, as Mr Menhinick, the head of the horticultural department, explains: 'There are always minor losses, and although replacements are made we are a dynamic garden and not a museum of set specimens.'

As befits a training college there is a very good irrigation system, but according to the

A charming millstone setting for herbs at Lackham College.

supervisor it is the generous mulch of compost and leafmould that keeps the soil in such good condition.

Other chequerboard styled beds in the walled garden contain collections of plants suitable for 'ground cover' or 'low labour' and one bed is set out with ornamental grasses.

Stone sinks are filled with thyme and marjoram; and along one wall, large modern heated glasshouses provide a controlled

75

environment for a range of tropical plants, early salad crops and plant propagation.

Unusual vegetables are grown such as endives, aubergines, Florence fennel, Hamburg parsley and the Japanese white celery known as 'pak-choi'. Tests are carried out on all these vegetables to see how they respond to cultivation, like the herbs and they too are used for cookery in the home economics department.

Bees are kept in a special unit and a special beekeepers' open day is held during the year. The main yield of nectar is said to come from the lime trees but judging by the number of bees working in the herb garden this too must play some part in the production of honey.

The full-time student at Lackham College is lucky to have the advantage of such beautiful surroundings. Equally fortunate are the thousands of visitors who come every year to study plants grown under controlled conditions and discover the answers to their own gardening problems.

Chequerboard style

For many people one of the most practical designs for a herb garden, as shown so well at Lackham College, is a chequerboard planting. It is a style that can be adapted to gardening on a small scale. The concrete slabs that form the basis of the pattern are easily obtained from garden centres and can be interchanged with other materials at intervals to provide variety. Occasional empty squares may be filled with gravel or cobblestones. Remember always that the herbs should be available for inspection and use without the need always to wear wellington boots.

Mrs Nixon at Farm Hill Herbs in Northern Ireland has planned a similar garden using this clever mixture of decorative, culinary, medicinal, annual and perennial herbs:

Space 1: Angelica, dill, peppermint
Space 2: Thyme, hyssop, sorrel
Space 3: Sorrel, southernwood, chamomile
Space 4: Chervil, anise, nasturtium
Space 5: Lavender, tansy, borage
Space 6: Rosemary, caraway, comfrey

The stones are laid in chessboard style with alternating squares filled in the above order.

LYTES CARY MANOR

Ilchester, Somerset

Owner: The National Trust

Situation: W side of the A37 (Fosse Way) 2½m NE of Ilchester signposted from the bypass A303.
Open: March–October, Wednesday and Saturday, 2–6pm.

This uncomplicated Somerset manor house was the home of the Lyte family for over four hundred years. In Elizabethan days plants grown in the garden here were studied to form the basis of Sir Henry Lyte's *Niewe Herball* published in 1578.

Lyte was a keen amateur gardener with a knowledge of botany but was not, as far as

Herbs where Sir Henry would have walked at
Lytes Cary.

we know, an apothecary. The author and historian Kay Sanecki describes him aptly: 'He appears as a typical neatly cropped Elizabethan gentleman with trim pointed beard and waxed moustache. A sleeveless cloak is worn over his ruff-necked tunic and in his left hand he holds a squarish book, presumably a herbal, and in his right a six-petalled flower.'

In 1578 Lyte translated freely into English the *Cruydeboeck* of Dodoens, and this became known simply as *A Niewe Herball*. He dedicated this to Queen Elizabeth from 'my poore house at Lytescarie within your Majesties Countie of Somerset the first day of Januarie MDLXXVIII'. An early copy with numerous marginal corrections and notes is kept at the British Library.

Henry Lyte cultivated a physic garden here and this is referred to by the seventeenth-century writer John Aubrey, who says of Lyte, 'He had a pretty good collection of plants for that age, some few whereof are yet alive.'

Now cared for by the National Trust there is little to be seen of the original garden. But since a visit here is of historic interest to herb lovers it is worth knowing a little about the present day layout.

All the Elizabethan plants which Lyte would have known and grown for their health-giving qualities, catmint, various lilies, lavender, rue, southernwood and the old-fashioned scented sweet peas grow in happy profusion along a south-facing border, and behind them a yellow Banksian rose, a passion flower and myrtle climb up against the house wall.

The garden, which extends to about 3 acres (1.2 hectares), is laid out as a series of carefully planned compartments. One contains a wide border designed by Graham Thomas and is full of scented flowers with herbal overtones. Plantings of purple sage backed by soft crimson-leaved *Rosa rubrifolia* illustrate the charm of using shades of one colour. Another group consists of white roses with clumps of silver-leaved artemisia, and behind them a cream-coloured honeysuckle appears over the wall. Opposite this colourful border is a well-trimmed yew hedge with clipped buttresses forming alcoves for ornamental stone vases. This adds to the classical setting.

The front of the house, complete with small chapel, has a quiet restful garden with stone flagged paths, extensive lawns and topiary yew bushes which lead the eye to a fine dovecote. And it is here, through a gap in the wall, that it would be no surprise to see the bearded figure of Sir Henry Lyte approaching ready to discuss the healing properties of sage or how to restrict the mint that will spread into all parts of the garden. Just the questions in fact which gardeners today concern themselves with.

Collecting old herbals

Most people who love herb gardening also love to study old herbals and the story of Lytes Cary may well inspire many to begin such a collection.

Collecting originals can be an expensive hobby but copies and later editions can often be found at the book markets, now being held regularly in large towns at weekends. If you are keen to begin collecting, study the local paper for dates and places. There are also specialist dealers who supply herbals by post and will forward their mailing lists. Just occasionally you see a herbal reduced in price because it has a page missing or the cover is damaged.

The revival of interest in the use of herbs has meant that many old herbals are being reprinted today. These new editions are worth buying because they contain explanatory notes concerning the author and interesting notes on his original work.

Herbs and the Fragrant Garden by Margaret Brownlow, first published in 1957, has been a bible to us in all our gardening activities. Margaret Brownlow also wrote *The Delights of Herb Growing*, which includes the story of the planning of the herb garden at Knole. These editions are still available at second-hand book shops and must increase in value if kept in good condition.

Other authors to watch out for include Mrs C. F. Leyel with her *Herbal Delights*. Mrs Leyel opened the first Culpeper shop in London in 1927 and with Mrs Grieve produced the best-selling *A Modern Herbal*. This book was first published in 1931 and is still a standard reference on herbs today.

Also look out for the works of Eleanour Sinclar Rohde, a distinguished scholar who spent much of her life studying and writing about herbs and herb gardens. One of her works was *The Old English Herbals*, published during the 1920s.

THE OLD BARN

Fremington, Nr Barnstaple, Devon

Telephone: Barnstaple (0271) 73873 **Owner:** Mr and Mrs A. Vousden

Situation: 4m W of Barnstaple on the A39 Barnstaple to Bideford road. **Open:** For charities including the National Gardens Scheme.

Hidden behind this delightful converted Devon barn is a treasure trove of herbs and scented plants in a garden which Mr and Mrs Vousden tend with love and care. The notice on the doorway to the garden gives some indication of the treats in store. 'There is beauty in this garden. If you crave for peace and pardon once through this door no need to want, for peace dwells in this garden.'

There is no carefully laid out herb garden at Fremington, but the discerning visitor will soon spot santolina, lemon balm, lavender, sage and other herbs in the richly planted border. As Mrs Vousden exclaims, 'What is a herb? Cottage gardens didn't have herb gardens in the olden days.' Here is a pot-pourri of all the much-loved plants and Fremington has become a mecca for herb lovers wishing to see herbs growing as nature intended.

The owners work in close partnership. Mr Vousden is responsible for the building work and has recently finished a mount or

Old-world elegance at The Old Barn.

One of the many happy surprises in store at The Old Barn, where secret treasures abound.

Tudor-style rock garden complete with catmint, ferns and a statue on top. Most of the stones for this were carried from a nearby beach.

It is Mrs Vousden who passionately loves old-fashioned roses and cannot resist adding yet another variety to the garden. The site of an old orangery has become a home for some of her favourites which climb happily up the brick pillars. Behind this is a Georgian gazebo which they have restored to make a look-out over their cottage garden plot.

Paths edged with heavily perfumed pinks guide eager feet on to fresh delights and round every bend there is a surprise in store. A fine nineteenth-century mulberry tree set in a brick rondel has a Kiftsgate rose rambling through the branches.

A stretch of lilies (*Lilium regale*) planted rather formally adds a further pleasure to this garden. 'Grow from seed,' advises Mrs Vousden, 'if you want to establish these lovely but unpredictable lilies.'

It is easy to believe Mrs Vousden when she says, 'I am always in the garden', and hard to imagine her having any time to cook

Roses, roses, all the way

The careful housewife of long ago would have thrown up her hands in horror if she could see us wasting our 'rose-power' today. Roses were grown then for their many uses in the still-room, for making rose vinegar to cure headaches, and for drying the petals to fill pillows to secure tranquil nights. In fact there remain even in this modern age plenty of ways in which we can use our rose petals instead of letting them wilt on the bushes.

For example, rose petals may be candied, the sweet results being used to decorate trifles and cakes. Pick the rose when it is dry and pull the petals apart.

Have two saucers nearby, one containing an egg white lightly beaten, and the other granulated sugar.

Handling each petal gently (a pair of tweezers is a help here), dip it into the egg white. When it is well coated dip it into the saucer of sugar. The rose petal should then be put on a baking tray lined with tinfoil. Dry the candied petals either in your airing cupboard or a very slow oven. If you dry them in the oven, do watch carefully that they do not turn brown or become too crisp. Store your delicacies between layers of greaseproof paper in an airtight container.

with herbs. But coriander is a favourite. She grows it to enjoy the frothy cloud of pinkish white flowers and then saves the seed for use in the winter months.

The secret treasures here can only be discovered slowly, and will reveal themselves when time is taken to enjoy the many scents and sights of this cottage garden to excel all cottage gardens.

Visitors are welcome. The Vousdens regard themselves as trustees of this very personal garden and share in the pleasure it gives to thousands of visitors.

ST MICHAEL'S MOUNT

Penzance, Cornwall

Telephone: Marazion (0736) 710507   **Owner:** The National Trust

Situation: ½m from the shore at Marazion (A394), connected by a causeway 3m E of Penzance.
Open: April–May, Monday, Wednesday and Friday; June–October, every day (except for Saturday and Sunday) 10.30am–4.45pm; November–March, Monday, Wednesday and Friday for conducted tours only, weather and tide permitting.

St Michael's Mount is a rocky pyramid-shaped island. Appearing, as it does, to rise from the sea at low tide, it presents a unique blend of nature, romance and architecture. At low tide the island can be reached by walking across the causeway, but at other times the ferry is the only means of access.

During the twelfth century it was the site of a religious foundation based on the Benedictine Abbey of Mont Saint Michel in Normandy. It then became a garrisoned fortress and finally in 1660 passed into the private ownership of the St Aubyn family. The present head of the family, Lord St Levan, lives at the Mount but in 1954 transferred the property to the National Trust.

It was Lord St Levan who decided to reconstruct a twelfth-century monastic herb garden for the enjoyment of tourists. He suggested to Peter Cook, who had a holiday job as a guide on the island while studying to qualify as a practitioner of herbal medicine, that he might like to draw up some plans.

Peter Cook studied many of the earliest of the printed herbals, including the Anglo-Saxon *Leech Books*, the development of the early church in England, and the practice of horticulture and medicine in the Middle Ages. He became totally absorbed in the study of the sort of garden one might have expected to find at a medieval monastery. For a small community like this, consisting of a prior and twelve monks, one plot would have been sufficient to provide pot herbs for the kitchen, medicinal herbs for the infirmary, and ornamental herbs for decorating the church and for refreshment of the spirit.

There were problems in deciding where to site the garden. The island is rocky and in bad weather gales cause the waves to lash against the walls. The present plot is about 70ft (21.6m) by 4ft (1.2m) and is backed by a 6ft (1.8m) stone wall. The garden is protected by the village and enjoys the maximum of sunlight and warmth.

Herbs were chosen which would have

been grown by monks in the thirteenth and fourteenth centuries for the needs of the monastic community, visiting pilgrims and the local inhabitants. They were also chosen for their ability to withstand the fierce winds and salt spray that blow over the island.

Many of the plants—comfrey, marjoram, sage, mugwort and rosemary—are grown today and used in the same way as they were in medieval times. Peter Cook hopes that his carefully researched garden will add to the considerable attraction and beauty of St Michael's Mount and also create a widespread renewal of interest in monastic herbs and their uses.

Plants for a saints' garden

Culinary, strewing and medicinal herbs for places of religion were grown in areas known as fields of Paradise. Here the monks walked and relaxed. There is some evidence of one in Oxford where it is possible to visit the site of Paradise, now a lost garden, but in the 1240s a fairly flourishing 6acre (2.4 hectare) garden of the Franciscans or Greyfriars. Full details are given by David Sturdy in his book *Twelve Oxford Gardens* (Ark Press).

The gardens were as often as not the open spaces at each end of the establishment and here among the more common plants would be herbs grown especially for decorations on feast days and to be carried in processions. Such herbs as rosemary were placed in corners or strewn around the floor to purify the atmosphere.

Flowers, mainly white as a symbol of purity, would include Our Lady's smock (a form of orchid) and Our Lady's tears or, as we know it now, lily-of-the-valley.

If the idea of a saints' garden, or garden of Paradise, appeals, here are four interesting plants to grow. Each has a link or two with a religious occasion.

Hyssop (*Hyssopus officinalis*), known as the holy herb, has small blue flowers, occasionally pink or white, and was one of the original strewing herbs used in medieval times for sanitary reasons.

Horehound (*Marrubium vulgare*) was a remedy for coughs and colds. Horehound candy can still be bought from some old-fashioned sweet shops.

Tansy (*Tanacetum vulgare*), another of the official strewing herbs, is associated with an Easter custom. Bishops and other church dignitaries used to play handball against the men of their congregation and a cake flavoured with the leaves of the tansy plant was the reward for the winners.

Meadowsweet (*Filipendula ulmaria*), commonly called queen of the meadows, was a major strewing herb which herbalist John Gerard said excelled all others 'for to decke up in the Summertime'. According to him, 'the smell thereof makes the heart merrie and joyful and delighteth the senses'.

EAST ANGLIA

CAMBRIDGE BOTANIC GARDEN

University Botanic Garden, Cambridge

Telephone: Cambridge (0223) 350101   **Owner:** Cambridge University

Situation: S of the city with entrances in Bateman Street, Trumpington Road, Brooklands Avenue and Hills Road. **Open:** Every weekday (including Saturdays) during all the hours of daylight, closing in the summer 7.30pm; Sundays, May–September, 2.30–6.30pm.

Botanic gardens are a development of the original herb or physic gardens where apothecaries could learn about the plants traditionally used in medicine. At Cambridge the garden was established in 1761 for the teaching of botany and science in general, and today it has two functions. It provides a place where plants can be grown for scientific research and is a garden where visitors can enjoy both instruction and recreation.

One of the important and unusual features of this attractive garden is a 'chronological border' containing a selection of the many plants introduced into British gardens from earliest times to the present day. Most visitors may find it surprising that many of

83

these plants, particularly the early ones, are herbs.

The early printed herbals were the reference for dating early discoveries but many of these, notably those with country names, may have been established much earlier. Bear's breeches (*Acanthus mollis*), hollyhock (*Althaea rosea*) and rosemary (*Rosmarinus officinalis*) are just a few in this section which were grown for medicinal purposes.

The saffron crocus (*Crocus sativus*) dates back to Roman days and may be seen in the Cambridge chronological bed. It was cultivated in about the thirteenth or fourteenth century and grown extensively around nearby Saffron Walden for some centuries. It was of course from this herb that the town derived its name. The yellow dye saffron is made from the dried stigmas of crocus. Since more than four thousand flowers were needed to produce a single ounce of the dye, it is not to be wondered at that in many quarters the chemical substitute was warmly welcomed.

Rosemary was grown by the Anglo-Saxons and used by them in rites to dispel evil spirits and prevent bad dreams. A sprig of rosemary twisted through the hair was said to promote memory. It was claimed that it had most powerful properties and it had a reputation, still held in some country towns, for curing colds in the head, preventing tooth decay and relieving the pain of gout.

The Cambridge chronological bed provides a sharp reminder that tobacco (*Nicotiana tabacum*) was one of the first plants to be brought over from the New World. Reaching England in 1586, it was first considered a panacea for all ills and was used to 'cure' respiratory problems. No government health warnings then.

Garlic (*Allium sativum*), an introduction of the seventeenth century, was known as 'molies' by the Elizabethans. Garlic bulbs were looked upon as magic charms rather

A Swede by any other name . . .

If you've trouble remembering and pronouncing the botanical names of your herbs, the man to blame is a Swede called Carl von Linne. Something of a genius—he was given the name 'the little botanist' at the age of eight—he began his system of naming plants well before the age of thirty and produced nearly two hundred works on the subject. Perhaps as a joke he called himself Carolus Linnaeus and so his method became known as the Linnaean system. It involved a division of the kingdom of animals, vegetables and minerals into classes, orders, genera, species and varieties according to various characteristics, and to each was given two Latin names—genus and species.

than used for the culinary and medicinal purposes for which the plant is cultivated today.

And so the fascinating chronological parade continues with plants such as nasturtium (*Tropaeolum majus*) from Peru, and bergamot (*Monarda didyma*). Bergamot, first raised in this country from seed sent by the American botanist John Bartram, is grown for its useful leaves which make a refreshing tisane. It also has extremely attractive deep red flowers. New species and varieties are still being discovered and will undoubtedly find a space here.

Cambridge has much else of interest, not least the systematic beds, referred to as 'herb borders'. They follow the normal pattern in that each bed is devoted to a specific family and each is well labelled. The beds are pleasantly informal.

A scented garden attracts many visitors with little or no sight for there is a raised bed and a seat that is easily accessible. Heliotrope, geraniums with scented leaves, mint, pinks, thyme, rosemary and scented roses all perfume the air of this exceptionally lovely

Shrub roses for small spaces

In June and July it is a pleasure to be overwhelmed by the sweetness of the scent and beauty of shrub roses. These fit neatly into the herb garden, provided the smaller ones are selected.

In the scented garden area of Cambridge Botanic Garden, shrub roses have been used as an aromatic and most attractive back-cloth to the low-growing plants, an idea to be considered when you wish to disguise an unromantic shed or completely cover a useful but unsightly fence. If you have a venerable tree, long past the fruit-bearing stage but still an old friend, put it to work supporting a sweet smelling rose or two.

Here are some to consider:

Rosa eglanteria (formerly *Rosa rubiginosa*), the common sweetbriar. This is a wild variety with single pink flowers followed by oval red hips and very fragrant foliage. Grows to about 8ft (2.4m) with a similar spread.

Rosa 'Blanc Double de Coubert'. A large white fragrant flower that blooms throughout the season reaching about 6ft (1.8m) with a spread of some 5ft (1.5m).

'Félicité Permentier'. A short bushy shrub about 4ft (1.2m) by 4ft (1.2m) with tightly packed pink petals.

'Fantin Latour'. Wonderfully fragrant, 6ft (1.8m) high spreading to about 5ft (1.5m), blush pink.

'Filipes Kiftsgate'. Here is a contender for the fence or cycle shed, fast growing and capable of reaching 50ft (15m).

'Gloire de Dijon'. An old cottage garden favourite with heavily scented biscuit-coloured flowers. It will tolerate a north wall and grow to a height of 15ft (4.5m) given favourable conditions.

semi-circular dell. A less sweet-smelling plant, that 'Herb of Grace', rue, has strangely also found its way here.

A new and most useful feature of the garden are eight rose beds which tell the history of garden roses right up to the present, time. They range from the first Apothecary's rose right through to today's popular hybrid tea and floribundas.

Cambridge Botanic Garden is a place for study or leisure. Students of all ages, heavy notebooks in hand, are to be found everywhere. And if you should chance to be there on a fine day, happy couples with plants far from their thoughts will be waiting for you to look the other way. It is as all good gardens should be, an enjoyable and stimulating place with a long history and a major contribution to make as scientists and common folk alike discover the treasures lying hidden in the green magic of the humble herb.

EMMANUEL COLLEGE

Emmanuel College, St Andrew's Street, Cambridge

Telephone: Cambridge (0223) 65411
Open: Every day, 9am–5pm.

Owner: The Master, Fellows and Scholars of Emmanuel College

The herb garden at Emmanuel College was designed on the basis that students hurrying to lectures are always ready to cut corners. So as the garden lay in their way, it provided straight paths with herbs in the areas least likely to get in the way of educational progress. That's the secret—and more of it later.

The college is right in the busy centre of this fascinating city and some imagination is required to believe that once it was the site of a Dominican priory. The herb garden, large and formal, is in New Court and is based on an early seventeenth-century design. Three triangular beds are surrounded by box hedges and are broken up into a number of small plots interlaced with more box hedges. A single herb species is planted in each plot—and to make an interesting change of texture and accentuate the design, coloured chippings have been added.

Plants have been chosen more for their

A box-edged garden

In the Emmanuel design box edges are used to outline a formal courtyard garden, whereas in gardens such as the Dower House at Badminton they are used to give shape and form to a large kitchen garden.

For low-growing hedges such as the one at Emmanuel College, choose the dwarf form of box known as 'Suffruticosa'. Another attractive form of this tidy hedging plant is 'Latifolia Maculata' which has delightful variegated golden leaves.

Box is expensive to buy and plants should be spaced 12in (30cm) apart. So if you want to enclose a rose bed or even plant a small knot garden, it is worth finding a friend with an existing box hedge and taking cuttings.

The slow-growing box makes a herb garden appear 'clothed' through the winter, when so many favourite plants such as mints, tarragon and chives have died down. It is therefore worth taking the trouble to acquire and cultivate this plant.

ornamental foliage than for their culinary uses. Some like rosemary, golden thyme, hyssop and lemon balm are among the more usual herbs you would expect to see, but look carefully and you will find unexpected treasures. The dwarf white lavender (*Lavandula spica* 'Nana Alba') which grows to only about 6in (15cm) high, the decorative sweet cicely (*Myrrhis odorata*) with large fern-like leaves, and elecampane (*Inula helenium*), an old established medicinal herb native to Great Britain, are just a few to discover.

Alongside and blending with the warm stone of the college buildings, there is a wide variety of scented shrubs and climbing roses. Among these, the Scotch or burnet rose (*Rosa spinosissima*) shows off its bristly thorns and creamy-white flowers which are followed by purple hips. The rose 'Crimson Glory', richly scented with deep red flowers, is often raided by students with romance in mind. When visiting, keep an eye open for the tree germander (*Teucrium fruticans*) and observe those odd funnel-shaped pink flowers; it grows well here.

Studying the important pathways running across the enclosed square, the visitor may well wonder if there is perhaps some deep religious significance in the plan. After all, it was once the site of a medieval priory! But the answer is much more practical, as already revealed. John Codrington, on the recommendation of Vita Sackville-West, designed the garden in 1961 to fill in an area which became available after temporary kitchens were demolished. He said: 'Having been an undergraduate myself, I knew that no undergraduate, when late for a lecture, could ever go round a corner without cutting it off so I drew straight lines from every door in the court to every other door.' Now this makes sense and when wondering how to start planning our own gardens perhaps it is a good idea to look at the doors and gateways first. After the walkways were established the three triangular areas were planted with herbs and a large paved area

The herb garden at Claverton Manor, home of the
American Museum in Britain.

The open knot garden at Cranborne Manor.

A delightful mixture of bright colours and quiet
greys in the peaceful walled garden at Sutton Manor.

An early photograph of the knot garden at the Tudor
Museum, Southampton.

was left in the centre of the square.

Mr Codrington drew three plans for developing the courtyard and the college selected the herb garden. The authorities feared that the garden might be damaged by undergraduates in the early years and not have a chance to mature. So some twenty years later it is encouraging to see that the garden is in immaculate condition and well worth visiting.

The paths, made of York stone bordered with brick and cobble, add an interesting change of texture. Mr Codrington arranged the edging bricks to resemble the painted lines of 'major road ahead' signs on a roadway and these can be clearly seen on the most important path through the garden. Walk the paths yourself and you will find that this most attractive courtyard can be traversed in at least ten directions.

Historical note

The founder of Emmanuel College was for many years Chancellor of the Exchequer to Queen Elizabeth I and established a college where Protestant preachers could be trained with the same thoroughness as their Dominican predecessors. Of the first one hundred graduates who migrated to New England fully one-third were Emmanuel men.

FELBRIGG HALL

Felbrigg, Norfolk

Telephone: West Runton (026 375) 444　　　　　**Owner:** The National Trust

Situation: Near Felbrigg village, 3m SW of Cromer; signposted off the A148 to Holt and Fakenham and the A140 to Norwich. **Open:** Daily (except Monday and Friday), 31 March–4 November, and bank holiday Mondays, 2–6pm. Closed Good Friday.

When visiting Felbrigg, it is easy to forget that North Sea winds and the high cliffs of Cromer are only two miles away. Felbrigg Hall has the advantage of being sheltered by a great wood planted by William Windham in the seventeenth century and maintained by successive generations.

The drive to the garden is through sweet chestnut, beech and lime trees that make an impressive entrance. A short walk through the park leads to a quarter-acre walled garden laid out as a 'potager', a French term for a garden that provides fruit, flowers, herbs and vegetables for the house. Altogether, more than half a mile of clipped box carries the eye along the paths to long, colourful borders and high protective walls.

Based on a previous garden cultivated here as early as the eighteenth century, the garden at Felbrigg was reconstructed by the National Trust during the latter part of the 1970s. It was from here that in August 1707 Katharine Windham, who lived at Felbrigg, wrote to a friend—'Felbrigg lookt like the land of Goshen, so full of everything that was good, abundance of fruit, the peaches not good anywhere this year, but the weather will make them better. I eat some excelent greengages, they are admirable, an excelent nectrine that comes from the stone, excelent white figes . . .'

With a little imagination the visitor will picture the old fruit trees growing against these same walls and the small square plots of herbs and vegetables lovingly cared for by generations of gardeners and their app-

Clipped box borders for the 'potager' at Felbrigg.

Golden sage, cotton lavender, a healthy rosemary and many other familiar herbs of Mediterranean origin do well in this fine sandy soil. A good collection of belladonna lilies (*Amaryllis belladonna*), with their funnel-shaped pink flowers, grows in front of two carefully restored greenhouses. And in one corner is a pleasing layout of crown imperials (*Fritillaria imperialis*) underplanted with the steel blue rue (*Ruta graveolens*).

There are plenty of attractive wooden seats on which to pause while enjoying the garden and contemplating the bees collecting pollen. You can even sit on a fascinating wheelbarrow seat. About the same length as a garden bench, this seat has pick-up handles and the traditional barrow front wheel with a hinged back. It was probably used to wheel pots of plants from one place to another, and would have been handy for taking them to the greenhouses in the winter months.

One of the many high brick walls has golden roses climbing right to the top interspersed with blue ceanothus bushes. At each end of the wall are two large bay trees, protected in winter with an 'overcoat' of wire netting plaited with straw. This ingenious idea could easily be adapted for the protection of all the Mediterranean shrubs that so often do not winter well. Underneath the climbers grow sweetly scented hyacinths which add a splash of colour in the spring before the roses and ceanothuses flower. In the summer this border is full of catmint.

Looking now at the orangery, the well-preserved woodlands and the parkland, it is difficult to believe that Felbrigg was totally dilapidated in the early part of the twentieth century, and the garden choked with thistles and nettles. The last owner, Richard Wyndham Ketton Cremer, has written the story of the house, and it is thanks to him and his father that work on the restoration of the walled garden was begun. But planting woodland was his great passion and as a

rentices. Today the walls have been planted with similar well-trained fruit trees and the beds are full of herbs and scented flowers set among restful stretches of well-kept lawns.

Framed by one of the many attractive brick archways, a large round pond decorated with a stone mermaid amid an island of lady's mantle (*Alchemilla mollis*) and surrounded by a wide border of lavender (*Lavandula angustifolia*) is as eye-catching now as it would have been many years ago. The large dovehouse, restored in 1937, would have been even more at home in the seventeenth-century herb garden, for at that time doves were an important source of food for the manor and the local community during winter months. The size of this fine octagonal dovecote, with places for some two thousand doves, is a reminder that for many years only the lords of the manor or the abbots of monasteries were allowed to keep doves.

tribute to VE day at the end of the Second World War he planted a large V-shaped wood consisting mainly of a mixture of conifers and beech trees.

Today, the highly trained gardeners here keep the garden and grounds impeccably. Visitors can appreciate the grand scale of herb, fruit and flower cultivation but still learn new ideas to carry out on a smaller scale.

A potager on a small scale

At Felbrigg you have a wonderful chance to study a potager, a place where fruit, vegetables, herbs and flowers all grow happily together. But can such a garden be created on a small scale? Of course, provided you have room. You need space to create at least four beds 10ft long by 5ft wide (3 × 1.5m). A grass path running around these beds of a width of 2ft (60cm) is essential to the design.

In the seventeenth century it was discovered that beds about 4ft (1.2m) wide were the ideal size for cultivation. This is as true today as it was then and beds laid out in this way can be looked after easily without treading on the soil during the wet winter months.

Edge the beds of the potager with herbs like parsley, thyme, sage or chives and plant small square blocks of quick growing vegetables such as lettuces, carrots and radishes. Runner beans can be grown decoratively up wigwams of tall canes, while gooseberry and blackcurrant bushes will conveniently fit into empty corners.

There is no sure way of fooling the birds short of enclosing the garden in a wire fruit cage which will, alas, destroy the appeal of the garden, but you *can* string your vegetables with black cotton and put nets over the fruit bushes. Try putting several children's plastic windmills, cheaply bought at seaside gift shops, in among your crops. The windmills last the season through and with their continual whirring really do seem to prevent the birds from reaping too much of the harvest.

GUNBY HALL

Burgh-le-Marsh, Nr Spilsby, Lincolnshire

Owner: The National Trust

Situation: 2½m NW of Burgh-le-Marsh, 7m W of Skegness on S side of the A158. **Open:** April–September, Thursday 2–6pm, Tuesday, Wednesday and Friday by prior written appointment.

Alfred Lord Tennyson, it is said, strolled quite often among the herbs, apple trees and roses in the walled gardens of Gunby Hall, which is not far from Somersby on the gently rising ground of the Lincolnshire Wolds. It would not have appeared strange that a poet of such stature should delight in picking a sprig of lovage or admiring the scent of the rosemary before being called in by his host for a supper of local pigeon with a slice of carp from the pond.

Gunby Hall has the smell and feeling of a

'. . . all things in order, all things stored' at Gunby Hall.

home and these qualities inspired Tennyson to write of 'an English home . . . all things in order stored,/A haunt of ancient peace'. The poem, so frequently quoted, hangs in a room of this mellow plum-bricked house in the poet's own handwriting above his signature and the date 1849.

The garden pattern has changed much since then, but on the east side of the house, built in 1700, weathered brick walls remain to enclose what in earlier days would have been a range of gardens devoted entirely to vegetables and orchards. There is much grass there now and little in the way of soft fruit. But Gunby Hall's famous orchard remains and a herb garden has been planted

as a new and attractive feature.

The herb garden has a central rectangular-shaped plot with six others around it to form a square of about 15 × 15yd (13.7 × 13.7m). Slabbed pathways, their edges softened by borders of chives and marjoram, contain and give access to each plot. A tapering border with many of the more vigorous herbs such as elecampane, balm, mint and lady's mantle runs alongside one of the ancient walls and is divided from the main herb area by a simple grass path. Here are many of the herbs cropped and enjoyed by villagers and owners of Gunby Hall and other houses on the site over the centuries.

In one plot wormwood, monkshood, catmint, marjoram, globe artichoke, balm and golden and common sage grow vigorously, while in another southernwood, parsley, tree onion, camphor, lovage, soapwort, sweet cicely, cotton lavender, tansy, bronze fennel, hyssop and sage present a gentle pattern of greys and greens. Elsewhere rosemary, lavender, curry plant, wild marjoram, tarragon, lungwort, thyme, alkanet, iris and many types of mint are planted in profusion.

In the 8.5 acres (3.4 hectares) of garden at Gunby Hall the visitor will find corner beds of lavender, honeysuckles and ancient roses, old-fashioned species of fruit trees arched and in pyramids, central beds of catmint accentuating the form of a sundial and a splendid pigeonry, applehouse and summer house.

Acquired by the National Trust in 1944, this house and its gardens with their homely mixture of herbs, seasonable vegetables, fruit and flowers provide most truly a 'haunt of ancient peace'.

Poetic bays

Bay trees and bushes are interesting enough in their own right but anyone with a literary bent and a taste for eccentricity could well make a complete garden of them and dedicate each one to a poet laureate or to a Greek god. 'There,' she (or he) would declare to startled yet admiring visitors, 'stands John Masefield (1930–67) and just to his left is jolly old Colly Cibber (1730–57) with Billy Wordsworth (1843–50) needing a bit of a trim.'

There would need to be a statue of Apollo, who fell in love with and pursued Daphne, the daughter of the river. To escape him she asked to be turned into a bay laurel tree and from that moment became even more lovable to Apollo, who forthwith decreed that poets and victors should be given the laurel as their prize.

Soon the poets and scribblers of the day caught on to the idea that possession of laurel could assist the creative spirit, so they kept leaves in their pockets and even put them under their pillows to aid the poetic process. Later, university graduates in poetry and rhetoric were called 'doctors laureate' and 'bachelors laureate' on accepting laurel wreaths. Then came the unofficial poet laureates—Chaucer, Skelton and Spenser—and eventually in 1668 the official poet laureate, John Dryden. The next poet to 'receive the bays' was Thomas Shadwell (1688–92) followed by Nuhum Tate (1692–1715), Nicholas Rowe (1715–18) and so on.

Some poet laureates came in for considerable criticism and their achievements or otherwise would make interesting reading during the long winter evenings when the herbs are taking a rest. For instance, Henry James Pye (1790–1813) was said to have wheedled his way into office by writing worthless nonsense about 'feathered songsters' in praise of George III. This infuriated a contemporary who wrote:

When the Pye was opened
The birds began to sing;
Wasn't that a dandy dish
To set before the king.

In America a number of states have designated poet laureates of their own, so perhaps the gardens of bays need not be confined to Great Britain.

NETHERFIELD HERBS

The Thatched Cottage, 37 Nether Street, Rougham, Suffolk

Telephone: Beyton (0359) 70452   **Owner:** Ms Lesley Bremness

Situation: Roughly halfway between Bury St Edmunds and Woolpit off the A45. **Open:** Most days, 10.30am–5.30pm. Advisable to telephone first.

The cottage where Lesley Bremness lives in rural Suffolk is straight out of the Goldilocks and the Three Bears fairy story, and it has a garden to match. Herbs are grown here for pleasure and for sale as container-grown plants.

Her interest in herbs began when she took part in a competition organized by the Herb Society and *Garden News* to find 'The Herb Garden of the Year'. Winning first prize for her entry, which was chosen because the layout was appealing in itself and sufficient evergreen herbs were included to ensure winter colours, she was encouraged to start a herb nursery.

The garden she has planted at Netherfield is based on her award winning one and is designed as a series of interlocking squares with brick and grass paths. Here are all the herbal conceits that might be found in the garden of a stately home.

A scented arbour surrounds a seat, and raised sink gardens cleverly display dwarf herbs. Plans are afoot to create a small knot garden which will be along traditional lines yet relate to the interlocking squares which form the backbone of the garden.

As well as the usual varieties of thymes, mints and marjorams there are some rarities. These include a pink rosemary, a dwarf curry plant suitable for rock gardens, a prostrate winter savory and a variegated rue. Seed is exchanged with the botanic garden at Edmonton so Canadian plants are in evidence in this garden. An avid plant collector, Lesley is always searching for new additions and defines a herb as 'There isn't a plant that does nothing'. This allows her a very wide range of plants in her small garden.

The outline of the garden, too, may vary. When she has a new idea she feels she must put it into practice straight away. The design of herb gardens is her particular interest and she will supply plans of gardens and draw up lists of plants for clients. And since her own four small sons love running round the brick paths in the garden, treating it as a model racing track, her plans will always be practical.

Herbs in pots

Rosemary, thyme, sage and parsley are just a few of the many herbs that will grow beautifully in pots. They are ornamental, useful and sweetly scented. On a warm summer evening they will add interest to your patio and are very much in keeping with the mood of today's gardening.

Another advantage of growing herbs in this way is that it is so easy to move the pots to catch the sun or, if necessary, shade during a hot spell. Attractive groupings can be planned to show the contrasting foliage and create interesting patterns. Creeping thyme planted near the edge of a pot will make an attractive arrangement with other herbs such as marjoram, lemon balm and spiky-leaved chives. Mint is an ideal subject for a pot as

continued

continued

its invasive runners are more easily contained.

Herbs, being simple plants, look very effective in plain unglazed pots. But if you wish to vary the pattern there are many other attractive containers. Consider the lovely large strawberry pots now sold in most garden centres. Try a different herb in each pocket.

Drainage is of vital importance so make sure you start the bottom layer with broken crocks and then brick rubble or even gravel. Then build up the pot with your chosen growing mixture. We find that a blend of John Innes No 2 and our own rather poor alkaline soil makes a good growing mixture for containers.

Firm the compost well down to a depth of about 1in (2.5cm) below the top of the container and water well. Plant out your herbs leaving room to grow. It is difficult to give a guideline, but five plants to a pot of about 20in (50cm) in diameter and 10in (25cm) deep seems to work very well.

Nearly all the herbs you wish to grow will thrive in a sunny corner, but try and provide some shade for mint and chives. Many plants dislike gusty winds. If this is your problem it might be a help to provide some protection. A length of trellis about 3ft (90cm) high should solve the problem. Painted white this can make an eye-catching feature contrasting well with the green foliage of the herbs.

Water your pots frequently during summer and give a liquid feed once a month. The plants should be carefully cut to shape and the trimmings used for flavouring in the kitchen or for pot-pourri.

If these pots are your only source of cut herbs, try growing two or three plants of each herb in different pots to give each one a chance to recover and grow again.

To make the patio as attractive as possible, why not include a few flowering herbs just to please the eye? Scented geraniums all have interesting leaves as well as small but pretty flowers. Nasturtiums grow easily from seed and contribute a bright splash of colour with their gay flowers.

Culinary herbs which do well in pots are basil, bay, chives, lemon balm, marjoram, mint, parsley, rosemary, sage, savory, tarragon and thyme. Among the ornamentals choose from bergamot, chamomile, hyssop, lavender, lemon-scented verbena, rue and scented leaved geraniums.

The expression 'pot herbs' refers to culinary herbs such as rosemary, thyme and bay which are used to flavour the cooking 'pot' and has nothing to do with herbs growing in pots in the garden. This can sometimes cause confusion.

NORFOLK LAVENDER

Caley Mill, Heacham, Nr King's Lynn, Norfolk

Telephone: Heacham (0485) 70384   **Owner:** Norfolk Lavender Ltd

Situation: In Heacham on the A149 at the junction with the B1067 to Sedgford, 13m N of King's Lynn. **Open:** End of May to end of September, daily 10am–6pm, including Sunday; from September to the end of May, 9am–4pm, Monday–Friday.

Caley Mill, built of carr stone, is a landmark in Norfolk where the blue, or often grey skies, ensure a peculiarly clear light, much appreciated by landscape painters. Is it for this reason that the blue of the lavender growing here seems an even more intense colour than the memories we carry of this much loved herb in our own gardens?

In the 6 acre (2.4 hectare) garden you can study the habits of different lavender plants which are cultivated here in rows planted 5ft (1.5m) apart. Your eyes will be opened to the differences between varieties with such intriguing labels as 'Munstead', 'Royal Purple', or the even more cryptic 'G.4' and 'L.6.'. There are other symbolic letters and figures which the friendly staff will be happy to explain to you.

Lavender grows in great profusion at Caley Mill, a real feast for your eyes, and you can delight too in the fragrance that fills the surrounding air, but there are also many other herbs in this unusual Norfolk garden which demand attention.

The main herb garden consists of separate beds approximately 6 × 4ft (1.8 × 1.2m) laid out in chequerboard style with gravel paths between. There are sixty-six different sec-

The lavender harvest at Caley Mill.

tions, each with a single specimen of a culinary, medicinal or ornamental plant. Wild flowers, too, are included because the owners realize the need for conservation of these plants—once rather derisively thought of as weeds—which grow happily in meadowland, wild areas and cultivated gardens. It is a source of amazement that so many different herbs can grow in such an exposed garden only a few miles from the east coast with just a shelter belt of Scotch pine and some leylandii trees.

Ideas are continually being developed and the new display garden consists of small shapes such as a square, triangle and circle. These show how in only a small space a variety of attractive and useful herbs can be grown to add a decorative feature to any garden. A small rock garden has been planted using local carr stone to demonstrate how well some herbs such as thyme, marjoram and chamomile grow in an alpine

setting. Here too is an attractive sales area, approximately 3ft (90cm) high and faced with timber palings, where customers can select herbs from those they have seen growing.

Recently a large Victorian-style rose garden has been laid out to give added colour in the summer months. The roses grow well, helped perhaps by the 8in (20cm) of rich compost forked in to give body to a very light soil.

The commercial side of the lavender farm, open to the public, is of especial interest in the summer. Then visitors can see lavender being reaped with a specially designed combine harvester. Also open are the distillery, where the valuable oil of lavender is extracted, and the drying shed, where lavender, fresh from the field, is dried for sachets, pot-pourri and other fragrant delights.

Delving behind the scenes

The origins of the lavender industry here are just as fascinating as the thriving commercial concern seen today. Back in the 1930s, a local nurseryman called Linnaeus Chilvers (usually known as 'Linn') realized that Norfolk, with its sunny situation and light, well-drained soil, would be a good place to cultivate lavender commercially. The tradition of using English lavender had at that time virtually disappeared. Existing farms had been destroyed either because of diseased plants or because the land had been sold for building development.

As so often happens with romantic tales that have happy endings, there were at first many problems. Anxious years were spent trying to breed a hybrid which was both resistant to disease and capable of producing the fine essential oils needed for soaps, perfumes and other scented cosmetics. The other problem was to find enough suitable land. Linn Chilvers had only a small nursery garden and realized he needed a larger acreage if he was to grow lavender as a commercial proposition. Luckily a local landowner, Mr F. E. Dusgate, could help and went into partnership with him. In 1932 6 acres (2.4 hectares) of land were planted with lavender and the foundations of Norfolk Lavender were firmly laid.

During these early days bunches of lavender were sold at the roadside to passing motorists. By chance one of the drivers who stopped to buy a bunch was a perfumery expert and gave Linn Chilvers a secret eighteenth-century recipe for making perfume. To cope with the increased demand, copper stills were acquired from France in 1936 and these remain in use some fifty years later.

Curiously the Second World War gave an immense boost to lavender production in this country. With the fall of France, England became virtually responsible for all the raw materials needed by perfumers, and English lavender earned valuable dollars when it was used in exchange for the war materials needed by this country.

The company continued to expand after the war. The original aims and ideas are still carried out as Linn Chilvers would have wished. Having no family of his own, he chose the Head family, who had always been friends, to carry on the lavender growing tradition in Norfolk.

OXBURGH HALL

Oxburgh, Nr Swaffham, Norfolk

Telephone: Gooderstone (036 621) 258   **Owner:** The National Trust

Situation: 7m SW of Swaffham, on the south side of the Stoke Ferry road. **Open:** 31 March–October, daily except for Thursday and Friday, 2–6pm.

Oxburgh Hall is a rather sombre Elizabethan moated house on the edge of a small Norfolk village which looks as though it has not changed for many years. But any visitor thinking the Hall is in a backwater should be prepared for a few surprises.

The 80ft (24.4m) medieval tower stretches into the sky and dominates the undulating countryside, giving the house a sense of mystery; indeed, you are very aware of ghostly presences hovering over the grounds.

The point of interest to herb enthusiasts is the extensive parterre, or 'French Garden'. A favourite type of planting over the water, it is in effect a large, elaborate bed constructed close to the house. It is really a development of the knot garden, but much larger and with more intricate patterns. Flowers were often in short supply in the seventeenth century when these gardens were at the height of fashion so chippings of granite, gravel and coal dust were used to fill the spaces between the box hedges.

The parterre at Oxburgh Hall fascinates scholars of both art and history. The design is very intricate with box edged scrolls and other detailed shapes. Punctuating the garden are sixteen neatly trimmed box domes about 6ft (1.8m) high.

The beds are filled with the silver feathery leaved cotton lavender (*Santolina chamaecyparissus*) contrasting with the steel blue rue (*Ruta graveolens* 'Jackman's Blue') and other plants appropriate to this formal design. When the National Trust restored this garden, traces of the coal and cement originally used were still clearly visible.

Records show that the idea for creating this garden came to members of the family when they saw a similar one in a garden near Paris around 1845. Returning home they decided to plant out the east garden at Oxburgh in a similar fashion. It is almost identical to one of the designs for parterres illustrated in *La Theorie et la Pratique du Jardinage* by A. J. Dezallier d'Argenville. This parterre is as fine an example as any to be seen in England and can be viewed to great advantage by climbing up to the top of the tower.

Oxburgh Hall has been owned by the illustrious Catholic family, the Bedingfelds, since the fifteenth century, and although it is now owned by the National Trust, members of the family still live here. They suffered great deprivations by remaining loyal to their faith as revealed in a letter written by one member of the family to another in 1830, which bore the address of 'The Ruin'.

The high wall round the kitchen garden was erected at the same time as the parterre was planted. Five towers were built into this wall to commemorate the five children of the family, rather than, as is often said, to imprison them.

Silver herbs for a special occasion

One way of celebrating a special family or even national occasion would be to plant a silver garden.

The most silvery herb of all is the decorative curry plant (*Helichrysum angustifolium*). This has a beautiful silver gleam to its leaves and is a most adaptable plant which can be trained for edging a border. The name comes from the spicy aroma of the leaves in summer. It is usually grown for its ornamental value, but some cooks use it for adding to salads and to give piquancy to a stuffing. The curry plant has a mass of small yellow flowers from June to August but it is the foliage that is its great attraction. Neat-growing, it usually reaches a height of 8–12in (20–30cm) and does well on light soil in a sunny place.

PETERBOROUGH CATHEDRAL
Peterborough, Cambridgeshire

Telephone: Peterborough (0733) 43342

Situation: In the centre of Peterborough. **Open:** October–April, every day, 9am–5pm; May–September, every day, 9am–7pm.

There are remains of the fine monastery at Peterborough to be seen today. And it is recorded that as early as 1302 the abbot 'had made a beautiful herber next to the Derby Yard (gardinum Dereby) and surrounded it with double moats, with bridges and very lovely plants (herbis delicatissimis)'. The area of this particular herber was about 2 acres (0.8 hectares) and the cost £25. In 1980 it was estimated that the same garden would have cost £15,000.

The reconstructed plan of Peterborough Abbey in John Harvey's book *Mediaeval Gardens* shows the siting of this herber, the infirmary, the monk's cemetery, the vineyard that later became an orchard and various pleasure gardens.

A new herb garden has now been planned for Peterborough. The site chosen is a 3ft (90cm) wide long border running the length of a south-facing cloister wall. Planting will be restricted to herbs used in monastic days and it is hoped that this will appeal to the many thousands of visitors who each year explore the cathedral and seek to learn more of its history and surroundings.

One of the plants chosen for the cloister garden is the pomegranate (*Punica granatum*), a popular plant with orange/red waxy flowers. The pomegranate is of special significance to Peterborough because the fruit was the emblem of Catherine of Aragon, the unfortunate wife of Henry VIII, who is buried in the cathedral. It was her reluctance to agree to a divorce that led Henry into the problems that culminated in the Dissolution of the monasteries. Peterborough surren-

dered in November 1539 but two years later was reconstituted as a cathedral.

Plants to be used at Peterborough Cathedral

ANGELICA (*Angelica archangelica*)
Plant reaches 6–8ft (1.8–2.4m) high with striking large leaves and globular umbels. Known as the herb of the Holy Ghost. 'This sovereign remedy' was believed to ensure long life and protect against the plague and spells of witches.

BAY (*Laurus nobilis*)
Dark green bush with shining leaves. Evergreen. Wreaths and garlands were made from the leaves.

CHAMOMILE (*Anthemis nobilis* syn. *Chamaemelum nobile*)
Low-growing perennial plant with white single or double daisy-like flowers. Leaves grow in feathery tufts and have a sweet apple scent. One of the sacred herbs and a strewing herb. Used for many medicinal purposes including the treatment of agues. It has a soothing and tonic effect on the system.

GERMANDER (*Teucrium chamaedrys*)
Low-growing perennial with small dark green leaves and small pink flowers. Ideal for edging. 'The drink used inwardly and the herb outwardly is good for such as are inwardly or outwardly bursten, and is found to be a sure remedy for palsy.'

HYSSOP (*Hyssopus officinalis*)
Neat-growing evergreen plant which

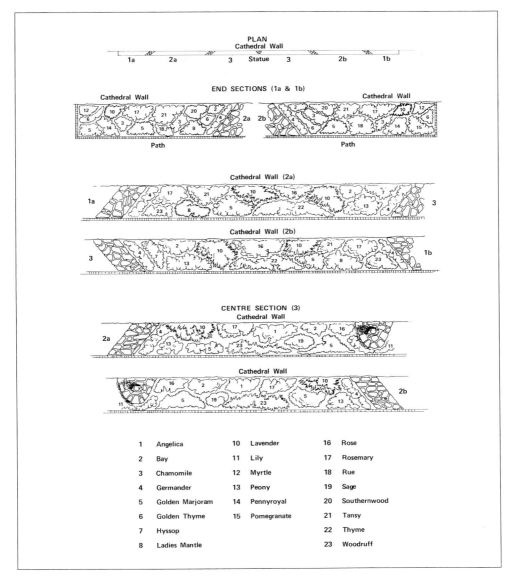

PLAN
Cathedral Wall

| 1a | 2a | 3 | Statue | 3 | 2b | 1b |

END SECTIONS (1a & 1b)

Cathedral Wall — Path

Cathedral Wall — Path

Cathedral Wall (2a)

Cathedral Wall (2b)

CENTRE SECTION (3)
Cathedral Wall

Cathedral Wall

1	Angelica	10	Lavender	16	Rose
2	Bay	11	Lily	17	Rosemary
3	Chamomile	12	Myrtle	18	Rue
4	Germander	13	Peony	19	Sage
5	Golden Marjoram	14	Pennyroyal	20	Southernwood
6	Golden Thyme	15	Pomegranate	21	Tansy
7	Hyssop			22	Thyme
8	Ladies Mantle			23	Woodruff

flowers most of the summer. 'Will heal all manner of evils of the mouth.'

LAVENDER (*Lavandula angustifolia*)

Silver-grey foliage and lavender coloured flowers in spike formation. 'Is of especial good use for all griefes and paines of the head and brain.'

LILY (*Lilium candidum*)

This is the madonna lily with white trumpet-like flowers in June and July. It would have been grown for decorating the chapel, making garlands and use in processions. Also grown for its healing properties. The leaves are good for burns, 'old ulcers' and new wounds.

MARJORAM (*Origanum onites*)
A true perennial with small heart-shaped leaves which forms low-growing clumps. Golden marjoram has gleaming gold leaves and pink flowers. 'The herb bound on the head would cure a cold.' Made into ointments for bruises and, Gerard writes, 'easeth such as are given to overmuch sighing'.

ROSE (*Rosa* spp)
Principal rose to use in herb gardens is the Apothecary's rose (*Rosa gallica officinalis*) with semi-double crimson blooms on upright stems. *Rosa gallica* 'Versicolor' 'Rosa Mundi' may also be used to commemorate the story of the Wars of the Roses. Syrup of honey and roses used to be given to feeble, sick, phlegmatic, melancholy and choleric people.

ROSEMARY (*Rosmarinus officinalis*)
An evergreen ornamental shrub growing to about 5ft (1.5m) high with spiky green leaves and pale blue flowers. 'Make thee a box of the wood and smell to it and it shall preserve they youth.'

MYRTLE (*Myrtus communis*)
Beautiful evergreen shrub with fragrant foliage and creamy-white sweet smelling flowers. Used in decorations for garlands and processions.

PENNYROYAL (*Mentha pulegium*)
Low-growing plant with dark green leaves and pale mauve flowers. Used as a strewing herb to keep pests away. 'Some affirm that they have found by trial that the pain and gout is cured by the Pennyroyal.'

PEONY (*Paeonia officinalis*)
Perennial with large attractive red, pink or white flowers.

SUFFOLK HERBS

Sawyers Farm, Little Cornard, Sudbury, Suffolk

Telephone: Sudbury (0787) 227247   **Owner:** John and Caroline Stevens

Situation: Just off the B1508 between Sudbury and Bures. **Open:** Saturday all day, throughout the year.

This commercial herb farm has 6 acres (2.4 hectares) of meadowland where the owners grow many English, North American and oriental herbs, wild flowers and grasses to provide seeds for private gardeners and for sowing in major development and conservation areas throughout the country.

Of special interest is the large area of display beds, a sheet of colour in the summer, while for the practical minded the propagation and potting areas (mainly polythene tunnels) are particularly absorbing.

In the field trials section, visitors will discover the effects of sowing different mixtures of herbs and grass. The common quaking grass (*Briza media*) and meadow foxtail (*Alopecurus pratensis*) are to be found here among such venerable herbs as oxeye daisy (*Chrysanthemum leucanthemum*), cowslip (*Primula veris*) and lady's bedstraw (*Galium verum*).

There is proof here that even when the soil is appalling, such seed scattered and just raked over will germinate and flourish.

WHITTLESEA MUSEUM

Market Street, Whittlesey, Cambridgeshire

Owner: Whittlesey Society

Situation: In Whittlesey on the A605, 6m E of Peterborough. **Open:** Friday and Sunday 2.30–4.30pm; Saturday 10am–noon.

On display behind the old Town Hall in Whittlesey (the alternative and former name is Whittlesea) is a collection of well-preserved agricultural items and a small herb garden about 10ft (3m) square on a raised concrete plinth.

Herbs cultivated here are the ones that would have been grown and used by farm-workers' wives a generation or two ago. Mint would have been used, as it still is today, to flavour the potatoes which are a principal crop of the fens. Sage, mixed with onions, helped make a tasty stuffing for the joints of pork enjoyed after a pig was killed and for the Michaelmas goose. Herbs such as parsley and thyme added seasoning to the savoury suet pudding, boiled in a bag, which the hungry menfolk would look forward to eating after a strenuous day in the field. The sweet scent of thyme and lemon balm would have been appreciated for attracting bees, and parsley would be chopped for the sauce to eat with the fish on Fridays.

All these herbs grow in this small raised garden which has a central diamond-shaped feature of bricks—brickyards were, and still are, an important industry in this town.

The museum is a tribute to the local inhabitants who work there on a voluntary basis and have collected in various rooms of the old Town Hall, all the mementoes that bring the history of Whittlesey up to date. Skates and other artifacts recall the pastimes of this fenland community on the nearby marshy Wash. One room has been set up as a brickworker's living-room complete with father, mother and baby.

Wines with herbs

Many different herbs are used to flavour wines and are the main ingredients of most country wines.

The famous quotation 'I borage bring always courage' used to refer to the alcohol and not the flower that decorated the wine glass! However, recently it has been found that borage does have invigorating qualities so perhaps we should think again about this beautiful blue flower that grows so profusely in cottage gardens.

Try this delicious cider cup with borage on a hot summer day.

1pt (500ml) cider, 1 lemon, 1 handful fresh borage leaves, half cup brandy, 1 tbsp sugar, 1 cup orange juice, 1pt soda water and a few borage flowers.

Pour the cider into a large jug and add the lemon cut into quarters. Chop the borage leaves coarsely and add to the mixture. Cover and after about an hour strain and add the brandy, sugar and orange juice. Chill. Just before serving add the soda water. Serve with plenty of ice and decorate with a few borage flowers.

Much work has been done to collect written records of Whittlesey, now rapidly changing. It is hoped that the small herb garden planted by the author, will inspire newcomers to learn a little about the traditions of using herbs.

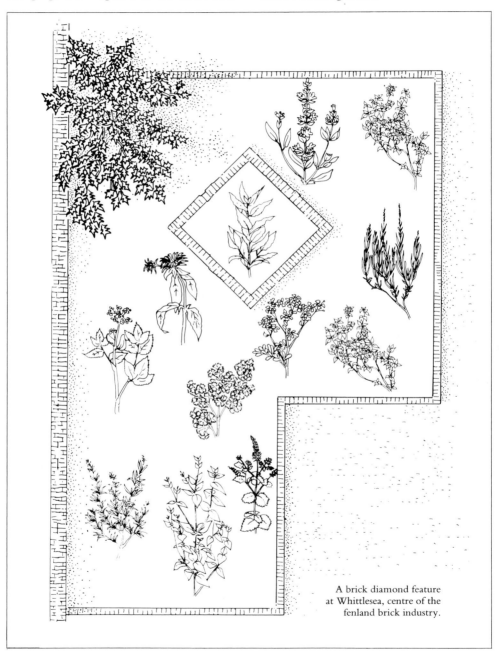

A brick diamond feature at Whittlesea, centre of the fenland brick industry.

Visitors to Lackham College will revel in the variety
of aromatic, culinary and medicinal herbs.

Hops grown in wigwam style make a good focal
point in the fascinating garden at Hardwick Hall.

Herbs for the connoisseur at Selsley Herb and Goat Farm.

A corner of the gardens at Barnsley House, a rare and
happy blend of the new and the old.

THE MIDLANDS

ABBEY DORE COURT

Abbey Dore, Herefordshire

Telephone: Golden Valley (0981) 240 419   **Owner:** Mrs C. L. Ward

Situation: 11m SW of Hereford, about 3m NW of the A465. **Open:** March–October, 10.30am–6.30pm.

As Herefordshire has claims to be the home of cider-making, the shape of the herb garden at Abbey Dore Court could well be that of one of the giant stone wheels used to crush cider apples in days gone by. Measuring 30ft (9m) in diameter, it has four spokes composed of a variety of discarded bricks, outer and inner rims of bricks and a hub also of bricks. Set in a lawn with a backdrop of shrub roses and clematis and with the burbling River Dore passing close by, this garden is an attractive feature of Abbey Dore Court.

The bay tree at the central point of the garden is surrounded with several varieties of thyme occupying space between inner rim and hub. One of the four areas between the spokes is set out with a collection of mints and the others contain varieties of marjoram, orris root, mercury, alecost, rue, winter savory, hyssop, horehound, lavender and many other herbs. Hedges and plantings of pink lavender, cotton lavender, artemisia, rosemary and catmint provide height and colour.

Planning a herb garden

Traditionally, a herb garden was always a square intersected with paths. In early monastery gardens this would have represented the shape of the cross. Today this plan still makes sense as it is possible to walk down the paths and pick herbs easily for later use or for rubbing immediately to release the scent. But if you need to cater for children's games, fruit trees and a vegetable garden in a small space, herbs can be grown in pots and tubs and look most decorative.

A chequerboard pattern looks effective in any garden and although some plants will grow more quickly than others, the formal look will suit the herbs with interesting foliage, and the finished, overall appearance should be rather like a Persian carpet with the different foliage herbs adding their particular shades and hues.

A circle of herbs planted round a small tree is the answer if you have just moved into a new house and are planning your garden from scratch. It adds character immediately to a new garden and could be planned round a small tree such as a flowering cherry or a lilac bush.

ALDERLEY GRANGE

Alderley, Gloucestershire

Telephone: Dursley (0453) 842161   **Owner:** Mr Guy and the Hon Mrs Acloque

Situation: Upton, Hawkesbury and Wooton-under-edge. Turn NW off the A46 Bath–Stroud road at Dunkirk. **Open:** Several times a year for the National Gardens Scheme and local charities.

The gardens at Alderley Grange, enclosed by brick walls and sheltered by fine trees, complete the picture of a west country house in the middle of an English village. Indeed, it is difficult to imagine anything more dramatic happening here than tea and cucumber sandwiches on the lawn followed by a leisurely game of croquet.

The house had been owned by the well-known garden designer Mrs Lees Milne, so it presented something of a challenge to Mr Acloque and his family to maintain such an idyllic setting. Luckily they had similar ideas and have continued to keep up the same high standards. At the same time they have introduced new planting schemes totally in keeping with the development of the garden.

The herb garden here has been described as 'simple in concept, original in design, superb in detail and meticulous in upkeep'. Indeed it lives up to these high ideals and is designed to resemble a star with eight separate segments. Narrow paths between the neatly clipped box edges lead to a sundial with an unusual gnomon acting as a focal point.

In this area, roughly 15ft (4.5m) square, there are all the herbs one could wish to see growing; alecost, bistort, borage, angelica, woodruff, bergamot and purple sage are just a few that delight the eye.

It is an orderly garden full of interest for herb lovers. To add symmetry, an 'Isaphan' rose has been planted in each of the segments. The clear pink flowers add colour

---

Profusion but not confusion

The aim of every herb gardener is to have generous clumps of mint, sage, thyme and parsley ready for use in the kitchen and yet still looking attractive in the garden without choking each other in their attempts to find sufficient space. Mr Acloque has achieved this at Alderley Grange and it is worth considering how.

The herb garden has the advantage of brick paths and box edges which gives it a tidy appearance and prevents some of the more exuberant plants from trespassing, an idea which could be employed elsewhere. The ground is so closely carpeted that weeds have little chance of survival but herbs are trimmed back several times a year and self-seeding plants are ruthlessly weeded out where they intrude into the general pattern of the border.

Another lesson to be learnt here is to keep lawns immaculately cut and the edges neatly outlined. This adds considerably to the overall appearance of a garden, making it look full of interest and yet beautifully cultivated.

---

right through the summer season. The plan includes the planting of smaller plants near to the sundial; these increase in height towards the outer perimeters of the garden.

Apart from the formal garden there is much else to admire at Alderley Grange. Perhaps it is the pattern of plants weaving through the borders that stays uppermost in the memory. Sweet williams appear at different intervals in a long border by the lawn; lady's mantle (*Alchemilla mollis*) spreads its yellow branched heads over the pathways; and everywhere there are evening primroses (*Oenothera biennis*) with fragrant yellow flowers that open in the evening. The whole garden illustrates well Mr Acloque's statement, 'My aim is profusion but not confusion'.

Shrub roses, too many to mention by name, cluster around this mellow stone house adding colour and fragrance to the scene. They are all much-loved favourites of the present owners of Alderley Grange.

A small orchard of medlars, filberts and quinces was planted to celebrate the jubilee of Queen Elizabeth II in 1977. All these trees would have been appreciated by the first Queen Elizabeth back in the sixteenth century.

The gardens here are at their best in the early summer, and this is when Mr Guy Acloque and his family like to share its beauty with friends and neighbours. At the end of August, preparations begin for the following year and all plants are cropped back, cuttings taken and seeds saved. By the end of October the aim is to have the garden completely tidied to get another chapter in the saga of the gardens at Alderley Grange under way.

BARNSLEY HOUSE

Nr Cirencester, Gloucestershire

Telephone: Bibury (028574) 281 **Owner:** Mr and Mrs David Verey

Situation: 4m NE of Cirencester on the Cirencester to Burford Road (A433). **Open:** All the year on Wednesdays from 10am–6pm (or dusk if earlier). Also first Sundays in May, June and July. Other days by appointment.

Built of warm honey-coloured stone at the turn of the seventeenth century, Barnsley House is a typical fine Cotswold dwelling on the edge of one of the many peaceful Gloucestershire villages. The yews and other trees are ancient, for the garden has been in existence for centuries. But for the keen visitor it will serve as a splendid example of how a dedicated gardener can employ her own skills and ideas to create a rare and happy blend of the new and the old.

Herbs abound at Barnsley House, clamouring for attention in a long border, cosy and at home in intimate corners and between the paving stones, and taking pride of place in the formal herb garden and the kitchen plots.

In planning her herb garden, Mrs Verey reasoned that although she thoroughly enjoyed wandering down the grassy paths collecting mint to garnish her lamb, parsley, chervil and chives for her salads and borage flowers to float in cool drinks it would be sensible to grow all these plants together and not too far away from the kitchen door. In consequence, she took over for this purpose a long and convenient border which ran at right angles to the house and enjoyed plenty of sun.

A feature is low well-clipped box forming diamond-shaped compartments, each containing a single variety of herb. The diamond points are emphasized with box bushes clipped into a ball shape while the corners of the garden are marked with small pyramids of box. Formality adds dignity to this small herb garden, with shapes and aromas compensating for what flower enthusiasts might regard as a lack of colour.

Growing here are mainly the culinary favourites such as chives, thyme, marjoram, winter savory, chervil and dill, and there are many useful and ornamental herbs including rue, dwarf hyssop, the statuesque tree onion and chamomile for soothing the troubled brow.

There is also the mandrake, looking remarkably innocent and friendly and not at all like the evil, magical root the old herbals

make it out to be. With a root shaped like the human figure and a reputation for bringing death and disaster to anyone who disturbs it, the mandrake at Barnsley House awaits the curious and adventurous visitor.

The wall behind the herb garden is covered with *Rosa longicuspis*, a mass of white single flowers in season forming a splendid backdrop to the orderly garden below.

The knot garden is for pleasure

There are many quaint rhymes and sayings associated with herbs and in viewing the knot garden at Barnsley House the visitor must consider Mrs Verey's own contribution to the lore as most relevant:

The Knott garden serveth for pleasure,
The potte garden for profitte.

Or in Latin as classical scholars were taught at Eton and Winchester in the sixteenth century:

Horti serviunt voluptati:
Hortus holitorius utilati.

Here the knot garden is much on the lines of the earliest form of pleasure garden which enjoyed a great vogue in the sixteenth century.

In an open knot garden such as you will see here the pattern is made by planting different varieties of clipped box and the neat growing wall germander. Clipped in the spring, and later if necessary, this evergreen garden is most attractive during the winter months. Traditionally the spaces should be filled with sand, chalk, coal dust or gravel to accentuate the design.

A short distance from the herb garden is a delightful potager adapted from a design in William Lawson's book *The Countrie Huswife's Garden* published in 1617. Like the book, this garden is a fount of ideas for the visiting gardener hunting about among the

A pot-pourri of ideas

The lovely gardens at Barnsley House comprise a mixture of all sorts of horticultural ideas, some culled from the pages of old herbals, some suggested by friends and others just ideas that Mr and Mrs Verey have experimented with themselves.

Here lies the secret of creating a successful herb garden. First you must work out the layout and basically the type of plants and trees you want to grow. From then on, the charm of the garden will grow in proportion to the time you can spend keeping your ears and eyes open and learning more and more about herbs and their associations.

Take advantage of holidays to look around for a bird-bath or a statue that will add style to a particular corner. Holidays also mean time can be spent visiting gardens searching for new ideas such as brick paths laid in unusual patterns, or simple but attractive nut arches. (We speak from experience, for we once returned from holiday inspired enough to dig up our front lawn and plant an Elizabethan-style herb garden there!)

Mrs Verey has learnt from many sources and these add to the overall beauty of her garden at Barnsley House. She does, however, feel that without the membership of the Royal Horticultural Society she would have found it difficult to acquire so much information on gardening matters. Membership is open to anybody and a modest subscription will bring a copy of the monthly journal through the post, free tickets for the Chelsea Flower Show and news of other exhibitions, lectures and use of their extensive library. There is, too, the important right to visit the society's show garden at Wisley as a member.

old brick and block paths which outline the beds of vegetables, sweet smelling herbs and fruit trees.

Following William Lawson's advice, Mrs Verey has in the main kept the width of the beds to 5ft (1.5m) so that the 'weeder woman' need not tread on them. Here too are delightful goblet trained apple trees and other multi-tier espaliers. It is indeed a garden full of good things to eat, delicious scented plants, and flowers that are a joy to the eye.

Thanks to the gift of a subscription to the Royal Horticultural Society and a garden-ing notebook from her family, Mrs Verey began attending the shows at Vincent Square and looking at other gardens. It was, as she now puts it, as if until that time she had been living with her eyes half closed. She became and still is fascinated by the historic and contemporary aspects of gardening. With her husband, she has created a garden which is full of interest, returns the love bestowed upon it and is a pleasure and privilege to visit.

CAPEL MANOR

Institute of Horticulture and Field Studies, Capel Manor, Bullsmoor Lane, Waltham Cross, Hertfordshire

Telephone: Lea Valley (0992) 763849   **Owner:** London Borough of Enfield

Situation: On the intersection of the M25 and A10 London to Cambridge road. There are regular trains from Liverpool Street and London Transport buses stop near the entrance. **Open:** May–October, weekdays excluding Mondays and public and municipal holidays, 10am–4.30pm.

Just outside the herb garden in the grounds of Capel Manor is a particularly fine walnut (*Juglans nigra*) which bears nuts much valued when green for their dye-making properties. It is said that the dye is good not only for all sorts of woollen goods but also for restoring colour to hair tending to turn grey.

Capel Manor is a Georgian mansion house surrounded by over 30 acres (12 hectares) of land ranging from mature woodland and wild habitats to carefully landscaped gardens. The many thousands of visitors seem little worried about the colour of what is or what is not under their hats and many stay for hours or days to learn more about the wonders of growing plants.

Tuition is offered on methods of vegetable dyeing using plants grown in the garden. Practical demonstrations include the basic methods of using colour, spinning, and the processing of home-dyed fibres.

Special importance is given to a small square garden formally laid out with a stone urn in the centre; it has mainly plants used for colour making either for cosmetics or fabrics. A tall-growing variety of chamomile (*Anthemis tinctoria*) with yellow daisy-like flowers, meadowsweet, marigolds, alkanet and lady's bedstraw are particularly attractive.

A small culinary herb garden is an excellent example of layout and construction and acts as an introduction to individual culinary herbs and their uses. The plants grown here form the background for instruction in the propagation of herbs, their individual uses and the ways of preserving them—drying, deep freezing and making vinegars.

The seventeenth-century style gardens,

planned in an enclosed area surrounded by high yew hedges, are full of plants of that exciting period in gardening history. There is the traditional knot garden with box hedges outlining the different compartments and a wrought-iron wellhead set in paving stones. There are plantings of a special and much-named favourite of the old country-garden writers, love-lies-bleeding, alias countrywoman's flower, alias Prince of Wales's feathers (*Amaranthus caudatus*). Grown for the brightly coloured tassel- or plume-like flowers which seemingly hold their colour for ever, they contrast well with the variety, 'Viridis', which has pale green flowers.

Another enclosed garden in the eastern section is referred to by the evocative title 'The Garden of Delight'. Here four identical beds surround a sundial, and an arbour fills one sheltered corner with climbing plants such as honeysuckle and old-fashioned sweet peas covering a wrought-iron framework to form a fragrant roof.

A collection of medicinal herbs arranged following the recommendations of Nicholas Culpeper in his *London Dispensary*, which he wrote in 1653, makes up yet another display garden at Capel Manor. Many of the plants are native and will be familiar as wild plants or weeds. The advice of Culpeper still carries weight. 'My opinion is that those Herbs, Roots, Plants etc. which grow near a man are far better and more congruous to his nature, than outlandish rubbish whatsoever, and this I am able to give a reason of to any that shall demand it of me, therefore I am so copious in handling them.'

Plants have been collected into groups according to their use, such as those which 'comfort the heart and chear the spirits'. Included in this section are angelica, balm of Gilead, clary sage, blessed thistle, lavender and others which have the reputation of acting as a tonic or more generally dispelling gloomy thoughts. In this square garden

Woad and woadmen

Molly of the Woad and I fell out
O what do you think it was all about?
For she has money and I had none,
And that is how the strife begun.

'Song of the Woad Harvesters'. Anon.

Julius Caesar wrote: 'All the Britons dye themselves with woad, which makes them a sky-blue colour and thereby more terrible to their enemies.' More than two thousand years later woad remains a much-loved and admirable member of the British herb tribe but is no longer used for dye-making. It had a good run, however, for in the Elizabethan era the growing of the herb was encouraged and continued in some areas to the mid-1930s. Its great rival was indigo from India, which gave a better blue and was cheaper.

Woad has a long history and in Anglo-Saxon times was called wad. The people who harvested and treated the herb—the woadmen—were called waddies. The production of the dye was a wearying complicated task involving much crushing of the leaves in a mill. (A painting of a fenland mill hangs in the Council Room of the Science Museum, London.) Although the dye was blue, it was often mixed with another plant dye to produce Lincoln Green and in the Middle Ages almost all cloth was coloured in this way.

Dye-making remains a fascinating subject and readers wishing to try their hand should ask around for details of local classes or groups. Capel Manor Institute organizes special weekend courses and demonstrations on the subject. There is a good collection of dye-making plants at the Chelsea Physic Garden.

surrounded by wide borders there are at least two hundred different varieties including poisonous plants. In the seventeenth century these would have been more familiarly known as purging herbs.

Apart from these carefully laid out gardens there is much of interest to see at Capel Manor including borders and corners where such herbs as morning glory (*Ipomoea*) show off their heavenly blue flowers which live only for a day and form a contrast to the more stately bear's breeches (*Acanthus mollis*) which spills over the pathway.

Rapidly becoming a horticultural centre of importance in this northern borough of London, Capel Manor has special facilities for disabled visitors. There is even a small garden laid out with raised beds suitable for working from a wheelchair.

CHENIES MANOR HOUSE

Nr Amersham, Buckinghamshire

Telephone: Little Chalfont (024 04) 2888   **Owner:** Mr and Mrs MacLeod Matthews

Situation: In Chenies, between Amersham and Rickmansworth where the B485 joins the A404. **Open:** April to October, Wednesdays and Thursdays, 2–5pm; parties at other times by appointment.

Should you be seeking a rare collection of dye-making, medicinal and other plants of the ancients and moderns then the gardens at Chenies will keep you fascinated for more than one long afternoon. If it is a sense of history you are after, a hint perhaps of romance and possibly royal scandal, a taste of adventure and an hour or so of perfect peace, then you'll find plenty of that there too. Chenies has a herb garden, a pattern of six plots called a Physic Garden, which provides a setting where the plants and their layout are a good deal less important than how the herbs were used—and by whom.

Visitors enter the Physic Garden by a path through other gardens where Henry VIII may have picked a posy for Anne Boleyn and, later, for Kathryn Howard (later to commit adultery with Thomas Culpeper). The garden has six plots, one of oblong shape standing apart from the others. There is a central bed containing a massive stone fountain surrounded with mullein and cotton lavender and four supporting beds forming a square with grass paths. On one wall there are perspex-covered notes on the uses of herbs in earlier times and detailed descriptions of the plants themselves.

A feature of the garden is a medieval well, 180ft (54m) deep, covered in about 1800 by an octagonal well-house containing a horse-driven pump. Items recovered from the well, dug about 1400 and explored just a few years ago, include a massive collection of clay pipes, a number of keys and part of a mortar no doubt used at one time by the house-physician for preparing his herbal remedies.

The several 'little gardens' of Chenies are at one turn a mass of colour and at another a gentle poem of green and white. On our visit lavender and tobacco plants were in strange but gentle harmony, attracting the interest of visitors passing by to view the Chinese 'weeping' ash planted in about 1770, the thousand-year-old 'Queen Elizabeth's Oak' in the small park and the smaller oak grown from an acorn taken from the branch on which the last Abbot of Woburn was hanged.

Chenies, just 25 miles from London and 35 miles from Oxford, is well placed for many visitors and is the ideal setting for the cookery demonstrations and flower arranging classes organized by the lady of the house, Mrs Elizabeth MacLeod Matthews.

How to propagate

If you are planning a new garden or replanning an old plot, you will require plenty of herbs for borders and perhaps to swop with other gardeners for plants they have available. You may even have a charity stall in mind.

Whatever the purpose, don't be put off by other people's tales of woe. Propagating herbs by cuttings is easy and unless you are going into business in a big way you don't need any out-of-the-way equipment. All you require in fact are sharp scissors or secateurs, rooting powder, a few pots, clear plastic bags, a quantity of compost made up of two parts gritty sand, one of peat and one of loam, and a tray of water.

Before taking cuttings, fill the pots with the cutting mixture leaving about 1in (2.5cm) at the top for watering.

Most woody and some non-woody herbs, such as mint, can be propagated by cutting about 5in (12.5cm) from the top of a branch or stem and then making a clean cut just below a leaf joint. Pinch or cut off all leaves except for a few at the top, brush the bottom of the cutting across the powder and insert it in a pot as near to the edge as possible. A thin pencil or stick is useful to make an initial hole should the cutting be tender or fragile.

Continue until the cuttings, roughly $\frac{1}{2}$in (1cm) or so apart, are all around the edge of the pot. Do not plant any in the centre. Stand the pot in a few inches of water until the surface of the mixture appears damp, place a plastic bag over the pot and cuttings and remove it to a warmish place where there is no danger of scorching by the sun. Within a few hours, the inside of the bag will be dripping with moisture; do not disturb it but in about a week stand the pot in water again for a few minutes. In about two to three weeks, with luck, white rootlets will appear through the drainage holes. The cuttings have 'taken'.

Heel cuttings may also be taken in this way; the cutting is torn back from the main stem and not cut. It is also called a slip.

The Royal Horticultural Society has published a most useful and well-illustrated book on propagation which is worth the small investment.

HARDWICK HALL

Chesterfield, Derbyshire

Telephone: Chesterfield (0246) 850430   **Owner:** The National Trust

Situation: 6½m NW of Mansfield and 9½m SE of Chesterfield on the A617. **Open:** Gardens, April–October, noon–5.30pm. Closed Good Friday. For times of opening of Hall, refer to National Trust handbook.

Plans for the building of Hardwick Hall at the end of the sixteenth century are still in existence and show that it was surrounded by four gardens of rectangular shape all enclosed by walls. The principal garden is situated to the south of the Hall. We know nothing of the layout in detail but can presume that this may have been the site for the herb garden where Bess of Hardwick's housekeeper would have gathered sweet herbs for the pot and for strewing the floors of the state rooms. Today there are shrub roses with plenty of room to spread their branches, a number of walnut and other nut-bearing trees and orchards full of pears, crab apples and many old-fashioned fruiting trees seldom seen in gardens today.

That remarkable lady, Bess of Hardwick, Countess of Shrewsbury, married and out-lived four husbands. Each time she became a widow she became more wealthy and by the fourth time she was widowed she was regarded as the second wealthiest woman in the land, beaten 'by a sovereign or two' by Queen Elizabeth. In her early seventies she began building Hardwick Hall and orga-nized all the details of interior decoration and furnishing. The popular rhyme of the day 'Hardwick Hall, more glass than wall' arose because the size of the windows increased with each additional storey. Her flamboyant taste is evident in the six towers that crown the building and carry her initials 'E.S.' 4ft (1.2m) high.

This most interesting herb garden is composed of two identical sections, each linked by a square central bed surrounded by a wide gravel path. The wide borders around these two square beds contain a rich mix of culinary herbs of the varieties most likely to have been used in the kitchens of the Hall.

Unusually in a garden so far north, many half-hardy plants thrive. The wind and cold hating pineapple sage, with its strong pineapple fragrance and soft green leaves decorates one of the borders and even the delicate lemon-scented verbena, *Lippia citriodora* (syn. *Aloysia triphylla*), bay (*Laurus nobilis*) and the aromatic myrtle (*Myrtus*

Hops

Hops (*Humulus lupulus*) growing up wigwams of poles to a height of about 6ft (1.8m) make a good focal point in the fascinating but rather flat garden at Hardwick Hall. It seems that cultivated hops were a novelty in Tudor times and this was one of the early ways of growing them. Although the addition of hops to the Royal Brew was not practised in the sixteenth century, the eating of young shoots and the inclusion of the dried flowers in sleep pillows was approved. Today hop leaves growing up the tripods of garden poles look most attractive and this is one more practicable idea for smaller gardens.

communis) appear to do well here. (They are of course protected in the winter.) Italian lavender (*Santolina neapolitana*), not a rarity but unusual enough, flourishes at Hardwick. Rather like the more common santolina, this plant has longer and more feathery leaves but has the traditional silver foliage and bright yellow flowers.

New ideas are always being tried in this garden although the original layout is care-fully retained. For instance, growing behind one of the garden seats on our visit were neat rows of bronze tipped lettuces.

It is worth walking round the rest of the 7 acre (2.8 hectare) garden which curiously and perhaps advantageously has not benefited from the attentions of landscape designers such as Capability Brown and Humphrey Repton.

HATFIELD HOUSE
Hatfield, Hertfordshire

Telephone: Hatfield (07072) 67872　　　　　　**Owner:** The Marquess of Salisbury

Situation: In Hatfield opposite the railway station. **Open:** Park and West garden, weekdays noon–5pm, Sundays 2–5.30pm; East garden, Mondays only, 2–5pm (but closed on bank holiday Mondays).

Built in Jacobean days, Hatfield is a very grand but charming house, bestowing on even the humblest visitor a sense of dignity and grace. Its gardens, clearly the pride and joy of the Marquess and Marchioness of Salisbury, are similarly gracious and disarming.

A large herb garden, one of the few of any consequence created this century, is full of scented and useful plants. Of traditional construction, it has four main paths leading to a centrally placed sundial. The paths are of stone flags with chamomile 'Treneague' providing a delightful apple scented walkway down the centre.

Designed about 1973, the herb garden achieves its purpose—a place to rest away from the cares of the day or to potter in contemplation. There are pleasant chamomile seats from which the visitor may watch the ever-busy bees at work among the thymes, lavender and sages. The garden has four large beds leading to eight circular plots encircling the sundial.

Large herbs, which often tend to be rather unruly, such as foxglove (*Digitalis purpurea*), rosemary (*Rosmarinus officinalis*) and bronze and green fennel (*Foeniculum vulgare*) grow in the four outer beds with many more scented and attractive plants filling the corners to create a tapestry of foliage.

Now regarded as the signature of Lady Salisbury's garden design, a standard honeysuckle (*Lonicera periclymenum*) protects each entrance to the garden from unwelcome spirits.

The circular plots are planted with old-fashioned roses and many varieties of herbs including thyme, hyssop and marjoram. The garden has as its surround a hedge of sweetbriar roses clipped to a height of about 2ft (60cm). Here among many varieties of old-fashioned roses are *Rubiginosa* varieties and the fine 'Lady Penzance' showing off its unusual coppery-pink blooms.

Here also are the original Apothecary's rose (*Rosa gallica* 'Officinalis'), which has small crimson flowers, the delicate red and

The knot garden—a work of art at Hatfield.

white striped 'Rosa Mundi' (*Rosa gallica* 'Versicolor') and, to complete the pattern, several different Alba roses including the richly perfumed 'Maiden's Blush' with flat shaped pinkish-white flowers. There are perhaps twenty other varieties all carefully labelled to make this gardening romance of the twentieth century a living legend.

Any spare corners are filled with tulips. The ones chosen are those brought back by Tradescant on his travels to Holland in the seventeenth century, which were the first tulips to be seen in England. There are also many old-fashioned pinks (*Dianthus*) —these were Robert Cecil's favourite flower.

Foreign novelties introduced during the Jacobean period were referred to as 'outlandish plants' as distinct from the native plants of this country, and were greatly valued..

Annual herbs are mixed successfully with the perennial herbs. The vigorous borage (*Borago officinalis*) with its blue star-shaped flowers, chervil (*Anthriscus cerefolium*) which

makes such a cheerful edging with bright green foliage, and pot marigold (*Calendula officinalis*) are all sown directly in the garden in their growing positions. The only seed raised under cover is basil (*Ocimum basilicum*) which needs warmth to germinate and will perish if planted outside before the cold spring winds have been replaced by gentle summer breezes.

Lady Salisbury describes the herb garden as not being very practical for the cook as it is so remote from the house. But as she says, 'It is agreeable when the weather is fine as the ways from the kitchen are green and flowery ones.'

The knot garden at Hatfield

Employing her talents in gardening and history to the full, Lady Salisbury has achieved another work of art with a large knot garden that fits perfectly in front of the original house now known as the Old Palace.

This is an open knot garden composed of herbs that would have been grown in the seventeenth and eighteenth centuries and although only planted a few years ago, it looks surprisingly mature. In true traditional style you look down from a pleached lime walk on to the enclosed garden enjoying the pattern made by the various herbs.

It is a sheltered area and there are many interesting scented plants growing in pots which add an extra dimension to the garden. One of the more remarkable is a small olive tree (*Olea europaea*). Pots of scented geraniums stand outside during the summer months and decorate any spare corner.

This type of elaborate knot garden is composed in a pattern that was popular at the time of Henry VIII and stayed in vogue for about a hundred years. It is one of the first examples of a pleasure garden, so often you will find a seat from which to enjoy the garden. You might also find a statue and a box hedge trimmed into a spiral or pyramidal shape. Paths of grass or brick divide the beds which contain flowers of the period such as primroses, violas, auriculas and cornflowers. Patterns forming the knot were taken from embroidery designs, carved leather books, carpets and wall tiles. Lady Salisbury aptly describes this as 'nature corrected by art'.

Although the herb garden and the knot garden have been added, to the great benefit of Hatfield, in this century, there is much to learn about the past which adds to the enjoyment of the gardens today.

And no doubt until the present happenings at Hatfield the great excitement must have been the time in the early part of the seventeenth century when Robert Cecil, the 1st Earl of Salisbury, was building his great house and establishing a family dynasty. The gardens were elaborately planned under the supervision of John Tradescant, Mountain Jennings and a Frenchman, Saloman de Caux. A vineyard was planted including a

A small knot garden

The fashion for growing herbs in ornate patterns called knots is with us again. But as Lady Salisbury says, 'It is a form of garden particularly suited to England and the English.'

If you want to try one yourself, select a closed knot where the herbs are planted in 'ribbons' and thread over each other to form a pattern resembling a piece of embroidery. Any spaces should be filled with sand, coal dust or gravel to emphasize the pattern. Good herbs to choose because they are evergreen (or ever-grey) are box, cotton lavender and rosemary.

The design can be taken from patterns in old herbals and simplified. You can create your own design by using a string stretched between two marking stakes and moving this about.

When marking out the design in the soil, use a pointed stick or the top of a hoe to make shallow drills. Sprinkle chalk or even flour into these and the pattern will stay even if you do have to walk all over it when setting out your plants.

The herbal hedges should grow to a height of approximately 8in (20cm) and will need shaping with scissors two or three times a year. The trimmings can be dried and used in pot-pourri mixtures or for scented bags.

collection of 30,000 French vines. A few fragments of the original vineyard remain to tell the story of this enterprising venture. Also remaining (in the West garden) is one of the four mulberry trees planted by James I and (in the park) the oak tree under which Elizabeth I was said to have been resting when she received news of her accession to the throne.

HOLME PIERREPONT HALL

Nottingham

Telephone: Radcliffe on Trent (06073) 2371   **Owner:** Mr and Mrs R. Brackenbury

Situation: 5m SE from the centre of Nottingham, just off the A52 approach past the National Water Sports Centre. **Open:** Easter Sunday, Monday and Tuesday, spring and summer bank holidays. During June, July and August, Sunday, Tuesday, Thursday and Friday 2–6pm; during September, Sunday 2–6pm.

Built in Tudor days this fine red-brick manor house, with its towers, alcoves and crenellation is a splendid example of those early houses designed for prestige and pleasure rather than as fortified castles.

Once a fine family home where generations of Pierreponts lived in princely style it was in a very bad state of repair when the present owners, Mr and Mrs Robin Brackenbury, took on the challenging task of restoring the house and replanting the gardens.

A large and colourful courtyard garden can be glimpsed through the hall doorway. Within is a grand box parterre which Mrs Brackenbury has replanted following the pattern of the original Victorian design. The compartments are filled with golden marjoram, thyme, cotton lavender, lemon balm and other herbs, and have a sundial as a focal point.

Along one wall of this completely enclosed garden is a wide herbaceous border with interesting plants, many of them herbal in origin. The colouring here is kept mainly to yellow, white and brown tones which contrast well with the mellow brick wall behind. Roses and clematis climb up other walls and a north-facing border is being developed as a shade garden where hostas and other plants can grow with little or no sun.

Although there is no herb garden as such, herbs are planted all over the garden in beds and borders where they grow most happily. As Mr Brackenbury says, 'This is partly

Herbs for the patio

In the last few years it has become the vogue for gardeners to create an area outside the living-room where the family can gather and enjoy the garden—a sort of outside living-room.

Here meals are eaten, books are read and informal summer parties are held. Herbs are very much a part of this scene. For instance, a lemon verbena plant growing in a tub can be appreciated for its scent and because it is decorative. Creeping thyme and chamomile grown in corners between the paving stones will release their scent when walked over.

But perhaps most important on the patio is the barbecue which is either a built-in feature or a portable piece of equipment. Around the barbecue herbs can be grown for use straight from the plant; for example, marjoram for flavouring kebabs, parsley to decorate steaks and grilled sausages, and lemon balm to flavour wine cups.

because I think creating a special herb garden nowadays is rather unoriginal; particularly if one cannot outdo Hardwick Hall.' He also finds that visitors seem to enjoy searching out the many different herbs growing here, and this often leads to a splendid discussion on the definition of a herb.

Until recently, Mr Brackenbury was High Sheriff of Nottinghamshire so much official entertaining was done in the house. The family also enjoy cooking for friends, and the kitchen help are said to 'dive into the courtyard garden to look for the appropriate herbs needed'. Rosemary is in constant demand to cook with lamb. The lamb too is homegrown as a flock of sheep graze on pastureland overlooked from the house.

Against the east wall a drift of Old English lavender rustles in the breeze, its gentle mauve hue blending well with the Tudor bricks. Other gardens are being replanted and admiration is unbounded for the bravery of the Brackenburys (she, a descendant of the original Pierreponts) in working to restore this house and fine garden with little outside help. Seeing this today is as fascinating as considering the former glories of the house.

IZAAK WALTON COTTAGE

Shugborough, Nr Stafford

Telephone: Stafford (0785) 760278 **Owner:** Staffordshire County Council

Situation: S of the A520 Stone to Eccleshall road. **Open:** April–September, Wednesday–Sunday and bank holidays, 10am–1pm and 2–5pm; October–March, Saturday and Sunday, 2–4.30pm.

Izaak Walton is remembered today for his book *The Compleat Angler*, although he wrote this book only for his own amusement, and is the author of other more learned works. His origins were lowly, but in his lifetime he became accepted as a friend by contemporaries of notable intellectual and social importance. He died a wealthy man leaving his farm at Shallowford to the town and corporation of Stafford for charitable purposes. This cottage is part of the estate although never his permanent home, and the aim of the museum is to show a typical late seventeenth-century house and garden such as Walton would have known.

His words in *The Compleat Angler* describe the idyllic surroundings:

'I could there sit quietly; and looking on the water, see some fishes sport themselves in the silver streams, others leaping at flies of several shapes and colours; looking on the hills, I could behold them spotted with woods and groves; looking down the meadows could see, here a boy gathering lilies and ladysmocks, and there a girl cropping culverkeys and cowslips, all to make garlands suitable to the present month of May.'

The cottage is enchanting yet small, and this should be remembered by herb lovers who hope the rest of the family will find plenty to amuse themselves while they concentrate on the garden.

Changed about ten years ago when it was decided to concentrate on plants known in this country before the eighteenth century, the garden is well worth a visit. It consists of a lawn and beds filled with early native roses and herbs surrounded by a yew hedge which has yet to reach mature proportions.

Borage, creeping jenny, thyme, valerian, tansy, sorrel, St John's wort, feverfew, periwinkle, germander, rue, vervain and meadowsweet are just some of the herbs that can be identified. During most of the season there is colour. Poppies and polyanthus

'Where there's rosemary, there's rue' . . . herbs from
the age of Shakespeare at Stratford–upon–Avon.

The herb garden at Knebworth, constructed from a
sketch by Gertrude Jekyll.

Flowers named after the Virgin Mary form an
unusual theme at this arcaded walk at Lincoln
Cathedral.

Izaak Walton's cottage at Shugborough.

show the flag in spring followed by roses and later in mid-July, bergamot, valerian and evening primroses are in full bloom. Many of these plants were given by local Womens' Institutes and it is through their generous gifts that the garden offers such a wide variety of scented herbs and unusual plants.

The present custodian, John Barnes, has only lived here for about a year and is still trying to re-establish order in the herb garden. His aim is to divide the different beds into medicinal, aromatic and culinary herbs, and he provides a fact sheet giving the different uses of each plant.

He makes his living from selling herbs and refreshments to visitors and is also a painter—some of his pictures are on display. Living here he has become an inveterate herb lover, a favourite plant being marjoram which he enjoys in different drinks. Gardening and herbal books are left out in the refreshment room for the interested visitor to browse through. The warmth and interest that he adds to a guided walk around the herb garden adds to the charm of the visit. And if time does dull the memory,

Types of compost

Most professional gardeners have their own methods of making compost and not all are prepared to reveal their secrets. However, all are agreed that, as one put it, 'there's compost and there's compost'. In other words, there's the compost you mix yourself or buy from the shops and there's the compost you produce from waste and decaying material alongside the bonfire and rubbish heap.

Dealing with the first, which may be regarded as the soil-containing mixtures, there can be little doubt that the winners hands down are the John Innes products. The two principal types are John Innes seedling and John Innes potting. Each contains sterilized loam, peat and horticultural sand. Fertilizer and lime are added according to the purpose of the compost, ie in accordance with what nutrients the plants will need.

The seedling compost is for seed sowing in trays and boxes and for striking cuttings; the potting compost is for growing on. Nos 2 and 3 contain two and three times respectively the normal amount of JI base, releasing nutrients in accordance with the time the plant is to stay in its pot.

There are now many types of compost on the market and many ingredients available for the keen gardener to use in a secret mix. The choice depends on the size of the gardening budget and time available for research.

plants bought here and growing happily at home will soon revive happy associations.

One point worth thinking about is that comfrey and horseradish grow on the railway embankment, only 30yd (27.5m) away, far more vigorously than in the garden he cultivates with such care.

KNEBWORTH HOUSE

Knebworth, Hertfordshire

Telephone: Knebworth (0438) 812661

Owner: The Hon David Lytton Cobbold

Situation: 28m N of London, 1m S of Stevenage. Road access from the A1 at Stevenage. **Open:** 11.30am–5pm. Bank holiday Mondays; April–May, Sunday only; June–15 September, daily except Monday; 16–30 September, Sunday only.

Knebworth House, a Tudor mansion, has been the home of the Lytton family since the fifteenth century, and the story continues into the twentieth century as it is now the home of the Hon David Lytton Cobbold and his family.

Fortunately for Knebworth, a young and enthusiastic gardener is busy working to restore the garden to its former glory. He is keen to inject the history of past events into the present day garden and you can appreciate his excitement when he found a plan drawn by the famous garden designer, Miss Jekyll, for a herb garden at Knebworth, dated 1907. This was perhaps a present for the Earl of Lytton, but no records are available and there is no evidence that the garden was ever planted.

To understand the significance of this discovery it is important to know that the well-known architect Edwin Lutyens married a daughter of the family, Lady Emily Lytton, in 1897. After initial disapproval, the family took advantage of his talents and examples of his work can be seen throughout the house and in the garden. Lutyens worked very closely with the garden designer Gertrude Jekyll, and it was no doubt because of this partnership that the original sketch was drawn. Although it was only a rough outline of what could be done, it inspired the gardener to plant the garden at Knebworth.

The quincunx, consisting of five equal circles, the basis of Miss Jekyll's design, was built with red engineering brick. A softer weatherworn brick might have been more appropriate, but would have needed more maintenance. This garden is very popular with visitors and as children tend to turn the brick pathway into a running track it was a wise decision.

Planting began in April 1982 and Miss Jekyll's instructions were followed exactly. She chose mostly perennial herbs, with lavender acting as a central feature for the middle bed, and rosemary for the surrounding circular beds. Clipped rosemary was used as a link to fill the spaces between the circular beds. The choice of the annual chervil is unusual, but since it seeds itself vigorously perhaps Miss Jekyll thought it would not need replanting each year.

Round the edges of this Jekyll garden, borders have been filled with interesting herbs to complete the picture. Golden and variegated herbs grow together adding welcome colour, and sweetly scented lavender and rosemary have been planted around garden seats.

More plans are in hand to make sure that this garden is of continuing interest, and in the next year or two the gravel paths will be replaced with York stone. Then thymes and chamomile can grow through the crevices.

Amazing discoveries came to light when restoring the overgrown garden. One was a Lutyens garden seat found in pieces in a neglected shrubbery. Dedicated to Anthony, Viscount Knebworth who was sadly killed when only thirty years old, this seat has now been repaired in the estate workshop, and a reproduction with the typical high back and curving arms has been

Knebworth House from the formal garden.

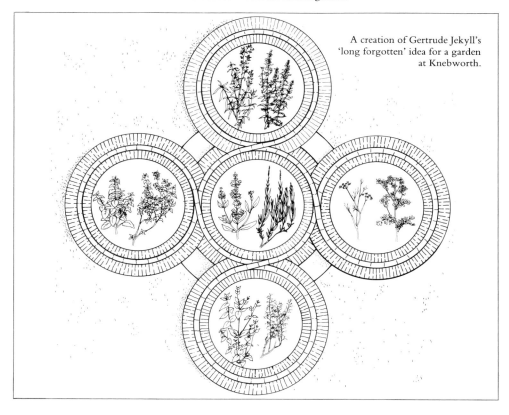

A creation of Gertrude Jekyll's 'long forgotten' idea for a garden at Knebworth.

made for the herb garden. This illustrates so well the Lutyens/Jekyll partnership evident at Knebworth and adds to the fascination felt by the visitor as he discovers more background information.

The gardeners appreciate the need to attract visitors to Knebworth with the pleasures of the funfair, the model railway and ice-cream stall, but they hope too that some visitors will pause and admire the garden. For they have resurrected a piece of horticultural history which will inspire herb enthusiasts and keen gardeners alike.

Gertrude Jekyll and her influence

The plans and writing of a gardener may be of more lasting significance than the actual planting of the gardens, and this is the case with Gertrude Jekyll. The herb garden she designed at Knebworth illustrates many of the points she emphasized in her work at the turn of the twentieth century.

Born in 1843, her early life was spent as a painter and designer of embroidery patterns, often using flowers and plants as an inspiration. Failing eyesight led her to plan gardens and she worked in partnership with the architect Edwin Lutyens. Their work is reflected in the design of many gardens today.

Miss Jekyll declared that groups of flowers, shrubs or trees should be allowed only the time during which they were at their most picturesque—and after that they should be allowed to leave the stage. She also recommended that one should draw up a plan and then buy plants to fit into a particular design, rather than rashly buy a plant and then search for a suitable site. Foliage plants were another love, as is evident from the careful use of herbs at Knebworth.

Not everybody has the good fortune to find a forgotten plan of a herb garden and build it in fine style as has been done at Knebworth, but the advice given by Miss Jekyll can still be put to good effect in any present day garden.

LATHBURY PARK HERBS

Newport Pagnell, Buckinghamshire

Telephone: Newport Pagnell (0908) 610316   **Owner:** Mrs Patricia Allen

Situation: ½m N of Newport Pagnell on the B526. **Open:** April–October, Thursday, 9am–12.30pm and 2.30–5pm. Or by appointment.

The herb nursery, in a walled garden of a large country house, is run by an enthusiastic amateur who has learnt through the years how to produce well-established container-grown plants for the wholesale trade.

Ask the owner, Patricia Allen, how she started and she will explain that, with her daughter, she began potting up a few herbs some years ago with the idea of trying out new recipes. A friend, who runs a garden centre, suggested they try their hand at growing for sale. This was considered a huge joke until he returned some months later asking for his herbs. Herbs were grown, and one satisfied customer led to another. Lathbury Park Herbs now supplies garden centres for many miles around.

However small the beginnings, sophisticated equipment becomes essential, with heated benches, irrigation systems and attractive scalloped plastic pots. Seed is sown in a peat-based compost and germinates in the large Victorian greenhouses, and the seedlings are transplanted into a soil-based mixture. Just before dispatch all plants have a phostrogen tablet slipped into the side of the pot. This acts as a sort of pep pill and keeps the plant looking green and healthy on the garden centre shelves.

Best sellers from this specialized nursery include basil for Italian dishes and French tarragon. Cuttings of this queen of culinary herbs were brought back from France so the aroma and flavour are particularly good.

All plants on sale commercially are displayed in an attractive 20ft (6m) border in front of a traditional kitchen garden wall. Lavender, thyme, sage and chives compete for attention with the more unruly angelicas, meadowsweet and foxgloves. An unusual white clary sage occupies a prime position in the front of the border. This garden is full of plants good enough to eat or to buy just for their sweet scent or decorative foliage.

Angelica, sweet and noble

Provided you can offer a fairly rich soil and a damp, shady position, a few plants of angelica (*Angelica archangelica*) will provide good things to eat, comfort you in sorrow and, so it is said, keep witches out of the garden. This majestic, soaring plant is the source of the angelica we see decorating cakes, sweets and other goodies. Here is a method for candying angelica, which should be done in spring when the shoots are young and tender.

Cut the stems into 3–4in (7.5–10cm) lengths. Simmer the sticks until tender, with very little water. Strain and peel the outside skin off; if stringy, boil again. Strain and cool. Add 1lb (450g) of sugar to the same weight of stalks and leave to stand for two days in a covered dish. Boil again until clear and a good colour. Drain again for the last time and sprinkle on as much sugar as will cling to the angelica. Let it dry (but not harden) in a cool oven. Store in airtight jars in a cool cupboard.

LINCOLN CATHEDRAL

Lincoln

Telephone: Lincoln (0522) 30320   **Owner:** The Dean and Chapter

Situation: in the cloisters of the Cathedral. Open: During the winter, 8am–6pm; during the summer, 7.30am–8pm

Dedicated to the Blessed Virgin Mary, Lincoln is the third largest and many would claim the most beautiful of all the cathedrals in the land.

Since it was never a monastery it is unlikely that herbs were grown here in the early days. But a small herb garden with a most unusual theme, built earlier this century, constantly delights visitors. The impressive pillars of an arcaded walkway designed by Sir Christopher Wren in 1674 is the setting for the garden planted with all the herbs of flowers traditionally named after the Virgin Mary, or associated with her name in biblical stories.

Paving stones have been removed giving all the familiar plants room to grow well together, their foliage bringing a touch of colour to the austere stone of surrounding buildings.

English history is full of tales of religious persecution: after the Reformation such descriptions as 'Our Lady' or 'the Blessed Virgin' were frowned upon where plants were concerned. So names were changed to the more prosaic lady's mantle, lady's smock or maiden pink, and these are the plants growing at Lincoln today.

In winter the imagination is captured by the common snowdrop, sometimes known as 'Our Lady's bells', which flowers at the feast of Candlemas during February. Later on, lungwort with blue flowers for Mary and red flowers for Joseph, and for this reason known as the 'Mary and Joseph flower', continues the story. Lily-of-the-valley has the delightful country name of 'Our Lady's tears'—how appropriate for those innocent sweetly scented bell flowers.

Lilies for May day

Legends abound about the uses of lily-of-the-valley and it is easily possible to believe that the subtle sweet fragrance will draw the nightingale from the hedge and lead him to choose his mate! Romantic Frenchmen give bouquets of lily-of-the-valley to their loved ones on 1 May. Grandmothers, mothers, wives and girl friends all walk around Paris proudly wearing buttonholes of the sweet smelling 'muguet de bois'.

Loved by all, the lily-of-the-valley (*Convallaria majalis*) is also a symbol of purity often associated with Whitsuntide festivals.

It is an easy plant to cultivate, preferring a well-drained rich soil and a shady position. Plant the roots at a distance of about 9in (23cm) apart, as they will spread very quickly to form a dense mat. Every few years dig up and divide the roots so as to give the plants more room to expand.

The common calendula or marigold (*Calendula officinalis*) has a place of importance here and represents 'Mary's Gold' or the golden rays of glory often shown around the Virgin's head.

The evergreen shrub rosemary is grown for a particular reason. Legend tells that the Virgin Mary, resting under the shade of a rosemary, took off her blue cloak and threw it over the bush. Since that memorable moment the flowers, originally white, have been the heavenly blue we associate with rosemary today.

In the Cloister Garden some plants have been substituted for the originals because it was thought they were more amenable to cultivation in this enclosed area, but it is by any standards a remarkable garden full of plants, if not actually herbs, very much associated with herbal traditions.

As John Codrington says, 'Just as Lincoln Cathedral preserves some of the finest flowering of Gothic architecture in England, and its choir and organists continue the equally important heritage of English church music; so it is also preserving from oblivion some of these ancient legends about the plants that are associated with the Blessed Virgin Mary.'

MAWLEY HALL

Cleobury Mortimer, Nr Kidderminster, Shropshire

Telephone: Cleobury Mortimer (0299) 270436 **Owner:** Mr and Mrs A. Galliers-Pratt

Situation: 2m NE of Cleobury Mortimer. On the A4117 Bewdley–Ludlow road. **Open:** Several times a year for charities. Consult the appropriate guidebooks. Also open by written appointment.

'There comes a moment when suddenly those meagre saplings can be called trees, and the twigs that passed for shrubs grow more exciting in every fresh season.' This quotation from a duplicated news-sheet which Mrs Galliers-Pratt gives to visitors on her open days will touch a chord in the heart of every true gardener.

At Mawley Hall plants are clearly there because they are loved and can be used. The immensely quotable Mrs Galliers-Pratt has regard too for other creatures of the herb garden; writing about this, which she created from an area of completely overgrown rubbish, she says:

During the first years it attracted a more interesting collection of wild life than plants. This is still a problem. Sharing is not exactly satisfactory, though butterflies are encouraged, and some of the residents hopefully eat each other besides the herbs . . .

Mawley Hall, a fine eighteenth-century house, was in a very neglected state when Mr and Mrs Galliers-Pratt came here in 1961

Rosemary hints

Brunettes can add lustre and body to their hair with a herbal rinse made from a small handful of rosemary sprigs, 2 pints (1.1 litres) of distilled or soft water and a couple of teabags. Put the rosemary sprigs and teabags into a large earthenware jug, pour on boiling water, infuse for 20 minutes, then strain into another jug and throw away the used herbs and teabags. Rinse your hair in the liquid.

A few rosemary sprigs thrown on to the fire at a barbecue will create a mouthwatering smell. Use the herb's long branches to baste steaks or sausages.

and started the mammoth task of restoring both house and garden to their former glory, at the same time creating a much-loved home.

Various other gardens secured priority but in 1969 it was the turn of the herb garden. Early years were spent clearing the area and preparing four large rectangular beds surrounded by gravel paths with six fine junipers as sentinels and overlooked by a range of interesting ornaments. Many culinary herbs are grown for use in the kitchen while chamomile and rosemary are dried for herb pillows. Mrs Galliers-Pratt uses thyme, rosemary and lemon balm as the basis for a delicious herbal cocktail.

Here clearly is a place where herbs, as in the past, earn their space in the soil by hard work. Elecampane has its root ground for healing purposes, black peppermint is used to flavour ice-cream, lovage flavours chicken dishes and chervil is used in salads.

There are now about thirty-two varieties of herbs in the new garden with more on the way.

MOSELEY OLD HALL

Wolverhampton, West Midlands

Telephone: Wolverhampton (0902) 782808   **Owner:** The National Trust

Situation: 4m N of Wolverhampton midway between the A449 and A460. Off the M6 at Shareshill then via the A460. **Open:** April–October, Wednesday, Thursday, Saturday and Sunday, 2–6pm; March and November, Wednesday and Sunday, 2–6pm. Also open on Easter, spring and summer bank holiday Monday and the Tuesday following, 2–6pm.

Moseley Old Hall lies only four miles north of the busy industrial town of Wolverhampton and with a new motorway lying literally at the back of the house it is difficult to imagine how remote it must have been in bygone days.

Famous in fact and fiction for the role it played in sheltering Charles II after his defeat at the Battle of Worcester in 1651, the house had fallen into a bad state of repair when the National Trust acquired the property in 1962.

The overall plan of the garden was designed by Mr Graham Thomas, garden consultant to the National Trust, and it has been reconstructed to look as it might have done in the seventeenth century using only plants then in cultivation. Dr Chand, who has been actively involved in the restoration of Moseley Old Hall, said there were many difficulties in laying out the garden as nothing was square. Other experts consulted included Miss Alice Coates on

herbaceous plants and Miles Hadfield on native trees.

At the front of the house are borders of old roses including the red rose of Lancaster and white rose of York, together with the blush striped 'Rosa Mundi' and other much-loved and renowned roses. Trimmed cones and spirals of box complete the seventeenth-century picture that Charles II would have seen from his bedroom during his eventful stay here.

The gateway on the left of the house leads into a wooden arbour or 'herber'. This is wreathed with the claret vine (*Vitis vinifera* 'Purpurea') and different varieties of clematis, the design being taken from *The Gardener's Labyrinth* by Didymus Montaine, published in 1577.

An authentic knot garden following one of the designs laid out by the Rev Walter Stonehouse in 1640 now forms a principal attraction at Moseley Old Hall. It is edged with dwarf box and different coloured

An authentic knot garden, an attractive feature of
Moseley Old Hall.

gravels are used in the compartments as would have been the case in the seventeenth century. According to Dr Chand the beginnings of this garden were fraught with difficulties. When the contractors first came to plant the garden it snowed so much they had to heat up the ground with flame-throwers before planting the box edging. And a troublesome few years followed before the plants were really established.

At one point of the knot garden is the hornbeam tunnel which, as Dr Chand explained, had been introduced to overcome a strange shaped corner to the garden. This tunnel leads to the beautiful nut walk, which runs the full length of the garden, past the knot garden, and past the orchard leading to the famous gate which is the way that Charles II, dressed as a woodcutter, first arrived seeking refuge.

Leading from the nutwalk to the house is a flagged path with paired fruit trees of Morello cherry, quince, mulberry and medlar. It leads to the enclosed herb garden which also has a central pathway finishing at a stone water trough bursting with different varieties of thymes. On either side of the pathway are borders of chives with a good assortment of herbs including marjoram, sage, spearmint, lemon balm, angelica, hyssop, rosemary, skirret and lady's bedstraw filling up the spaces.

At the entrance to the herb garden a Morello cherry tree has seeded itself and tends to encroach on the plants depriving them of sun. But it seems that nobody has the heart to uproot this rather beautiful tree.

At Moseley Old Hall the small herb garden may disappoint some visitors. But since an interest in herbs inevitably seems to be interwoven with a love of history there is much to be seen and enjoyed here. The knot garden, arbours, nutwalk and delightful roses all add up to a wealth of seventeenth-century features that takes the escape of King Charles II right out of the pages of the history books.

Myrtle for the bride

Among royal brides, the Queen had myrtle in her bouquet and so did Princess Anne. Later, Lady Diana Spencer kept up the royal tradition.

It is thought that Queen Victoria started the custom; the sprig from her wedding bouquet was planted at Osborne House on the Isle of Wight where it grew into a fine bush. It is from this bush, or perhaps now from a bush grown from cuttings of the original, that myrtle is supplied for royal brides.

It is a delightfully fragrant plant for any sheltered garden. It will grow to a height of 8–10ft (2.4–3m) and makes an attractive bushy shrub with glossy leaves which are small and oval. Hundreds of small, white, scented flowers with long golden stamens turn the bush into a vision of beauty in the latter half of summer.

This very special shrub does need rather special care. The best place for it is against a south-facing wall or fence. It will also grow well in a large pot on a patio and can be brought under cover in winter. If you are growing myrtle in this way, 'Tarentina' is a good variety to choose because it is more compact and therefore suitable for growing in a pot.

Cuttings of myrtle should be taken in June or July. Take 3in (7.5cm) lengths from non-flowering branches and insert them in a mixture of peat and sand. Extra warmth may be needed to encourage rooting. If you don't have a propagator, cover the pot with a polythene bag and try your luck on a sunny window-sill or in the greenhouse. When rooted, plant the cuttings out in single pots containing a good potting compost. Keep in a warm, draught-free place during winter and water very sparingly. Sadly, myrtle grown outside is not always successful.

OAK COTTAGE HERB FARM

Nesscliffe, Nr Shrewsbury, Shropshire

Telephone: Nesscliffe (074381) 262   **Owner:** Mrs Ruth Thompson

Situation: In Nesscliffe on the A5 NW of Shrewsbury. Turn down a narrow lane opposite the Nesscliffe Hotel. **Open:** Visitors are 'very welcome' but as there are no fixed opening hours a telephone call is advisable.

For the pedantic gardener keen on plucking out an offending weed and on keeping plants in order, a visit to this delightful garden near the Welsh border will at first prove a shock. Mrs Thompson calls it a 'controlled wilderness' and it is the control rather than the wilderness that provides the interest. Herbs grow in unfettered abundance and in such profusion that any matchbox size patch of bare earth is a discovery to be remarked upon. The casual stroller is waist and often head high in foliage while the earth beneath is as stuffed with roots and ground cover as an old sofa is with horsehair. But the Thompsons know where everything is and follow each flowering plant and herb through from seedling stage to the day when the seedheads burst and the cycle begins all over again.

They moved to Nesscliffe in the early 1970s and were faced with a maze of concrete paths and the conventional cabbage patch and sloping strip of lawn. The saving grace was a paddock and a view. They kept the paths, using them as natural divisions and for access to a series of small terraced gardens that have been created over the years. Small walls were made from the remains of old pigsties, and a yew hedge has now reached sufficient height to confound a neighbour who asked at planting time if the Thompsons planned to live forever.

The emphasis now is on English cottage gardening with culinary, medicinal and other herbs surviving well in the light sandy soil alongside the old-fashioned plants beloved of flower arrangers.

The Victorian favourite masterwort (*Astrantia major*) and the giant scabious (*Caphalaria gigantea*) grow cheek by jowl with common broom (*Cytisus scoparius*) and Our Lady's milk thistle (*Silybum marianum*) to provide texture and colour rarely seen elsewhere; and on a lower level the thymes, four-leaf clover and pinks share common ground. The old cottage garden musk (*Mimulus moschatus*) and the mints, particularly pennyroyal (*Mentha pulegium*) and the tiny Corsican mint (*Mentha requienii*), vie with the Old English lavender (*Lavandula angustifolia*) to bring the greater perfume to the air.

John Thompson's special interest in seeds, insects and conservation subjects in general is evident, as is Ruth Thompson's knowledge of historic plants. They have created for themselves, and their visitors, a garden which can fairly be called unique.

The violet revival

A bunch of damp sweet smelling violets is the very essence of an English spring. How lovely to go out on a rather bleak March day and see these small vividly coloured flowers nestling close to the ground. Like the shrub roses and other cottage garden flowers, violets are enjoying a welcome return to fashion.

Cultivated violets (*Viola odorata*) thrive in a rich loamy soil and the ground should be carefully prepared before planting by adding compost and, most important of all, plenty of moisture.

The most popular way of propagating violets is by pegging down the runners that the plant throws out in the spring as soon as it has finished flowering. They should be firmed into a rich compost mixture and will quickly establish themselves. As soon as they have rooted they

can be moved into their growing position and will flower the following spring.

OXFORD BOTANIC GARDEN

High Street, Oxford

Telephone: Oxford (0865) 242　　　　　　　　　**Owner:** University of Oxford

Situation: In the High Street by Magdalen Bridge. **Open:** March–October, weekdays 8.30am–5.00pm, Sunday 10am–noon and 2–6pm; October–March, weekdays 9am–4.30pm, Sunday 10am–noon and 2–4.30pm.

For those visitors with a special interest in plants that are in some way different yet not so rare and outlandish that they could never be cultivated at home, Oxford Botanic Garden is invariably a delight. It has, for example, the world's largest collection of variegated plants, a mouth-watering feast of leaves patched, striped, tipped and of most colours under the sun. Labels help the inexperienced to find their way about and to acquire rudimentary but useful knowledge about the causes of colour variation and changes in texture and pattern. Clues to inherited tendencies, transmission of a virus during grafting and the role of the pollinating insect provide hours of fascinating research which could well be carried on at home.

Research into variegated plants is a speciality of the garden and there are plenty of specimens to see. The collection includes a variety of iris (*Iris pallida* 'Variegata') with striped leaves, a strawberry (*Fragaria ananassa* 'Variegata') with gold and green leaves and the tricolour sage with purple, green and cream leaves known to Gerard as 'painted sage'.

This happy hunting ground for the herb enthusiast is small but of great historic significance. Established in 1621 by Henry Danvers, Earl of Danby, it is the oldest of the physic gardens in Great Britain. Danby leased from Magdalen College 5 acres (2 hectares) of meadowland just outside the city wall which had formerly been a Jewish cemetery. The garden was to be used for the tuition of students, for research, and to cultivate plants for sale to local doctors and apothecaries.

Financial struggles in those early days left little money to spare for paying the salary of a professor. Lord Danby was lucky enough to contact Jacob Bobart, a practical gardener and at that time tenant of a nearby hostelry. He agreed to take on the work and became 'Horti Praefectus'. The terms of his contract

---

Patched and striped

As a change, try creating a border of herbs with variegated foliage. Golden thyme (*Thymus citriodorus aureus*) has leaves that are a dappled gold and green during most of the summer months and it goes well with one of the lovely golden sages (*Salvia officinalis* 'Icterina'). Another interesting variety is purple sage (*Salvia officinalis purpurea*).

A rather fine variegated rue that has leaves splashed with cream is definitely a collector's item. You may have to search hard to find this treasure. Also include in your collection golden lemon balm and marjoram.

There are many reasons for variegation, ranging from mosaic infection to a mixing of the green and white pigment-bearing plastids. You will learn as much as there is to know about the subject at Oxford Botanic Garden, with its fascinating collection of plants with leaves patched and striped.

were 'to dresse manure preserve and keep the said Garden', and 'plant the same with such herbes, settes and plants as shall be thought requesit and necessaries'. This Jacob Bobart did with enthusiasm and skill during the years of the civil war. The salary agreed was £40 per annum.

Even so, some seven years later Jacob Bobart was to report that as yet he had received no wages. There must have been an unspoken agreement that he could have the profits from the sale of medicinal plants and other herbs, for in later years he became a man of great wealth and influence in Oxford. The layout of the garden, as shown in an engraving of 1675, is thought to be his work.

After Bobart's death in 1680 his son, another Jacob, became gardener and professor of botany and the reign of the Bobarts lasted another forty years. The following lines of verse recall the high esteem that the name Bobart enjoyed in Oxford circles:

All Plants which Europe's Fields contain;
For Health, for pleasure, or for Pain;
(From the tall Cedar, that does rise
With Conic Pride, and mates the Skies;
Down to the humblest Shrub that crawls
On Earth or just ascends our Walls),
Her Squares of Horticulture yield:

By Danby Planted, Bobart Till'd
Delightful scientifick Shade.
For Knowledge, as for Pleasure made.

(*Vertumnus*, an Epistle to Mr Jacob Bobart Botany Professor to the University of Oxford and Keeper of the Physick–Garden 1713.)

The Physic Garden was completely re-planned in about 1725 and continued to provide plants for the various doctors and apothecaries in Oxford. However, in 1840 the name of Physic Garden was dropped in favour of Botanic Garden. Plants were now cultivated for teaching and for scientific research rather than for use by practitioners.

This is very much the situation today. During our visit we learned that seed supplied by the garden was being used at the Radcliffe Infirmary during trials to find a new plant-based method of coagulating blood.

The garden is laid out in a series of long rectangular beds demonstrating the different families (following the Hooker and Bentham classification system) and naturally there are many herbs which may be readily identified without reference to labels or books. A bed in the south-west corner is devoted to culinary herbs such as lovage, thyme, a variety of mints and several marjorams. More intriguing for many are the beds of so-called economic plants—those used for making various fibres and creating dyes and which yield important oils. Here a handsome castor oil plant (*Ricinus communis*) with large glossy leaves claims attention. Nearby is caraway (*Carum carvi*) which provides oils for the catering industry.

One ancient yew survives from a central avenue planted before 1650 during the days of Jacob Bobart, and among other fine and interesting trees are a Glastonbury thorn (*Crataegus monogyna* 'Praecox')—it has no thorns and it flowers at Christmas—and a maidenhair tree (*Ginkgo biloba*).

SELSLEY HERB AND GOAT FARM

Water Lane Farm, Selsley, Stroud, Gloucestershire

Telephone: Stroud (04536) 6682   **Owner:** Mr and Mrs P. Wimperis

Situation: Approach via Stonehouse on the A419 then take the Kings Stanley road, following signs for Selsley. Immediately opposite Selsley church is a track leading over common land; take this and watch out for Water Lane straight ahead of you. Water Lane Farm is at the bottom of the lane.
Open: Tuesday–Sunday 2–5pm, or by appointment.

Selsley—it means 'clear view'—lies on one of the last escarpments of the Cotswolds before the vale of the River Severn, and occupants of Water Lane Farm have enjoyed the sight of the dawn light over the Malverns, May Hill and the Black Mountains since 1550. The hills provide a dramatic backdrop to a small and much-loved formal garden and an impressive array of potted herbs on a south-facing bank with views to Stroud. Taking advantage of an exceptionally attractive site, Gill and Peter Wimperis have set out a nursery of herb plants in sections covering bay and sages, scented geraniums, culinary herbs, lavender, rosemary and thyme, mints, the onion family, hedging herbs and 'old medicinal' herbs.

Herbs difficult to find in many gardens —balm of Gilead (*Cedronella triphylla*), Jerusalem sage (*Phlomis fruticosa*) and myrtle (*Myrtus communis*)—tempt the connoisseur, while in a coverted stable there are scented pillows, pot-pourri made on the premises, pomanders, dried flower arrangements and herbal creams.

Goats, sometimes with their young, ducks and geese form part of a brave venture for the Wimperis family, who have brought a touch of romance to the business. In such an atmosphere, even the most casual visitor testing and tasting the wide range of mints or coming face to face with woad could hardly fail to be transported for a moment back to the days when such plants were vital in the kitchen, the sick room, the byre and on the field of battle.

A clear view over an impressive array of pot plants at Selsley, where the Wimperis family have brought a touch of romance to the herbs business.

Why parsley can be a devil to grow

Whenever the conversation gets round to herbs, someone refers to the reason of growing parsley. It can be a difficult plant and quite often the reason is that parsley seed soon loses its germinating power. Also, it likes a nice, warm, friable soil with some shade and moisture and does not like the cold at all. Consequently, a late summer sowing can often prove very successful and guarantee a good picking even through the cold frosty days ahead.

For best results when growing parsley outside, dig a trench about 16in (40cm) deep and line the bottom with well-rotted manure or compost. Fill this in with garden soil and plant the seed in drills about ½in (1cm) deep. The area should be kept well watered, particularly if there is a dry spell.

When the seedlings appear they should be very carefully pricked out in a row about 8in (20cm) apart. In autumn —or the first week in November at the latest—each row should be covered with cloches for protection against bad weather and to ensure that you will be picking your own supplies with a good flavour from Christmas to the following spring.

There are many sayings about parsley, and one is that the seed goes to the devil seven times before appearing. This is probably because it often takes six to seven weeks for any green tips to appear. When nothing happens at all, gardeners comfort themselves with the belief that the herb grows for the wicked and not for the just. When a good crop shows, there are those who indulge in the belief that parsley only grows well when the lady of the house wears the trousers.

STONE COTTAGE

Hambleton, Oakham, Leicestershire

Telephone: Oakham (0572) 2156 **Owner:** John Codrington

Situation: Just off the A6003 Uppingham to Oakham road. **Open:** For various charities during the year. Consult the appropriate guide or write for an appointment.

Stone Cottage, as its name suggests, is a true picture-postcard house in a quiet village of the old county of Rutland, bordering on a very recently built reservoir called Rutland Water.

The owner John Codrington describes his garden as 'A Garden of Memories'. Is this true? Amazingly enough he was born, or so he says, in the reign of Queen Victoria. But to see him walking round the garden with secateurs at the ready, you realize that his outlook on horticultural matters is very much of the 1980s. The answer then will depend to a great extent on the attitude of the visitor. If you are keen on wild gardens and botany there is much to discover, but if you want to see only a tidy patch all neatly labelled, you will certainly not share in the adventure happening here.

The aim is to create a garden where all the herbs known to man can ramble as they wish. It is in accord with present day thinking—the wish for conservation of plants and wild life in their natural state having superseded neatly trimmed lawns edged with bedding plants.

However, there is a specific herb garden at Stone Cottage which is charming in all aspects. Spilling over on to the paving stones but enclosed on two sides by a honeysuckle (*Lonicera nitida*) hedge, a variety of herbs are grown and used for culinary purposes —lovage, thyme, marjoram, chervil, bay and many others.

A statuesque tree onion (*Allium cepa viriparum*) with clusters of small bulbils at the top of the hollow stems grows in one section, and although not fond of onions, John Codrington finds he does enjoy the flavour of this useful herb.

An Agatha Christie garden has been devised as an altogether different type of herb garden. The idea came to this original thinker when a bird dropped a seed of deadly nightshade (*Atropa belladonna*), and it grew. Now the Agatha Christie garden has a collection of poisonous plants with red labels giving the appropriate drug such as atropine, aconitine, conine, stramonine, digitalin, hyoscine and colchicine.

Every plant in this garden has a story to tell and none more fascinating than the liquorice (*Glycorrhiza glabra*). This plant from the Leguminosae family is not particularly beautiful but the root is renowned for making liquorice sweetmeats and is used medicinally. John Codrington went to Pontefract, the home of liquorice, when he wanted a plant for his garden. It was a great disappointment when an official at the Town Hall told him that it no longer grew in the neighbourhood, and all the liquorice used was imported.

Coincidence now enters the tale which, surprising as it is, is quite true. Returning home he gave a lift to a young hitch-hiker and told him of his plight. The lad replied, 'That's a lot of rubbish. There's plenty of liquorice growing at Pontefract. Come and see me at my dad's pub and we'll get some.' Sure enough John Codrington called at the pub a few weeks later and this is where he was able to dig up a root from a large patch of liquorice growing on a nearby piece of waste ground.

There are many such stories to be related, and the garden is as the owner says 'Not only of beauty, but includes interest and the evocation of memories'. Could there be a better description of a herb garden?

Plants have been carried back from many places, including a rubbish dump behind the Generalife Garden at Granada, Sri Lanka, the Imperial Park at Tokyo and the Greek temples of Sicily.

New ideas are constantly being developed. In the gravel garden for instance, plants grow straight out of the gravelled surface and look quite at home. Seats have been placed on the outer perimeter of the garden and windows have been cut from the bordering shrubbery so that a vista of Rutland Water and the surrounding country can be enjoyed.

Herb lovers will treasure this garden for the opportunity it gives them to study wild plants growing in natural conditions. If at first you think it is just a jungle of plants gone to seed, weeds, overgrown plants and self-sown seedlings, look a little closer and treasures will soon reveal themselves. And like the owner, a keen amateur botanist since childhood days, you will come to appreciate that cow parsley is not an obnoxious weed but an interesting wild plant called *Anthriscus sylvestris*. Seeds are saved of plants both wild and cultivated and kept for the garden or given with true generosity to appreciative friends.

A dragonfly, enjoying its brief span of life, circles over a shady pond where foxgloves, meadowsweet, campions and oxeye daisies all grow in happy profusion. Impossible here not to be caught up in the miracle of life itself. 'Look and discover', says John Codrington, 'because I have not made them respectable with Latin names on labels.'

It is difficult to describe this garden. It is a place one must find for oneself and having found it the memory will linger on.

A weed is a plant out of place

The wild garden complete with drifts of bluebells, yarrow, dandelions, cowslips and primroses, sheltered by banks of foxgloves and topped by crab apple trees and elder bushes is fast becoming a form of herb garden much appreciated in the present era.

Such a garden is the one that John Codrington cultivates. Although few will have a garden as large as his and in such ideal surroundings, many tips can be given for starting a similar garden on a smaller scale.

Before beginning to plan your wild garden, dig over the soil and clear the ground of all existing weeds. Strange as it sounds, this is important as you only want to establish the wild flowers of your choice.

The four structural requirements of such a garden are a winding path, a garden seat, a pond and a tree. First establish places for these and then draw up a plan to find out how much space will be left for growing ground cover plants.

Seeds of mixed meadowland flowers, herbs and grasses can be obtained from specialist dealers and sown on the prepared ground. Please do not uproot plants growing in the wild to grace your garden. Since so many people are now following this pattern of horticulture it should be quite easy to beg a root or two of comfrey, forget-me-not or giant hogweed to include in your garden. Waterloving herbs such as the mints, bistort, meadowsweet and sweet cicely will grow amicably around the pond.

Once the garden has been established, maintenance can be kept to the minimum by cutting back too vigorous growth and handweeding invasive ground elder, nettles and bindweed. Perhaps it should be emphasized here that this is no form of gardening for the neurotically tidy person who does not feel happy unless he takes a hoe out every few weeks!

The charm of this form of gardening is the pleasure of sharing its attractions with butterflies, birds, toads and hedgehogs and of showing others the joys of conserving wild life in all its many aspects.

SHAKESPEARE'S BIRTHPLACE GARDEN

Henley Street, Stratford-upon-Avon, Warwickshire

Telephone: Stratford-upon-Avon (0789) 204016   **Owner:** Shakespeare's Birthplace Trust

Open: April–October, weekdays 9am–6pm, Sunday 10am–6pm; November–March, weekdays 9am–4.30pm, Sunday 1.30–4.30pm.

This half-timbered Elizabethan house where Shakespeare was born is a good place to begin a tour of the Stratford gardens. You can wander down the paths studying the flowers, herbs and trees growing in profusion. Familiar herbs such as 'hot lavender', mints, savory and marjoram, are neatly planted in semi-circles and all are carefully labelled.

Trees associated with this period such as mulberry, quince and a medlar grow here, as do a grape-vine, pomegranate and fig. Trees of English origin include the cedar,

oak, lime, hawthorn and silver birch. Bringing events and plants right up to this century is a rose ('Ena Harkness') presented by Her Majesty Queen Elizabeth II to commemorate her Coronation year.

Apart from minor alterations, the garden layout has not been changed—save that in the centre there now stands the base of what was Stratford's medieval market cross. This garden was purchased for preservation as a national memorial to William Shakespeare in 1847.

NEW PLACE

Chapel Street, Stratford-upon-Avon, Warwickshire

Telephone: Stratford-upon-Avon (0789) 204016   **Owner:** Shakespeare's Birthplace Trust

Open: April–October, weekdays 9am–6pm, Sunday 2–6pm; November–March, weekdays only, 9am–12.45pm and 2–4pm.

By far the most important and beautiful of the gardens in Stratford-upon-Avon is the Great Garden at New Place where Shakespeare spent many happy hours tending his plants and enjoying the company of his friends. Today you can walk through the gardens and marvel at the velvet smooth lawn, the long border and the wild bank, quoting perhaps from *A Midsummer Night's Dream.*

I know a bank where the wild thyme blows
Where oxlips and the nodding violet grows
Quite over-canopied with luscious
   woodbine,
With sweet musk-roses and with eglantine

Box hedges decorated with clipped domes divide the border into compartments containing cottage-garden flowers such as hollyhocks, canterbury bells, larkspurs,

pansies and the famous 'streaked gillyvors'.

As you reach the wild bank, look out for the eglantine, a wild rose resembling our sweetbriar (*Rosa rubiginosa*). It has distinctive pink petals and attractive round leaves. You will also find oxlips, a popular flower in Shakespearian days; the bright yellow blooms are similar in shape to those of the cowslip but are more robust in appearance. Woodbine, the country name for the honeysuckle clambering over the hedgerows, was grown in Elizabethan times to provide shade. It was also used for secluded bowers where lovers could sit and hold hands away from prying eyes.

The highlight of the garden is the venerable and beautifully preserved mulberry tree. See it when it is surrounded by banks of spring flowers and time will stand still for you. Research shows that this could well be the spot where Shakespeare planted the first mulberry tree in 1609 in response to King James I's decree that loyal supporters of the monarchy should plant mulberry trees and

help promote the silk industry in this country.

This tree became famous after Shakespeare's death and caught the imagination of pilgrims to Stratford who came to look at it and cut souvenir pieces from the bark. Then in 1758 an unsympathetic parson, the Rev Francis Gastrell, came to live in New Place; after two years of putting up with knife-wielding visitors he took an axe to the tree and chopped it down, selling it not for souvenirs but as firewood. The handsome mulberry you see today is thought to have grown from a cutting taken from the original tree and so earns a place among Shakespearian legends.

The knot garden occupies the part of the garden which Shakespeare is thought to have cared for personally and has been described as 'one of the most enchanting sights of Warwickshire'. The stone for the paths that divide this typically square-shaped garden came from Wilmcote (the home of the poet's mother).

The beds are edged with low-growing box and the familiar savory, hyssop, cotton lavender, thyme and other sweet-smelling herbs of today, which Shakespeare would have known.

There is a shady tunnel of trees and crab apples to transport you back into *A Midsummer Night's Dream*: 'And sometimes lurk I in a gossip's bowl'. The small sour fruits were frequently roasted and used to flavour a mug or 'bowl' of ale. 'Gossips' was the name given to godparents and no doubt ale flavoured with crab apples would have been a popular drink at christenings in those days.

Ernest Law's *Shakespeare's Garden*, first published in 1922, tells the story of the replanting of this very special garden. Little was known of it until Victorian times when New Place was purchased, thanks to the efforts of scholars of the day. The garden was opened up so that 'Shakespeare's countrymen could enjoy it for all time'. After the end of the First World War the trustees were moved to appeal for plants and funds to support a restoration project—and the response was incredible. King George V and Queen Mary sent roses and cottage garden flowers, as did other members of the royal family. Gifts of plants and money flooded in from castles mentioned in the Bard's plays, from cottage gardens and from the East End of London, as well as from overseas.

The knot garden was modelled on a pattern from Didymus Montaine's book *The Gardener's Labyrinth* published in 1577. Perhaps Shakespeare studied this very book

I know a wild bank

A wild bank can be a most successful feature in any garden. Although more in keeping with a country cottage garden, there is no reason why a small part of a town garden should not be given similar treatment.

Choose a south-facing slope and plant the herbs associated with Shakespearian days. A garden such as this should not be too tidy and virtually the only cultivation needed will be vigilance with the secateurs in cutting back too vigorous growth.

Some Shakespearian plants suitable for a wild bank are:

Wild rose, eglantine (*Rosa rubiginosa*)
Fragrant pink flowers followed by brightly coloured hips.

Woodbine, honeysuckle (*Lonicera periclymenum*)
Blooms in early summer and is sweetly scented.

Thyme (*Thymus vulgaris*)
Forms cushions of tiny dark green leaves and mauve flowers in the summer.

Heartsease pansy (*Viola tricolor*)
Small dainty pansy-like flowers which appear right through the summer.

Fennel (*Foeniculum vulgare*)
Growing to 5ft (1.5m) this attractive plant with yellow flowers and green lacy leaves is excellent for adding height to the top of the bank.

Wormwood (*Artemisia absinthium*)
Has silver-grey leaves which are deeply indented and small yellow flowers. Reaches 4ft (1.2m) and gives off a strange, rather bitter perfume.

Primrose (*Primula vulgaris*)
The well-known and much loved pale yellow flowers are truly the harbingers of spring. Plants will establish themselves well in a wild bank garden.

when laying out the original knot garden. He may also have met and talked with Gerard and would certainly have consulted his herbal. Is it too romantic and fanciful a thought that Shakespeare walks there still? 'The bard lives on' scratched on a wall will be the truth for most visitors to New Place. It's magic.

HALL'S CROFT

Old Town, Stratford-upon-Avon, Warwickshire

Telephone: Stratford-upon-Avon (0789) 204016 **Owner:** Shakespeare's Birthplace Trust

Open: April–October, weekdays 9am–6pm, Sunday 10am–6pm; November–March, weekdays 9am–4.30pm, Sunday 1.30–4.30pm.

The home of Shakespeare's daughter Susanna and her husband Dr John Hall, this fine Tudor house is near the parish church where Shakespeare is buried. Enclosed by walls on all sides, the garden is a picture-book revival of an olde-time country garden. It is spacious and although it was designed as recently as 1950, it conveys the sense of formality of the Tudor style.

A fine mulberry tends to dominate the scene, tempting the visitor with its shade. The garden is, as one visitor remarked, a place for lingering in—and there is much to linger for. The shrub roses and cottage-garden flowers in wide borders deserve more than cursory inspection as does the quite small but fascinating plot of herbs grown by Dr Hall to help him treat his

A garden of simples

Dr Hall cultivated 'simples'—herbs used for medicinal purposes—in his garden at Hall's Croft, and today many gardeners could follow his example by growing medicinal herbs and at the same time learn a little more about the habits of such useful plants.

It should be emphasized here that if you have been ill for some time you should seek expert advice. But for the grazed knee, the irritating sore throat and the occasional sleepless night, herbs picked from your own patch can often help.

The oval ridged seeds of dill, an attractive feathery leaved annual with umbels of yellow flowers, can be made into dill water to bring up wind from an unsettled stomach. Sage leaves chopped and mixed with oil make a soothing rub for aches and pains. And a relaxing tea or tisane to ensure dream-free nights can be made from the dainty daisy-like flowers of chamomile.

Having tried a few of these homely remedies, keen gardeners wanting to learn more about herbs and medicine should apply to The Registrar, The School of Herbal Medicine, Tunbridge Wells, Kent TN2 5EY. Many different training courses, including a one year correspondence course as a general introduction to herbal medicine, are offered by this professional organization.

patients for every complaint under the sun.

A well-respected physician and apothecary of the day, Dr Hall would have needed a large supply of medicinal herbs—or 'simples' as they were called then—as his practice extended to Worcester, Ludlow and Northampton. The good doctor also carried out research on the treatment of scurvy. This unpleasant complaint, which we now know to be caused by vitamin C deficiency, was very prevalent after the winter months. Fresh vegetables were difficult to find in those days and Dr Hall discovered that green herbs and fruit juices would help to ease the symptoms.

Spare a few minutes to go into the house and look at the room furnished in the style of an Elizabethan dispensary. The pestle and mortar, apothecaries' jars, dried herbs and herbal potions seem almost to be waiting for use today.

ANNE HATHAWAY'S COTTAGE

Shottery, Stratford-upon-Avon, Warwickshire

Telephone: Stratford-upon-Avon (0789) 204016   **Owner:** Shakespeare's Birthplace Trust

Situation: At Shottery, 1m N of Stratford-upon-Avon. **Open:** April–October, weekdays 9am–6pm, Sunday 10am–6pm; November–March, weekdays 9am–4.30pm, Sunday 1.30–4.30pm.

The picturesque thatched cottage where Shakespeare's wife Anne Hathaway lived before her marriage is world-renowned today and worth seeing to appreciate the story of Stratford.

Visitors will enjoy the beauty of the typical cottage garden with an interesting medley of trees, shrubs, flowers and herbs growing together. Many favourite herbs can be discovered including 'bold oxlips' and the crown imperial, rosemary 'for remembrance', pinks, milk thistles, foxgloves and mulleins.

An orchard full of venerable fruit trees and wild flowers completes the picture of an Elizabethan garden.

Fact and fantasy

For many herb lovers, the apparent devotion of some folk to the sayings of the past is strange and somewhat irritating. But there is a fascination in the beliefs held by the herbalists of the sixteenth and seventeenth centuries, among them John Gerard and John Parkinson. They will probably be quoted for many centuries to come, not because they have any real authority but because they tend to underline the gullibility of mankind.

For instance, it was declared that stinking horehound (*Phlomis herba-venti*) 'cureth the biting of a mad dog' while the madonna lily (*Lilium candidum*) 'bringeth th haire againe upon places which have beene burned or scalded'.

A purgation of Christmas rose (*Helle-*

continued

continued

borus niger) was considered good for mad and furious men and for those troubled with the falling sickness or leprosy. French lavender (*Lavandula stoechas*) was much sought after, for a decoction of the husks and flowers 'openeth the stoppings of the liver, the lungs and the bladder, and in one worde all other inwarde parts, clensing and driving foorth all evill and corrupt humours, and procureth urine'.

It is sad to read of the faith placed in such herbs as angelica (*Angelica archangelica*) as plague and pestilence swept the country. Said Gerard: 'The roote of garden Angelica is a singular remedie against poison, and against the plague, and all infections taken by even and corrupt aire.' He declared that a piece of root held in the mouth or chewed 'doth most certainly drive away the pestilentiall aire'.

THORNBY HERBS

Thornby Hall Gardens, Thornby, Northampton

Telephone: Northampton (0604) 740090   **Manager:** Mr Stanley Barton

Situation: In the village of Thornby, 10m N of Northampton just off the A50 Northampton to Leicester road. **Open:** All through the year on Tuesday, Thursday and Sunday, 2–5pm.

Head gardener at Thornby Hall for many years, Mr Stanley Barton found himself in an unusual position on the death of his employer: he was offered the chance of running the walled garden as a commercial proposition.

Deciding to take advantage of this, he transformed the old kitchen garden, which must cover about $\frac{3}{4}$ of an acre (0.3 hectares), into a herb nursery. Plants are grown for cutting and for sale in containers, and Mr Barton has become a confirmed herb lover. The garden is run on organic principles using a soil-based compost of his own manufacture which keeps the container plants green and healthy looking.

A white form of Jacob's ladder and a white hyssop are two of the more unusual plants on sale. Another herb here, not often grown commercially, is witch hazel (*Hamamelis virginiana*). With twisted yellow flowers appearing on bare stems during the winter months, this is a valuable medicinal

Two of the stone gargoyles illustrating various forms of suffering—all to be cured with herbs!—at Thornby.

plant, and an extract is used to soothe bruises, sprains and strains.

The well-arranged shop is a veritable Aladdin's cave, and all manner of dried herbs, herbal teas, books on herbs and other associated goods will tempt the purchaser. And it will be a problem to resist buying one of the amusing stone gargoyles to take home. Each one illustrates a different form of suffering. The poor fellow with a headache has a crow pecking away at the top of his skull. Melancholy is the complaint of the weeping lady with a fish drowning in her tears. Bad eyesight, stomach problems, toothache, bites and stings are also dramatically illustrated. These troubles, it may be superfluous to mention, can all be cured by herbs.

A short distance away from this commercial area is a display herb garden planted in the original Victorian rose garden at Thornby Hall. The layout is almost unchanged.

Plants are grown here for their decorative, culinary or medicinal uses. But as they are cared for by a professional gardener of many years standing they are not allowed to spill over the paths but are obliged to grow in neat and orderly cushions. Discipline is the order of the day and the edges of the turf paths are all immaculately trimmed. And yet just an occasional weakness does creep in. For rambling over the high yew hedge, topped with topiary peacocks and similar birds, is the flame creeper (*Tropaeolum speciosum*) with brilliant scarlet flowers. This is one of Mr Barton's favourites and grows to a height of 10–15ft (3–4.5m).

Other favourites include pineapple sage (*Salvia rutilans*) with soft green leaves. When bruised the leaves really do smell of pineapples. This variety has scarlet flowers in bloom from June to September and makes an attractive indoor plant.

The training of a skilled gardener is evident in the attractive grouping of the herbs. Bronze fennel, silver thistle leaves and purple sage form a satisfying display in one corner and in another section golden marjoram, golden sage and golden feverfew add a splash of sunshine.

Root division

Many herbs such as chives, mint, marjoram and other low-growing plants can be propagated by root division in the autumn. After watering well a few days beforehand, dig up the whole plant and divide it by pulling the roots apart into small bunches. In cases of extreme stubbornness, you may have to use two forks to prise them away from each other or attack the clump with a sharp knife. Remove and destroy the rubbish by burning and return the selected portions to the soil. Root division may also be done in the spring.

A hedge of Hidcote lavender runs along a wide asphalt path and against this grow the various scented-leaved geraniums and bright clumps of the pretty little heartsease pansy.

After a lifetime of pulling out weeds Mr Barton is now transferring his interests to cultivating them. Along a wide north border in front of a mellow brick wall are shrub roses, meadowsweet, teazles, foxgloves and many other wild herbs growing in an unrestricted fashion. This has become a happy hunting ground for all the bees in the neighbourhood and it is hoped that butterflies will also find their way here.

THE NORTH

ABBEY HOUSE MUSEUM
Kirkstall, Leeds

Telephone: Leeds (0532) 755821   **Owner:** Leeds City Council

Situation: On the Abbey Road (A65) from Leeds to Ilkley. **Open:** Museum, April–September, weekdays 10am–6pm, Sundays 2–6pm; October–March, closes at 5pm. Garden open any time.

One of a series of terraced gardens leading down to the busy Kirkstall Road, the herb garden was designed and planted in the early 1960s as a memorial to a former Lord Mayor, Mrs Mary Pierce. The Abbey House itself was, from 1162 until 1539, the great gatehouse to Kirkstall Abbey. After the Dissolution of the monasteries it was converted to a dwelling-house by the last Abbot, John Ripley, who died in 1568. It was acquired by the city council in 1925.

Thus, although of recent construction and containing as yet no plants of special interest, the garden is the ideal place for a newcomer to begin a study of those herbs used by monks and townsfolk of old to give flavour to their soups, mask the odour of unwashed bodies, cure the bites of vipers and provide the dyes for clothing and tapestries.

Little old ladies bring their knitting to seats overlooking the garden and catch a glimpse over the fennel of the ruins of the abbey in the near distance. Children in their scores are frequent visitors among the comfrey, the rue and the lovage, some learning the first principles of botany from the busy bees and the seedheads while others, excited by the mix of fragrances and shapes, mill about like young colts in a field.

For many visitors the Abbey House itself will be a special attraction, not least because of the special folk collections arranged to show how the 'ordinary' people of the region lived. For many years the Castelow family have had their chemist's shop in Woodhouse Lane and here at Abbey House is a reproduction containing representative examples of the type of equipment used in the days when herbs and herbal preparations were much in demand. An inn, a pottery, a grocers, a clay-pipe maker, a saddler and a tin-tack maker are also on view. Domestic appliances are a feature of the collection and

no seeker after knowledge in the world of herbs should miss a chance to see the trivets, the peelers and the squeezers used to prepare dishes in which herbs were such an essential part.

Herbs in the candy store

The influence of herbs on the young is quite considerable yet few will admit it. Take a party into a sweetshop, however, and they are soon convinced. Spearmint this, peppermint that, mint fresh whatnots and tasty mint such and such abound. Anise (*Pimpinella anisum*) may seem a strange plant at first—but aniseed is a flavouring most will know about. A few minty surprises to hand, a paper and pencil and instructions to visit the local shops and note down as many herb-based preparations as can be found will illuminate many a dull afternoon for a bright youngster.

ACORN BANK GARDEN

Temple Sowerby, Nr Penrith, Cumberland

Telephone: Ambleside (096 63) 3883

Owner: The National Trust

Situation: Just N of Temple Sowerby and 6m E of Penrith off the A66. **Open:** April–October, every day, 10am–5.30pm.

Scented magic surrounds this small walled garden, full of herbs, on the fringe of the Pennines. Although it is off the beaten track, visitors will find it well worth their while to make their way here and become captivated by the garden's charms. Most remain for longer than they intended.

There are tales that when the Romans came as far north as this, they brought herbs for their festivals and rites and ever since then herbs have been grown in the area. The climate is surprisingly favourable for a garden so far north. Luckily, because of its position the garden escapes the biting cold wind, known locally as the helm wind, that blows from the Pennines.

The garden is planned to run from east to west and contains a long middle bed with wide borders running down each side which finish in a thick holly hedge. On the north side there are extensive views over open country and ancient damson trees protect the more delicate plants growing underneath. The fine brick wall on the south side is thought to have been one of the original hot walls with a flue running through it to protect fruit trees from the frost.

There are opportunities to grow herbs that prefer shady conditions as well as those that like full sun. The climate is good with a

An ancient water tank—the date marked as 1778 —makes a useful container for herbs at Acorn Bank.

high rainfall and the soil drains well and is therefore suitable for Mediterranean plants.

It is difficult to know which of the 240 plants reputed to be growing here to describe, but mention should be made of a few in detail. After all they are the raison d'être of this garden.

Marsh mallow (*Althaea officinalis*), a favourite border plant with broad toothed leaves and pretty pinkish-white flowers, was much employed by apothecaries for treating bruises, aches and pains and for the manufacture of cough sweets.

Mountain spinach (*Atriplex hortensis*), sometimes known as orach, has beautiful deep red leaves which were formerly eaten as a vegetable. The seeds were reputed to be a remedy for 'yellow jaundice'.

Then there is the giant elecampane (*Inula helenium*) with golden daisy-like flowers that soar to a height of 6ft (1.8m) above large shaggy oval-shaped leaves. Once used in cough medicines, elecampane now plays a supporting role as a useful plant for the back of the border.

Monkshood (*Aconitus napellus*), with dark green glossy divided leaves and striking violet-blue clusters of flowers, is a poisonous herb and care should be taken not to touch it. Trained herbalists sometimes prescribe it in minute quantities to be used externally for relieving sciatica.

Bergamot (*Monarda didyma*) with its lovely scented plumes that flower throughout the summer, attracting bees, is well represented. Also growing is an unusual wild variety known as 'Snow Maiden' (*Monarda fistulosa*). The leaves and flowers of bergamot make a soothing and refreshing drink known as oswego tea, a popular drink in many American households after the Boston Tea Party of 1773.

These few details reveal just a tantalizing glimpse of the numerous plants to be seen, and the enthusiast will be able to spend many worthwhile hours studying here and enjoying the peaceful atmosphere that pervades this unique garden.

The house is occupied by the Sue Ryder Foundation. The inhabitants are all severely handicapped, but paths have been designed so that they can easily manipulate their wheel-chairs around the garden, enjoying the many scents and different textures of the herbs throughout the seasons as well as a chat with visitors.

A trophy garden

Just as some people collect silver cups and their grandparents collected stuffed animals, a gardener of today could be forgiven for starting a trophy plot or border with cuttings from other people's plants. We once had a rosemary border collected in this manner and it was remarkable how each plant differed in one way or another. Of course, we always asked for a cutting and were usually given two or three; removing them by stealth is easy but unforgivable. Which leads on gently but naturally to this little rhyme, the source of which is apparently unknown.

> I know a cheery woman
> And every time she calls
> She leaves my carpet on the floor,
> My pictures on the walls.
>
> She doesn't steal my silver,
> Or ask me for a loan,
> She doesn't use my fountain pen,
> She always brings her own.
>
> But, show her in the garden
> The treasures you have got,
> And if you turn your head away,
> She'll pinch the blooming lot!

ARLEY HALL AND GARDENS

Nr Northwick, Cheshire

Telephone: Arley (056 585) 284   **Owner:** The Hon Michael Flower

Situation: 6m W of Knutsford, M6 junctions 19 and 20, and M56 junctions 9 and 10. **Open:** April–9 October, Tuesday–Sunday and bank holidays, 2–6.30pm.

Arley Hall, with its complex of ancient buildings and gardens, lies at the heart of an estate which has been owned by the same family for many centuries. And because it has been and still is so much loved, the visitor is indeed hard pressed to take an objective view and distance himself from the people who have lived and worked here over all these years. An epitaph to a long-expired hunter—'I laid his bones beneath the greenwood tree And wept like childhood o'er my ABC'—is one of many gentle reminders that despite the buttressed yew hedges, the magnificent ilex avenue and the long sweep of the herbaceous border this is essentially a family garden.

The herb garden itself was very much a family affair, the site having been a depository of rubbish from the large kitchen garden during the 'Dig for Victory' years of

---

Helping hands

For those busy most of their lives with the soil, a couple of begrimed hands as hard as leather are the symbols of the trade. But most of us using hands for other purposes prefer the softer approach.

To keep hands—those most useful tools—in top condition, many herb growers wear gloves or use a barrier cream. Also, they take care to dry them well after washing. And they have a special hand cream which they apply immediately after washing. To make this you need: 2 tablespoons of ground almonds; 1 egg yolk; 1 teacupful of milk; 1 teaspoon almond oil (bought from the chemist); 1 tablespoon of dried herbs, eg lavender, rosemary, thyme.

To make: Bring the milk to the boil and let the dried herbs steep in it for about half an hour. Strain and pour the milk back into the pan. Put in the ground almonds and stir until the mixture thickens. Add the beaten egg yolk. Remove the pan from the heat and stir in the almond oil. Beat well and when cool put in a jar.

Another trick of the trade is to make a herbal hand bath for hands which are in need of care and attention. For this you need comfrey leaves, or failing these, leaves of rosemary, lavender or thyme. Marigold petals may be added to help heal cuts or sore places. Another essential is a cupful of vegetable oil. Steep the herbs in the oil and leave in a warm place for a fortnight and then strain, keeping the oil. You will then need half a teacupful of the oil, a tablespoon of castor sugar and the juice of a lemon. Mix these together. To use: sit comfortably with your herbal hand bath in a flat dish and soak your hands (backs and palms) for about five minutes each side. Do not rinse off excess oil. Gently pat dry with a soft towel. It works miracles.

the war and later as a busy market garden up to 1960. Not a pretty sight, dominating as it did the entrance to the herbaceous border and other attractive areas. The area was gradually cleared and under the guidance of Viscountess Ashbrook was turned in 1968 into a garden of herbs and useful or scented plants. The nearby Flag Garden, so called because of the paving-stone pathways, was created from a rubbish dump in 1900.

The herb garden is paved with gravel with well weathered square paving sets and has as a centre piece a stone finial removed after the war from a demolished building in Piccadilly Circus. It is bordered on three sides by a yew hedge—with an entrance

The Lady's mantle brings joy to the heart at Arley Hall.

gap—and the brick wall of the kitchen garden.

Created 'more by ear than design', the herb garden at Arley Hall has an interesting formal shape consisting of ten principal rectangular plots with paths of flagstones and gravel. The central plot has the stone ornament and there is a ball-shaped bush of box at each corner. A wild form of bugle and creeping deadnettle have been used most effectively to provide colourful ground cover.

The planting now is as much to give pleasure to visitors as to conform to any rigid historical pattern and the more popular herbs such as rosemary, rue, the sages, angelica, lovage and chives are in abundance. Thyme is well represented in gold,

silver and deep green patches while mints, hyssop, bergamot, fennel, vervain, sorrel and tree onions also claim attention.

The adjoining scented garden, made in 1977 and planted with aromatic shrubs and flowers to provide scents and some colour throughout the year, is a series of raised plots of irregular shapes contained by square blocks of local granite from demolished buildings or from the 'Coronation Streets' of the north after modernization.

The Flag Garden, ablaze in summer with the blooms of floribunda roses softened by the blue of dwarf lavender, has in family tradition long been regarded as the personal garden of the lady of the house—a place of quiet retreat—while in the walled garden the curbed pond, copied from one in the

Vatican Gardens in Rome, is guarded by four heraldic beasts rising most fearsomely from vast plantings of lady's mantle.

An interesting feature at Arley Hall is a short avenue of holm oaks (*Quercus ilex*) planted about 1840 and clipped annually each spring. The herbaceous borders were probably among the first to be established in England.

Rowland Eyles Egerton-Warburton, who was largely responsible for the tranquil beauty of Arley Hall and gardens, died in 1891 having made it his home for nearly eighty years. Affectionate and warm-hearted, yet wise and practical, he has left upon it the imprint of his personality, as have his successors to this day.

ELLY HILL HERBS

Elly Hill House, Barmpton, Darlington, Durham

Telephone: Darlington (0325) 64682 **Owner:** Dr and Mrs Pagan

Situation: 1m from the A66 Stockton roundabout and 3m NE of Darlington. **Open:** By arrangement. Telephone for an appointment.

Elly Hill House is a mellow farmhouse dating from the seventeenth century and is still surrounded by fields. The herb garden and glasshouses contain about a hundred different varieties of herbs with more being added each year.

The main herbal display is in a border against an old barn wall, with a background of espalier-trained nectarines and apricots. Towering angelica, comfrey and lovage, as well as bergamot, borage, marjoram, thymes, a variety of mints, lady's mantle, mace, chervil, rosemary, sage, valerian and feverfew are to be found in abundance.

Self-sufficiency is the aim and each year

the Pagans provide more growing space for fruit, vegetables and herbs. A mixed blessing, perhaps, for as Nina Pagan says, 'This makes for less mowing but more weeding'.

Herbs are grown all around the garden as crops for harvesting and in the summer the airing cupboard is evacuated to make room for drying herbs. These dried herbs are used for making pot-pourri, sleep pillows, herb sachets and flower candles.

As Nina Pagan is a Cordon Bleu trained cook she enjoys trying out different herbal recipes and using herbs as garnishes to decorate the dishes she prepares. Her view is that you 'take the first bite with your eyes.'

Herbs fascinate this enterprising lady and she is now training to be a medical herbalist. When qualified she hopes that Elly Hill will become a healing centre with the emphasis on herbs.

The garden at Elly Hill is cultivated by a keen cook who likes to include herbs in her recipes and as decorations. Here are two culinary combinations which you can make from your own garden.

Bouquet garni: This consists of a bay leaf, two sprigs of parsley and one sprig of thyme. Tie together with thread or place in a muslin bag and add to a casserole just half an hour before cooking is completed. Remove before serving.

Fines herbes: These are fresh herbs used to garnish a salad or flavour an omelette. Take equal quantities of chervil, parsley, chives and tarragon, chop finely and scatter over the dish.

Pot-pourri and dried mixtures

Pot-pourri means a mixture of petals, spices, herbs and essential oils, and is used to sweeten rooms or made into sachets to hang among your clothes.

Pot-pourri is often blended to suit the scent of your own particular garden flowers. The recipe here is very simple and based on rose petals.

Rose pot-pourri
6 cupfuls dried rose petals
1tsp dried mint leaves
1tsp ground cinnamon
1tsp ground allspice
3tsp ground orris root powder
6 drops oil of roses

Combine the dried rose petals with the other ingredients in a plastic container with a tight-fitting lid (such as a plastic ice-cream box). Keep in a warm, dry place for about six weeks shaking the container gently every other day. The pot-pourri is then ready for use and can be transferred to an ornamental bowl or used as a filling for sachets.

Herb pillows

These come in all sizes and are easy to make using the recipe above. Look out for remnants of attractive materials on market stalls.

LITTLE MORETON HALL

Congleton, Cheshire

Telephone: Congleton (02602) 2018   **Owner:** The National Trust

Situation: 4m SW of Congleton off the A34, Newcastle-under-Lyme road. **Open:** April–September, daily (except Tuesday), 2–6pm; March–October, Saturday and Sunday, 2–6pm. Closed Good Friday.

One of the best examples of half-timbered architecture anywhere in England, Little Moreton Hall was originally built in 1480 and was owned by the Moreton family for over six hundred years. During the last hundred years it was used as a farm and sadly the original furniture is no longer there and the records of the house have been lost.

Spirals, stars and balls—all manner of fascinating
shapes at York Gate.

The terrace at Mount Stewart, starting point of a
garden that will keep visitors fascinated and amused
for hours.

The Hall is surrounded by a moat forming an almost perfect square. One section is planned as a knot garden, based on a design from Leonard Meager's *The Complete English Gardener*, first published in 1670. This garden was planted in 1975 to the design of Paul Miles and is in the form of an open knot with gravel used to fill spaces between the box edging, which forms the outline. Problems in recent years have made it difficult to keep this garden under control, but now that a full-time gardener is employed the high standards of the National Trust are being maintained.

Elizabethan herbs to be found here in the borders include thrift, London pride, wall germander, peony, marjoram, hyssop and

Signalling a 'cure'

An interest in herbs can lead you in very many directions, from a keener interest in ancient history to a deep study of how plants got their names. On the way you will almost certainly come across what is known as the 'Doctrine of Signatures' and an examination of this aspect alone could take a year or two. This doctrine was in vogue in the sixteenth century, just before the apothecaries and others began cashing in with their herbal cure-alls and when scientific analysis of medicinal preparations was still something of the future. It was founded upon the supposition that plants had special signs which showed the diseases they were intended to cure.

For example, lady's mantle (*Alchemilla mollis*) was regarded as a magic herb because, among other attributes, it collected dew and held it on its leaf long after other plants were dry. Two and two being put together, it was considered that the dewdrop was a tear from above and signalled a cure for sick eyes. The yellow juice of the greater celandine (*Chelidonium majus*) was thought to be a certain cure for jaundice, and because the leaves of lungwort (*Pulmonaria officinalis*) look like spotty lungs, the plant was used in connection with chest problems.

Of course, as the most excellent *Guide to Glasgow Botanic Gardens* points out, although many of the earlier herbs have had their efficacy discredited or have been replaced by synthetic products, others remain important. Feverfew (*Chrysanthemum parthenium*) is still regarded as efficacious when dealing with migraine, while foxglove (*Digitalis purpurea*) continues to be used in the treatment of heart disorders.

The word *officinalis* which crops up so frequently is accorded to many herbs of medicinal significance as an indication that they were once, and in some cases still are, included in an official pharmacopoeia.

chamomile. Lavender is trained on short standards as it would have been in Elizabethan days.

At the time of our visit the plants were labelled in Latin only. This may suit a learned gardener who can identify the botanical names with ease, but without this knowledge it may prove difficult to appreciate the delights of the garden. As one visitor said, 'There is probably an abundance of interesting plants in this garden, but for the amateur we need some help, some stepping stones to the past. With these missing the idea is lost to us and it becomes merely another garden.'

However, lack of the English names may start some visitors off on a trail of learning. The whole field of naming plants is one worthy of exploration.

NESS GARDENS

Botanic Gardens, Ness Neston, Wirral, Cheshire

Telephone: Liverpool (051) 336 2135   **Owner:** University of Liverpool

Situation: On the Neston road between Ness and Burton and within 2m of the A540, Chester to Hoylake road. **Open:** Daily, 9am–sunset, except on Christmas Day.

Tennis has suffered at the expense of herbs at Ness, home of the University of Liverpool Botanic Gardens. The remarkable and comprehensive Ledsham herb garden was laid out in the spring of 1974 on the site originally levelled for tennis courts. The aim has been to bring together in one area all the culinary herbs, most of which have essential oils in their tissues imparting flavour and scent.

The area is well paved, the herbs being confined to a series of square and oblong beds, and yet is attractive, and the range of plants should give even the most timorous cook a sense of adventure. Here are herbs for every taste, from balm, for making a soothing cup of tea, to tarragon, queen of the culinary tribe.

Although the herb garden alone is worth travelling a distance to see, there are also many other gardens of interest at Ness. The history of the gardens is itself worthy of study, for it was here that Liverpool cotton broker Arthur Kilpin Bulley turned his gardening hobby to such profit that he founded the nurseryman's and seedsman's firm of Bees. Bulley sponsored many planthunting expeditions to China and the Himalayan province of Bhutan.

Fresh herbs in the winter

Although herbs come very much into their own during the summer, they can also be potted up and kept going through the winter. They will be popular in the kitchen for decorating and flavouring salads—and as a bonus they make lovely house plants.

Few people have the ideal place—a heated greenhouse—but an unheated area under glass, such as a conservatory would do very well. There is much to commend a living-room or bedroom, but the kitchen is not so suitable because warm steamy air and sudden changes of temperature produce the wrong sort of environment.

continued

continued

Choose any type of pot that provides good drainage and use the best compost you can afford; one with a John Innes No 2 base would be fine. The plant should be well watered when it is potted and then kept fairly dry throughout the winter. Be careful with your watering—too much water has been the death of many a good herb. The herb's best friend is a mist sprayer, which should be used frequently to provide moist conditions and to keep the foliage clean.

Remember that however carefully you tend them, your herbs are not going to grow as freely as they did in the garden during the summer months.

Top priority should go to parsley and chives which are the ones you use for winter salads and flavouring; I would recommend at least four pots of each. Herbs you do not need so often are sage, tarragon and thyme; two pots of these should ensure an ample supply for the cook.

Use the plants in rotation and give each pot a feed with liquid fertilizer after it has been cut back.

Herbs are not only useful to the cook, they look very beautiful in their own right grown as house plants. Follow the rules for plants in the greenhouse or conservatory and you will be rewarded with a colourful display.

ROBIN POTTERY, CRAFT AND HERB CENTRE

Spring Acre Farm, Thorpe-in-Balne, Doncaster, S. Yorkshire

Telephone: Doncaster (0302) 882565   **Owner:** Mr and Mrs E. L. Robinson

Situation: Near Askern on the A19 N of Doncaster. **Open:** Weekends, 2–6pm or by arrangement.

Here is a truly functional herb garden, specially laid out for large groups of visitors to move about freely and for a lecturer to extol the virtues and properties of the many plants to those within earshot. It has no claims to beauty or grace, scores of standard concrete paving stones having been placed like the white spaces of a chessboard, the black spaces being soil. But it works, and as the creeping thymes and pennyroyal grow quickly to blur the sharp concrete edges, and as the comfrey, angelica and lovage provide height and bulk, it is becoming an admirable place to visit.

The garden was planted on a warm day in May 1983 with herbs brought in from a Cambridgeshire garden and within weeks was a centre of interest for those attending a fair in the grounds. Fishermen visiting the large man-made lake nearby call for a sprig of insect-repelling southernwood for their hats and good cooks from a wide area are taking a new look at recipes requiring herbs that are not always easy to find in the supermarkets.

The Robinsons are making plans to open the garden in the evening to local groups and to provide home-made herbal cordials and snacks for a small charge. As the garden features many herbs from the Bible and from the works of Shakespeare, subjects for talks should not be hard to find.

The herb that cheers

Known as tisanes or infusions, herbal teas are made in the same way as the more usual Indian or China tea. Use either a glass or china pot and pour the boiling water over the fresh or dried herbs and infuse for five to ten minutes. Use a strainer when serving. Some people like their tea with a little honey and a slice of lemon. Here are some of the herbs worth trying.

Lemon balm. A very soothing drink particularly at bedtime.

Mint tea. A good tea as a tonic. Also delicious served iced and decorated with borage flowers on a hot day.

Nettle tea. A very good drink in the spring, being full of vitamins. Boiling water will take the sting out of the nettles, but wear strong gloves when picking them. Follow this example:

If they would drink nettles in March
And eat mugwort in May
So many young maidens
Wouldn't go to the clay.

STOCKELD PARK

Wetherby, N. Yorkshire

Telephone: Wetherby (0937) 62376 **Owner:** Mrs Rosamond Gough

Situation: On the Harrogate Road (A661) from the A1 through Wetherby. **Open:** 17 July–19 August (except Mondays), 2.30–5.30pm.

Originally designed by James Paine in 1760, this attractive sunken garden with its five wheels of differing circumferences was in the early days composed of box hedges containing fragrant roses. They died in one of England's big frosts and John Codrington, the designer of the herb garden at Emmanuel College and many others, drew on his vast experience to compose what we see now.

The design is the strength of the garden, and a good thing too for the herbs in their season provide excellent pickings for collared doves and rabbits. Being sunken, with beautifully proportioned stone steps leading down to it from a gravel path across the front lawn and with grassy access all round, the garden can be viewed to advantage from a height and from many angles.

The circular plots are edged with warm-coloured concrete set in gravel and contain most of the herbs used by the lady of the house in Elizabethan and later times. Indeed, the domestic quarters of the house are but a few steps away for a housemaid bent on finding comfrey for her swollen knees or for a cook seeking rosemary and thyme. All the herbs are grown by Mrs Gough from seeds and cuttings.

Getting ready for winter

If you've ever wondered how owners of well-kept herb gardens manage to start the season with such healthy, neat and productive plants, think well on an old East Anglian saying: 'An hour spent in the garden in the Autumn will be two hours saved in the Spring.'

Mints should be dug up and a few runners planted for next year's crop. A change of position helps. Add a little well-rotted compost to the trench. Unless you are growing it as a commercial crop, treat tarragon in the same way, cutting it back to about 3in (7.5cm) from the ground. As an insurance, strike cuttings or plant runners in a tray of compost under cover.

Bay bushes will need a good mulch and a cover of fine netting. Those that are clipped should be brought under cover.

Rosemary may die for no particular reason even if the weather does not seem specially severe. So take precautions and have a few cuttings in pots.

YORK GATE

Back Church Lane, Adel, Leeds

Owner: Mrs Sybil Spencer

Situation: Behind Adel Church on the A660, Otley Road, between Otley and Leeds. **Open:** For various charities including the National Gardens Scheme. Consult appropriate guidebooks.

Many aspects of gardening can be discovered in this rather austere Yorkshire house on the outskirts of Leeds. There are to be found in just 1 acre (0.4 hectares) of extensively cultivated ground, a nutwalk, peony bed, iris border, white and silver garden, pavement maze, miniature pinetum and an unusual herb garden.

The herb garden is formal in outline and the plants here are grown more for decoration than for use. It measures only 30ft (9m) long by 10ft (3m) wide and forms an enclosed leafy walkway backed by high yew hedges.

The symmetry of the garden is accentuated by a central pathway leading to a classical summerhouse complete with pillars. On either side of the path, borders contain trimmed box globes and spirals to give the firm outline necessary during winter months. Red sage, giant alliums, bronze fennel, angelica and golden balm complete the picture, their foliage creating a restful tapestry.

The owner of York Gate, Mrs Sybil Spencer, says of her garden, 'There is a surprise around every corner.' Looking from the summerhouse in the herb garden double vistas can be enjoyed in both directions. One leads the eye to a most unusual 'wobbly' sundial. There are many outstanding points of interest in this owner-maintained garden, but it is to the herb garden that the pilgrim will return for that rare sense of harmony between plants, landscape and sky.

Aromatic herbs, delightful little containers and even the hint of herbal teas at York Gate.

NORTHERN IRELAND

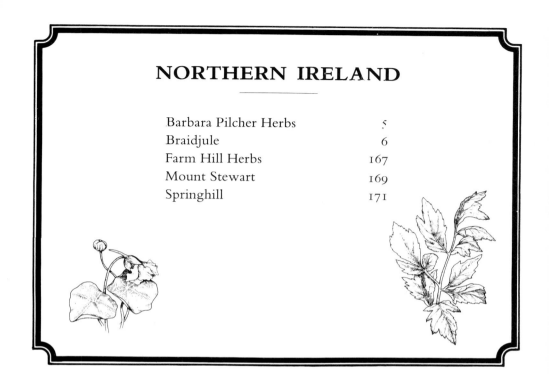

BARBARA PILCHER HERBS

98 Belfast Road, Lisdoonan, Saintfield, Co Down, Northern Ireland

Telephone: Carryduff (0232) 813624   **Owner:** Mrs Barbara Pilcher

Situation: On the outskirts of Saintfield, just off the A21. **Open:** Nearly all the time.

Barbara Pilcher cultivates herbs on the fringes of this small Ulster town, developing into a thriving commercial concern what was once the hobby of what she terms 'a compulsive plant lover'.

Her garden is on a steep slope to a busy road, the noise and fumes being screened to some extent with lovage, comfrey, angelica and other tall herbs. To Barbara Pilcher, this is home with a capital 'H', for the family has moved several times and the precious herbs have moved with her. Now she and they are settled, there are plans to establish several types of garden for her own pleasure and to show customers different ideas they can use themselves.

Trained as a botanist and having now a special interest in wild flowers, she particularly wants to know more about those of local origin which might have had herbal uses in the past—and with this in mind she is studying a large patch behind the house. She has been delighted to discover early purple orchids growing, as well as many other rare hillside plants. Since ground elder threatens to make a takeover bid her main concern is 'how to get rid of the unwanted and keep the wanted'. Being an organic gardener she does not use herbicides and has to rely on hard work with the hoe.

Her other interest is bee-attracting plants such as lemon thyme, mint, hyssop, rosemary and sage. These she plants decoratively together in lead water tanks, wooden half barrels, large terracotta pots and any other container that happens to catch her eye. These catch the attention of visitors, for arranged sympathetically outside a door or in front of unsightly drainage pipes, they give a home a sense of maturity.

Although in an isolated spot and not easy to find, it is worth making an effort to discover this small Ulster garden where herbs are cultivated with a great understanding of their needs and growing conditions.

Herbs in pots

Consider growing herbs in pots as Mrs Pilcher does to camouflage an eyesore such as a pile of rubble or even to give a sense of homeliness in front of a newly built garage.

Herbs grow well in all sorts of tubs, troughs, pots and other containers so it is worth looking out for a disused coal scuttle, chimney pot or even pig-trough. Once you have the idea, it is comparatively simple to sort out which herbs to grow. Mint, parsley, sage, thyme and rosemary usually do well in such restricted areas.

Since herbs are mainly of Mediterranean origin and have no liking for soggy conditions, ensure that the container has drainage holes. Layer the bottom with coarse sand or pebbles and a handful or two of peat before filling it with a good peat-based compost.

BRAIDJULE

120 Knockan, Broughshane, Ballymena, Northern Ireland

Telephone: Broughshane (0266) 861202   **Owner:** Mr and Mrs Brian Gunn-King

Situation: On the B94 between Broughshane and Clogh. **Open:** By arrangement on Sundays.

This most unusual garden, dug out of an old quarry, is run by an enterprising couple who believe in gardening on veganic principles. Basically this means that all compost is made from vegetable waste. No animal manure, artificial fertilizers or herbicides are used at all.

The Gunn-Kings are vegetarians themselves and grow a splendid selection of culinary herbs to flavour their food and to provide a balanced and healthy diet. Wherever possible they aim to eat food raw, which they believe provides all the nutrients needed by man.

This is compatible with the belief of the Greek philosopher Hippocrates—'Let food be your medicine, and medicine your food'. Mrs Gunn-King says it is extremely rare for any of the family to need the services of a doctor. She believes the use of fresh herbs from the garden plays a large part in ensuring their health and well being.

Herbs, vegetables and fruit bushes are all grown in long narrow beds, no wider than 2ft (60cm). Once established, these beds are not dug over but additional compost (based on vegetable matter from their own compost heap) is just forked into the top surface. Companion planting is practised which,

they feel, helps to keep away unwanted garden pests.

Herbs are sold at a yoga class Mrs Gunn-King runs, and to health food stores. In the past few years they have found a tremendous upsurge in the use of herbs in Northern Ireland. More and more of the people they meet want information and recipes for using herbs as part of a varied and healthy diet.

Companion planting

In keeping with their principles of growing plants veganically, Mr and Mrs Gunn-King believe in companion planting as a way of combating garden pests. It can be tried in any garden and is a matter of choosing plants which help each other reveal their full potential.

Chamomile, frequently referred to as 'the plant's physician', is often planted among vegetables or flowers that appear sickly. Many herb growers report success time and again, the sick plant recovering and the disease or attacker being routed.

Members of the onion family—chives is one of them—are thought to have the ability to repel blackfly and to help roses recover from an outbreak of the dreaded blackspot. It is also said that the scent of

the flower improves. The Gunn-Kings firmly believe that their soft fruits are especially good when they plant chives nearby.

Nasturtiums have long held a reputation for doing nothing but good to tomatoes, and marigolds have a similar effect on crops of potatoes. Summer savory at both ends of a row of broad beans will, it is said, help pest control. Pennyroyal has the power to send the ant scuttling, country folk believe, while white fly is supposed to succumb to French marigolds in the greenhouse.

Scientists are getting near to the heart of the matter. For more information, contact the Henry Doubleday Research Association, 20 Convent Lane, Bocking, Braintree, Essex.

FARM HILL HERBS

Farmhill Road, Co Down, Northern Ireland

Telephone: Holywood (02317) 2196   **Owner:** Mrs Katherine Nixon

Situation: A short distance from the A2 and on the S side of the Belfast Lough. **Open:** April–October, Thursday, Friday and Saturday, 9am–5pm. Or by appointment.

The artistic abilities of Mrs Katherine Nixon are evident in the hand-painted sign of the apothecary's accoutrements and the visitor is at once keen to discover what surprises

from the present and the past lie behind the high brick walls. For the lover of good clean garden design there are indeed pleasures in store. The large, rambling garden contains a

Good garden design at Farm Hill where the plants are also for sale.

The tussie mussie

The scented nosegays of herbs which Mrs Nixon is skilled at arranging make charming thank-you presents or get-well gifts.

Known for centuries by the delightful name of tussie mussies, nosegays were carried by ladies of noble birth when venturing out of doors among the common people. They protected them from the odours of uncleansed streets and unwashed bodies and, it was thought, from the diseases in the air.

As Mrs Nixon will demonstrate, a tussie mussie can be made from many types of herbs. Start with a small central flower such as a rose bud and build up the posy outwards in ever-increasing circles. Select the aromatic leaves of rosemary, sage and scented geraniums if you have them, and introduce pinks, lavender or bergamot to provide a splash of colour. Surround your nosegay with a paper doily and a bow of ribbon.

Nosegays received as gifts were often dried and kept over the years as a present of more lasting significance than, say, a box of candies.

square-shaped herb garden which is a model for those wishing to display their plants to greater advantage.

Based on a lover's knot, the pattern illustrates the petals of a flower starting at the four corners and meeting in the centre. The pattern is outlined with hyssop and the petals are filled in with lungwort. Ground cover between the petals is provided by chamomile. In the centre is a cartwheel filled with various thymes, balanced by a further circle of cobbles. A wide brick path follows the square of the formal garden. Behind this are herb filled borders.

A collection of low-growing herbs, often classed as alpines, grow happily together in a sink. These discarded white glazed sinks still have another life to live as herb containers. Covered with a mixture of cement, sand and peat the final result has the same neutral colouring and texture as stone.

The container-grown herbs on sale at Farm Hill are arranged in a display area beside the garden. When deciding which herbs to buy it is a great help to be able to see the mature plants growing in the garden.

Mrs Nixon specializes in making up tussie-mussies (bouquets of scented leaves and flowers), and one of these would make a fragrant reminder of an inspiring garden in Northern Ireland.

MOUNT STEWART GARDENS

Newtonards, Co Down, Northern Ireland

Owner: The National Trust

Situation: On the E shore of Strangford Lough, 5m SE of Newtonards on the A20. **Open:** April–October, every day (except Friday), noon–6pm. Open on Good Friday.

Lady Londonderry who loved and created the gardens here wrote, 'When my husband and I first came here on a visit in the winter some time before he succeeded to the property, I thought the house and surroundings were the dampest, darkest and saddest place I had ever stayed in.'

Yet as Graham Thomas reflects in the National Trust guide to the garden, 'The garden at Mount Stewart is a magnificent memorial to a remarkable woman, who lived and enjoyed life to the full. This garden on the grand scale could only have been created by some one with initiative,

imagination and an intimate knowledge of other great gardens.'

There is no formal herb garden at Mount Stewart but herb lovers will delight in finding herbs and scented plants growing profusely in every corner. There is so much space and the setting is so grand and yet strangely romantic that the extravagant planting seems exactly right.

On the terraces containers of clipped bay (*Laurus nobilis*) provide a framework for the house and are much admired. They are

Mount Stewart—with clipped bay on the terraces.

about 10ft (3m) high with the tops trimmed to a width of about 6ft (1.8m). These bay trees were imported from Belgium in 1923 and some were thought then to be easily fifty years old. Planted in large square stone containers they must surely be the finest mophead specimens growing today.

Mediterranean plants like bay flourish here because Mount Stewart enjoys a sub-tropical climate. Heavy dews at night compensate for a low rainfall, and many half-hardy shrubs normally found in Cornwall and Devon grow well in this fine Ulster garden.

Herb enthusiasts are always searching for unusual garden layouts, and better still if there is a story attached to the idea. The shamrock garden must be quite unique in this respect.

Reached from a raised walk through the sunken garden, a large area is planned in the outline of the national flower of Ireland. Accentuating another legend is a bed of red daisies (*Bellis perennis*) planted in the shape of a man's left hand. The story behind this symbolic planting is that many years ago two rival Scottish clansmen were sailing from Scotland to Ireland with the intention that the one who touched Irish soil first would possess the land. The McDonnell, an ancestor of the Londonderry family, realizing he was losing the race, rashly cut off his left hand and threw it on the shore thus claiming the land.

Work started in the shamrock garden in 1924 when a yew hedge was planted. One year later the first bed in the shape of a hand was designed and planted with four hundred red roses. This has now been altered to resemble a much smaller left hand, but plants of red colouring will always be grown here.

Foliage and scented plants, including a collection of shrub roses, soften the outlines of the garden and lead the eye away from the rather macabre centrepiece. As in other parts of the garden, elegant containers are

Beautiful bay trees

The beautiful bay trees at Mount Stewart, neatly clipped and grown in large stone containers, are the envy of any visitor whose much-loved specimens returned to their maker in a recent frost.

Known as mopheads, they are often seen in scaled down versions outside smart restaurants. Traditionally they are planted in pairs and really do add style to any garden. You may train your own bay into a mophead but since this could take at least twelve years, depending on the size of the plant, it is probably worth investing in an off-the-shelf specimen.

Once established, mopheads need little maintenance except for careful watering. The leaves should be kept free of dust and given a spray of water occasionally; trimming should be carried out once or twice a year to maintain a good shape.

Unless you live in a very warm area, it is a wise precaution to give the tree protection against frost and cold winds. A shed or conservatory will do very well.

filled to overflowing with quite simple plants. Pots large enough to swamp a normal-sized terrace are filled with artemisia (*Artemisia arborescens* 'Powis Castle') and the soft silver foliage adds a fitting sense of mystery. These stone containers set in small triangular pools of water are just one of the many features that contribute to the theatrical setting of this amazing garden.

Looking at the splendid clumps of golden marjoram (*Origanum vulgare aureum*) and hellebores (*Helleborus corsicus*) growing together so companionably, it is difficult to believe that it was not planned as a decorative herb garden.

Mount Stewart is made up of many different gardens, each one fascinating and full of original ideas that could be adapted in smaller spaces. The Mairi Garden where Mairi, the youngest daughter of the house slept in her pram, is designed in the shape of a Tudor Rose and planted with blue and white coloured flowers. Small bells wave in the breeze around the fountain and cockle shells add extra emphasis to the well-known nursery rhyme which begins 'Mary, Mary, quite contrary'.

Along the aptly named Dodo Terrace all sorts of amazing stone animals make the visitor stop, stare and pause open-mouthed, before realizing the joke. The dinosaur, hedgehog, mermaid, monkey, dodos and other creatures, complete with Ark, all have a right to belong in this garden. They are a reminder of Lady Londonderry's political friends who met each week in London during the First World War. Their gatherings were known as meetings of the Ark Club and members were given nicknames of living or imaginary animals.

SPRINGHILL

Moneymore, Co Londonderry, Northern Ireland

Telephone: Moneymore (064 874) 48210   **Owner:** The National Trust

Situation: On the Moneymore to Coagh road, 1m from Moneymore. **Open:** April–September, every day except Friday, 2–6pm.

Springhill is a white rough-cast house, sturdily built and flanked by numerous outbuildings that tell in a nutshell the story of the Conynghams.

A well-respected family in County Londonderry and Ireland their lives revolved around the army and managing their estate. The first Colonel William Conyngham supported Cromwell, and the last Captain William Lenox-Conyngham fought in the Second World War. He died in 1957 having secured the future of Springhill with the National Trust.

But the spirit of the family lives on, particularly in the herb garden which is still referred to locally as Miss Charlotte's garden. And indeed this small garden, enclosed by walls on three sides, which leads on to a wide pathway, has all the attributes of a lady's garden.

Sometimes known as privvy gardens these small gardens were tended entirely by the lady of the house and were secret retreats where she could escape and sit in the sun away from the prying eyes of servants and estate workers.

A surprise here is a lovely aromatic chamomile lawn large enough to walk over.

Measuring approximately 9 × 4yd (8 × 3.6m), this rectangular piece of ground is closely covered with a mat of bright green chamomile that gives the characteristic 'bounce' and sweet apple scent when trodden on. The lawn has to be clipped by hand and renewed periodically when the weeds begin to take over. This is one of the drawbacks of chamomile as a turfing medium.

Whether or not there was originally a chamomile lawn at Springhill is unknown. This one was planted by the National Trust quite recently. However, in the seventeenth century chamomile was often grown as a low creeping cover for banks, walkways and seats. It is a plant Shakespeare knew; in *Henry IV*, Falstaff mentions 'The more it is trodden on the better it grows'.

The variety here is 'Treneague' which is non-flowering. It is propagated by splitting up the little plantlets which grow quickly, making it is quite easy to establish a chamomile bank or a seat.

Herbs are grown more for ornament than use at Springhill and there is a good selection of plants with decorative foliage. One of these is the curry plant (*Helichrysum angustifolium*) with gleaming silver leaves and a strong curry aroma. In his book *Gardens of the National Trust* Graham Thomas tells how this plant causes many a chuckle when visitors are taken on a conducted tour at Springhill. 'Do you smell anything special just here?' enquires the very Irish guide. The visitor sniffs appreciatively and says 'Why yes. Curry I think.' 'Ah', replies the guide, 'I have often wondered about it. They tell me there was once an Indian cook at the house. He died one day and nobody seems to know where he was buried.' Graham Thomas concludes, 'Irish embroidery is not necessarily worked with needles and silks.'

On every side of the house are the rambling shrub roses that grow so well in Northern Ireland. And it was on the north wall that Lord McCartney, Ambassador to

Making a chamomile lawn

As the gardeners at Springhill will tell you, a chamomile lawn can be a mixed blessing. Certainly, it fits very well into a herb garden and the aromatic plants do perfume the air in a most delightful way when trodden upon. But there are problems. A lawn of this nature needs hand weeding and must be cut with shears or scissors. Also, it will never achieve the green sward effect of turf.

Drake, the popular historians would have us believe, was bowling on a chamomile lawn when called to his famous battle with the Spaniards—but in those days labour was not hard to come by. However, why not plant just a small area and see how it comes on? Perhaps you have a suitable space around a garden seat, between paving stones or on a wild bank.

A chamomile lawn is impressive when planted at the entrance to a herb garden. In this case it should be considered in terms of a door mat and be no larger than this.

Before planting, remove any weeds and work a top dressing of general fertilizer into the soil.

Choose the 'Treneague' variety and space the plants 4in (10cm) apart. During the first few weeks weed most carefully by hand and water regularly to give the creeping tufty leaves a chance to become established.

China, planted the first of the roses to bear his name. Luckily it survived and since that time McCartney roses have always climbed the mellow brick walls of Springhill.

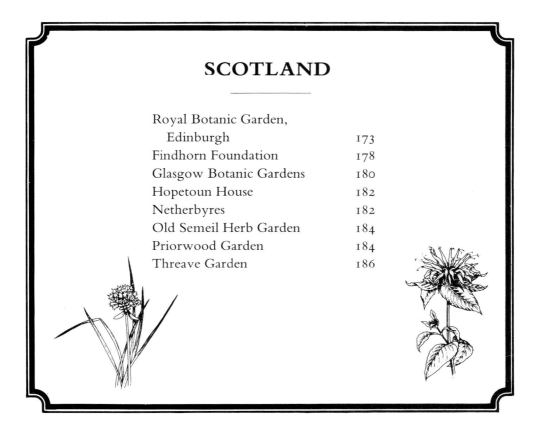

SCOTLAND

ROYAL BOTANIC GARDEN, EDINBURGH

Inverleith Row, Edinburgh

Telephone: Edinburgh (031) 552 7171

Owner: Department of Agriculture and Fisheries for Scotland.

Situation: Inverleith Row (E Gate). **Open:** Every day of the year except for New Year's day. Weekdays 9am until sunset, Sundays 11am until sunset. (During the operation of British Summer Time closing time is one hour before sunset.) The plant houses and exhibition hall are open from 10am–5pm on weekdays and 11am–5pm on Sundays or until sunset when this is earlier. During the Edinburgh International Festival the garden opens one hour earlier on Sundays.

The origins of this garden date back to 1670 when medicinal plants were grown on a small plot of land, about 14yd (12.6m) square, near the Palace of Holyroodhouse, making it the second oldest botanic garden in Britain. The oldest, at Oxford, was founded in 1621.

The present site was acquired in the nineteenth century and the work of transferring the plant collection was organized by William McNab, a leading horticulturist of the time. One of his inventions, a transplanting machine, meant that fully grown trees could be moved with great success.

173

Stone troughs are a handsome feature at Edinburgh.

A botanic garden is designed principally for horticultural research and accurate identification and classification of plants; so a visit to the Royal Botanic Garden is a good way to learn a little more about herbs and their uses. It also provides an opportunity to enjoy a leisurely walk through a beautifully maintained park in the middle of this busy city.

Culinary, medicinal and poisonous herbs are all in the demonstration garden on the northern side of the grounds. Here an extensive lawned area has been divided into sections, each shielded by high hedges. Backing the area is an impressive beech hedge which runs the length of the garden and adds strength to the geometrical design.

Well-known pot herbs such as sweet cicely, sorrel, lemon balm, angelica and thyme are all here for study. Each is labelled with the common name, botanical name and country of origin. One bed is devoted to annuals—dill, green purslane, summer savory, coriander, sweet rocket, borage and chervil. The herbs are sown in their final growing position and thinned out when about 2in (5cm) high.

Cottage garden plants such as cornflower, calendula, sunflower, night-scented stock and Californian poppy are flowers associated with traditional herb gardens and these fill another bed. Short rows of seeds are sown at regular intervals in diagonal lines across the corners of the beds. This emphasizes the geometrical precision of the beds, making a welcome change from the usual random planting of these vigorous self-seeding flowers.

Medicinal herbs feature prominently, as they would have done in early days when medicines were derived from plants and botanic gardens were a source of much plant material and knowledge. Well to the fore is rhubarb (*Rheum officinale*), an important drug for the early apothecaries and differing only slightly from garden rhubarb (*Rheum palmatum*). Roots of the mature plant were dried and used as the base of a purgative.

The magnificent oval walled garden at
Netherbyres—result of a caring partnership.

At Threave Garden, the Himalayan blue poppy is
one of a collection of rare and interesting plants from
many countries.

Henbane (*Hyoscyamus niger*), one of the hallucinatory 'magic' plants used by witches to brew love potions, is another prominent plant, growing to a height of approximately 2ft (60cm) with ovate pointed leaves covered with a velvety down and funnel-shaped flowers that are a creamy yellow colour with distinctive brown markings. Herbalists used it to soothe and relieve pain. As it is a highly toxic plant, no attempt should be made to use it without medical guidance.

Among other plants with medicinal uses growing here is the poppy (*Papaver somniferum*). The handsome flowers are pink, red or white. The paper-thin petals soon fall and leave a large oval seedhead which contains traces of opium.

The attractive valerian (*Valeriana officinalis*) with large clusters of pinkish-white flowers is cultivated for the value of its rootstock. When dried this is used in stress-relieving drugs. The seeds and leaves are highly poisonous. In folklore it was thought that to fall asleep in its shade was to invite death because you would be breathing the poisons given out by the plant.

This large collection of plants with powerful toxic properties, all correctly labelled, may well have been the inspiration for many a thriller writer searching for a different way of disposing of his victim!

A short walk from the demonstration garden is a wide raised bed full of silver plants, which are much loved by the Scots. 'Silver Queen', 'Valerie Finnis', 'Schmidtiana' and 'Lambrook Silver' are just a few of the many different artemisias that make attractive clumps of gleaming silver foliage. The enthusiast has a good chance to identify the different varieties of this confusing family.

The native thistle growing here is *Onopordum acanthium*. This variety has broad silver-grey spiny leaves and grows to a height of approximately 6ft (1.8m) with pale purple thistle-like flowers. Another

A personal botanic garden

Botanic gardens were established primarily for the study and use of different plants. Important ones in Great Britain are found at Edinburgh, Glasgow, Cambridge, Oxford, Swansea, Birmingham, Liverpool and other towns, generally where there is a university to take on continuing study and research into the habits of the plants.

But whether you are academically inclined or not, there is no reason why you too should not start your own botanic garden. Study a few selected plants such as the mint family or different varieties of sages, thymes or lavender.

All you need is a small area where plants are accurately labelled with their country name, botanical name and country of origin. Use a notebook to record such details as the date the herbs were planted, how they were propagated, when they flowered, and whether the seed was collected for sowing the following year. Note also any special uses the plant might have for culinary, medicinal or cosmetic purposes

plant that would add interest to any herb garden with plenty of sun is the decorative *Anthemis montana*. Reaching only about 8in (20cm) in height it has pretty, small, daisy-like flowers growing abundantly, and it makes neat cushions.

The glasshouses tell the story of plants raised in temperate and tropical climates. Many of the provisions we eat or drink, such as bananas, cocoa and coffee, become more interesting when seen as attractive plants actually growing, even if under artificial conditions. And as botanic research continues all the time careful study of the labels will reveal that quite a few of these plants have been collected on expeditions organized by the Royal Botanic Garden in the last few years.

The Exhibition Hall, given by an anonymous benefactor, opened in 1970. Displays arranged here make study a pleasure and the ever-expanding world of plant life a source of wonder. The story of plants and medicine is outlined from early days when all physicians were good botanists. Then their livelihood would depend on their ability to grow and prepare plants for remedies for the rheumatics, lung complaints and other disorders that plagued their patients. This exhibition was arranged to celebrate the Tercentenary of the Royal College of Physicians of Edinburgh in 1981. One section shows modern medicines with packs of well-known drugs which contain plant extracts. It underlines the fact that about a quarter of all prescriptions today contain plant material in one form or another. It illustrates too the revival of interest in herbal medicine. New information has become available, and earlier works of importance are being reprinted. The bond between physician and botanist which gradually weakened over the centuries is becoming closer, and once again plants are of importance in the search for healing medicines.

FINDHORN FOUNDATION

The Park, Forres, Grampian

Telephone: Findhorn (03093) 2311   **Owner:** Findhorn Foundation

Situation: 4m from Forres off the A95 road. **Open:** Every day. Guided tours of the foundation at 2pm daily in the summer; in the winter on Mondays, Wednesdays and Saturdays only. The foundation also runs study courses which are open to the public.

The Findhorn Foundation, situated on the coast of the Moray Firth in northern Scotland, has developed in the last two decades from a small group of people keen on establishing a garden into an international community of around 200 permanent members. It now embraces many aspects of communal living and pioneers new approaches to ecology, education and appropriate lifestyles.

It is a working community and thousands of guests who come each year to take part in one of the residential courses look upon it as their spiritual home.

The members of the community seek to co-operate with rather than dominate nature, so a sandy soil has been made fertile—and vegetables of high quality and flowers of brilliant hue can now be cultivated. As part of this work a herb garden has been established. Designed by the Scottish writer and herbalist Dawn MacLeod, a circular pattern was created for aesthetic and practical purposes. Each herb is clearly visible and accessible for harvesting.

Over a hundred different plants are grown including annuals such as basil, chervil, coriander, cumin, dill and summer savory. Chamomile, elecampane, lady's mantle, clary sage, wormwood, yarrow, hyssop and lungwort are just some of the medicinal herbs grown. Fragrant, cleansing and dye herbs fill any empty spaces in the wheel-shaped garden, which is surrounded by a cotoneaster hedge and forms a central point for the caravan community.

Harvesting herbs

At Findhorn, herbs are grown to be enjoyed freshly cut in salads and other dishes during the summer months. But they are also harvested and dried for culinary and medicinal uses during the winter. Here is the way to do it.

Choose a sunny dry morning when it is a pleasure to be outside and cut your herbs in small bunches. Aim to pick about half the plant so that the garden does not look too bare.

Tie the herbs into small bundles and hang them in a dry warm place for a few days. Ideal places are the kitchen, a garden shed or the airing cupboard.

Within a few days the herbs will feel crisp and papery to the touch. The next step is to rub them into a rough powder and store this in airtight containers. If you are harvesting small quantities, coffee jars are ideal. Label and seal each container carefully and keep it in a dry cupboard until needed.

Without doubt home-dried herbs have a better flavour than shop bought herbs. However, do not dry enough to feed an army. Think small. A pound jar of each dried herb should last an average family throughout the year.

A community of herbs at Findhorn.

Harvesting is done in a balanced way so that the beauty of the garden is not disturbed. Freshly cut herbs are always in demand for the kitchen and are also dried for use in the winter. They are needed too for medicinal purposes as an apothecary works with the community.

The foundation recognizes the part that herbs play in the context of the living earth and see these useful plants as gifts given by nature for the healing of humanity.

GLASGOW BOTANIC GARDENS

Great Western Road, Glasgow Strathclyde

Telephone: Glasgow (041) 334 2422 **Owner:** City of Glasgow District Council

Open: Gardens, 7am to dusk all year round. Kibble Palace, 10am–4.45pm in the summer; 10am–4.15pm in the winter. The main range of glasshouses, 1–4.15pm all year round. Students who wish to visit at other times may apply to the curator's office.

The herb garden here is modelled on traditional lines and situated in a south-facing corner of the botanic garden. On three sides it is sheltered by the vast Kibble Palace which is one of the largest glasshouses in Britain. On the other side is a large ornamental pond which backs on to the busy Queen Margaret Drive.

The layout resembles a maze with walkways of turf leading to a centre point. Here there once stood a sundial, but now only the millstone base remains. This is of local interest as it was taken from a flint mill on the nearby River Kelvin and is surrounded by flints also from the mill. The herb beds are raised to a height of approximately 3ft

(90cm) and this makes it easy for visitors to see the plants as they walk along the wide pathway which runs the length of the garden.

Culinary herbs grow in the outer beds and both common and botanical names and the uses of the herbs are given. Sometimes these plants also have medicinal uses and in this case an additional label can be discovered on the inner side of the bed.

Angelica (*Angelica archangelica*), caraway (*Carum carvi*), coriander (*Coriandrum sativum*), fennel (*Foeniculum vulgare*) and dill (*Anethum graveolens*) all belong to the Umbelliferae family and have several different uses. The stems of angelica are crystallized to decorate cakes and trifles, but the seeds are also used medicinally as stimulants. Dill is used to make dill water to relieve indigestion and soothe windy babies, but it is also useful for flavouring salads and is included in traditional Scottish salmon recipes.

Growing well here is Scots lovage (*Ligusticum scoticum*) which as the name implies is native to this part of the country. Its dark green leaves and celery flavour are similar to common lovage (*Levisticum officinale*) and it grows to a height of approximately 3ft (90cm) with attractive pink flowers.

Among the medicinal herbs it is worth taking a careful look at bryony (*Bryonia dioica*). This is a plant of the cucumber family with rough hairy five-lobed leaves and small greenish-yellow flowers. It is sometimes called the English mandrake because of its enormous rootstock that roughly resembles the human form. One of the many poisonous plants, it is seldom prescribed today but was formerly used as a remedy for persistent coughs and lung diseases.

Of particular interest is the bed filled with plants used for making natural dyes. In

Walkways cut from grass turf form a 'maze' of gardens of unusual interest.

Scotland it is thought that the colours in the different tartans were designed with a view to the dyes which could be obtained from locally grown plants. Today there is a renewal of interest in the colouring properties of plants and research is being carried out into traditional methods of natural dyeing.

Here you can see among others, dyer's greenweed (*Genista tinctoria*) which, as its name implies, yields a greenish-yellow colour; dyer's rocket (*Reseda luteola*) which produces a rich yellow colour; and of course the fascinating madder (*Rubia tinctorum*) which, according to the mordant used, gives different shades of red varying from a light scarlet to a deep wine colour.

Like all botanic gardens, Glasgow has a vast range of glasshouses and in one part of the main range is a section devoted to those useful economic plants grown in tropical countries. Here the different plants from which jute and other fibres are obtained can be studied in detail. The panama hat plant (*Carludovica palmata*) has thick leaves which are cut into strips and bleached to make the panama hats so popular with English gentlemen in the 1930s and traditional wear at that time for schoolgirls. Camphor (*Cinnamonum camphora*) is well known for its medicinal uses for coughs and colds, but few people are aware that chips of the bark are distilled and used in the manufacture of celluloid. And those who believe in using natural methods of destroying pests invading the cabbage patch will be interested in derris (*Derris elliptica*).

Kibble Palace, which provides the sheltered background to the herb garden, is named after the clever and eccentric designer John Kibble who built it as a conservatory for his own house at Coulport, Loch Long, in the nineteenth century. It was then dismantled and brought up the River Clyde on a raft before being erected on the present site. In its heyday concerts and large political gatherings were held here and both

Gladstone and Disraeli spoke to vast audiences under the enormous glass dome.

Like all true eccentrics John Kibble lost interest in his glasshouse and the Botanic Garden authorities purchased the property for ten thousand pounds. This payment led to financial difficulties and necessitated the garden being taken over by the City of Glasgow Corporation. Today the 40 acre (16 hectare) gardens are maintained as an educational resource and for the enjoyment of local residents and visitors who come from as far afield as Germany, India, Japan and Canada to extend their knowledge of plant life.

HOPETOUN HOUSE

South Queensferry, Lothian

Telephone: Edinburgh (031) 331 2451   **Owner:** Hopetoun House Preservation Trust

Situation: On the A904 near Forth Road Bridge; from Glasgow the M8, from Stirling the M9.
Open: Walled garden centre, all the year round, 10.30am–5.30pm; house May–September, daily, 11am–5.30pm.

While some people drop their H's, the gardeners at Hopetoun House have dropped their O's in a novel way to create a garden of three interlocking circles of brick. The planting varies from year to year, season to season, but the witty design is there to stay.

The house was originally designed for Charles, 1st Earl of Hopetoun, by Sir William Bruce and building began in 1699. Enlargements were made by William Adam from 1721 onwards, and after his death in 1748 the interior decoration was carried out by his two sons Robert and John. Much of the original decoration of the main apartments still survives today.

Scotland's greatest Adam mansion is set in a hundred acres (40 hectares) of magnificent parkland on the shores of the Forth and is a treasure house, well worth a visit. But see the herb garden first and wonder on your subsequent tour if Adam and his sons would have appreciated the joke.

NETHERBYRES

Netherbyres, Eyemouth, Borders

Owner: Lt-Colonel S. J. Furness and Flower, Lady Furness

Situation: On the A1107, ½m from Eyemouth. **Open:** Occasionally, consult the booklet issued by the Scotland's Gardens Scheme.

The gardens at Netherbyres are situated in a thickly wooded estate only a short walk from the east coast of Scotland. Full of interest, they are the result of a caring partnership between Lady Furness and her son Lt-Colonel Furness.

It is hard to believe today that Lady Furness, passionately fond of gardening, was not allowed to take a horticultural training. Then it was not considered a suitable career for a girl in her position. However, as a child she watched and worked with a particularly good head gardener who did not mind her persistent questions.

Now she puts to good use all her gardening expertise for she and her son run the garden with very little outside help. Luckily he has inherited his mother's love for plants and they spend many happy hours working together.

Herbs grow well in this sheltered environment, and a small square herb garden enclosed by a low-growing lonicera hedge makes an enchanting corner that is both a joy to look at and full of useful culinary plants. A surprise gift for her on her return home from holiday about eighteen years ago, Lady Furness finds it a great help to have plants growing within easy reach of the house—and the care of this garden is her own particular interest.

It is rather like playing at gardens here and new features are continually being added. Pot herbs such as parsley, thyme, tarragon and a bay tree grow well. Lavender grows in stone tubs and a sundial is surrounded with thyme plants. A clump of chamomile has been labelled by a member of the family with the endearing inscription: 'To the Saxon a sacred herb, now used to colour fair tresses.'

The attractive white clapboard summerhouse, built by the family firm, looks the perfect place to relax and enjoy the various scents and pleasures of this garden within a garden. Alas, Lady Furness finds it difficult to do. Her words will have a familiar ring to other busy gardeners: 'If you do go and sit down you always see something that needs doing.'

A short walk from the house is a magnificent oval walled garden which dates back to the eighteenth century. The walls were built by a well-known local engineer, William Crow, and are made of Scottish stone faced with Dutch bricks. Originally the section of the wall near to the house was much lower than it is now so that a view of the garden could be enjoyed. Later on it was built to the same height but faced with slightly different bricks. This great walled enclosure measures approximately 200yd by 100yd (182m by 91m) and has trained fruit trees growing around the perimeter.

The curved wall makes a most unusual setting for the knot garden which is designed to fill a wide border and stretches for a quarter of the oval. Box edging outlines the different compartments which are filled with plantings of separate herbs. Velvet textured red sage fills one space and contrasts well with the cheerful glowing golden marjoram in an adjacent section. Parsley and tarragon fill other compartments and a statuesque angelica enjoys the protection of these fine elliptical walls. French tarragon, bergamot, thyme and other plants that are seldom found so far north grow well here. In this intensely cultivated wall garden the owners' love for herbs and scented plants is apparent everywhere.

The combination of informal plantings of different varieties of mint in large clumps under ancient apple trees is a joy to the eye. In the pink and silver garden scented plants spill over the edges of the paths. Here the Scottish thistle, *Onopordum acanthium*, or one of its relatives, seeds itself vigorously and fortunately there is plenty of room for it to grow to its full height. A huge yew hedge stretches right across the garden dividing it into two halves, and a wide archway has been cut through so that you can see the garden framed from different angles.

Gardening partnerships

Many of today's outstanding gardens are the results of a partnership. At Netherbyres it is a mother and son partnership which has contributed to an oval walled garden full of interest to herb lovers and to a small square herb garden which was a gift from son to mother.

A famous partnership is that of Vita Sackville-West and Harold Nicolson who together created a garden at Sissinghurst. It was Harold who did the planning and structural work and Vita who loved all the different plants and spent her days working in the garden. The garden was an extravagance and a hobby for them both and it provided a quiet meeting place for two very cultivated, enterprising yet different people.

On our visits to herb gardens up and down the country we have been struck by the success of gardening partnerships. Many of the most stimulating gardens are run in this way and each garden is generally the richer for such an association between different minds giving and taking on the way to a unity.

OLD SEMEIL HERB GARDEN

Strathdon, Aberdeenshire

Telephone: Strathdon (09752) 343

Owner: Mrs Gillian Cook

Situation: Near the junction of the A97 and B973 between Mossat and Strathdon. **Open:** May–October, 10am–5pm. Closed Thursday.

In the Tornashean Forest (Hill of the Faries) in the heart of the Grampian district, Old Semeil Herb Garden is one of many which disprove the old saying that you can't grow herbs above Scotch Corner. Here, in what might be termed a traditional garden of four plots with a cartwheel in the centre, Mrs Cook cultivates a very wide range of culinary, medicinal and aromatic plants, mainly so that visitors can see the mature herb before purchasing from her nursery. Dyer's broom (*Genista tinctoria*), which when mixed with blue-producing woad (*Isatis tinctoria*) results in a green colour, and dyer's chamomile (*Anthemis tinctoria*) for a yellow dye are among the more unusual herbs on display and are listed in a comprehensive catalogue.

PRIORWOOD GARDEN

Melrose, Borders

Telephone: Melrose (089 682) 2555

Owner: The National Trust for Scotland

Situation: In Melrose by the Abbey. **Open:** Mid-May to the end of October, every weekday 10am–6pm, Sunday, 1.30–5.30pm. End of October–24 December and mid-April–mid-May, Monday–Friday, 10am–1pm and 2–5.30pm.

Next door to the ancient building of Melrose Abbey is a newly established garden now creating considerable interest among flower arrangers and gardeners alike. Here flowers and herbs are grown for drying purposes and sold in the National

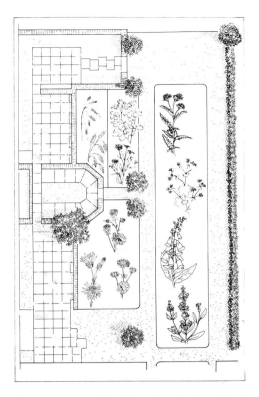

Flower arrangers and gardeners in particular will find great delight in this formal herb garden at Priorwood.

mantle (*Alchemilla mollis*), bergamot (*Monarda didyma*) and the lovely Jerusalem sage (*Phlomis fruticosa*) are just a few to delight the eye. Most popular of all is the globe thistle (*Echinops ritro*). The deep greyish-green leaves of this variety are without spines while globe-shaped blue flowers, which dry beautifully, can reach 2in (5cm) across. This is a real contender for the title of Scottish thistle.

Other borders are filled in a most attractive manner with annuals, shrubs, a collection of decorative grasses, everlasting flowers and shrub roses. In a sheltered patio area by the house grow the more tender plants such as hydrangeas, a fig tree and love-lies-bleeding, the lovely little plant with distinctive tassel shaped flowers.

At the back of the garden a large wooden structure (who would dare call it a shed?) is used for drying plant material. Here flowers, leaves and seedheads are hung up in bunches to dry or laid in boxes of sand. Sand has been used for drying flowers for a long time and at Priorwood trials have shown that this produces good results if the sand is carefully prepared beforehand. The finished dried flowers look very colourful and are transformed into floral ropes, floral balls and all sorts of fascinating arrangements.

Apples through the ages

Leading from this useful but rather formal garden is a fine collection of well-matured and some fairly new apple trees arranged in a walkway with picnic tables to encourage rest and contemplation. This important collection of fruiting trees leads from Roman times to the apples of the present century.

The Romans are credited with responsibility for bringing the first cultivated apples to this country and were accustomed to enjoying the best of table apples and to drinking excellent home-brewed cider. 'Court Pendu Plat', one of the varieties introduced by the Romans, is still in use

Trust shop next door and at local markets.

Tucked away in a quiet corner is a formal herb garden designed by Jean Meikle, who runs the adjoining shop. Plants growing here include woodruff, comfrey, *Iris florentina*, golden marjoram and rosemary. Most of them were given by friends in Scotland and can be cut for drying. In Scotland, dye plants are often grown and there is a fast-growing interest in the employment of leaves, flowers and roots for colouring.

The herb garden is part of an extensive collection of plants cultivated in separate beds, the principal one being an herbaceous border stretching the length of the garden and containing about fifty varieties. Lady's today and a tree can be seen growing here.

'Old Pearmain', one of the first English apples to be recorded, dates back to the thirteenth century. At that time the orchards of Melrose Abbey would have been of great importance in the community and Pearmains may have been cultivated by the monks on this same orchard site all those centuries ago. Apples were highly esteemed in monasteries being grown for food, medicine and cider-making.

In taking the visitor up to the present day the walkway ends with 'Discovery', a lovely red fruit with a sweetish taste, a twentieth-century introduction.

A dried flower garden

A dried flower garden can be very attractive and useful as the cut flowers, leaves and seedpods can be made to give pleasure right through the winter. A garden such as this is in reality an extension of a herb garden, and colourful blooms such as delphiniums, marigolds and larkspurs blend well with mint, sage and thyme when grown for the appeal of their foliage.

Should you wish to establish a dried flower garden, choose a border or corner that enjoys plenty of sunshine and select plants you can appreciate for their scent and charm during the summer. The following have been chosen because they are good garden plants, will dry well when hung in small bunches and keep their colour during the winter. The part of the plant suitable for drying is also listed.

Bear's breeches (*Acanthus mollis*): flower spike.

Bergamot (*Monarda didyma*): seedhead.

Foxglove (*Digitalis*): seedhead.

Lady's mantle (*Alchemilla mollis*): flowering spray.

Lavender (*Lavandula angustifolia*): flowerhead.

Tansy (*Tanacetum vulgare*): flowerhead.

Thistle (*Echinops ritro*): flowerhead.

THREAVE GARDEN
Castle Douglas, Dumfries and Galloway

Telephone: Castle Douglas (0556) 2575 **Owner:** The National Trust for Scotland

Situation: 1m W of Castle Douglas and just off the A75. **Open:** All the year, 9am–sunset. The walled gardens and glasshouses are open daily, 9am–5pm.

One of the most popular tourist attractions in south-west Scotland, Threave Garden is the training school for National Trust gardeners. Fifteen young people live here and receive both a practical and theoretical training in all aspects of horticulture.

The garden consists of about 65 acres (26.3 hectares) set in beautiful woodland and within easy reach of the sea. All kinds of horticultural work are carried out and students get experience in the care of azaleas, herbaceous beds, rock and rose gardens, and work in the large walled garden where they cultivate herbs as well as fine Scottish raspberries and other good things to eat.

The herbs are planted in a wide border backed by a lofty brick wall. Half-hoops of paving stones stretch from the path to the wall and allow the gardeners access to the different herbs without getting muddy feet. All the plants grow within easy reach but do not look too regimented.

Herbs, mainly the culinary ones, are cultivated as they would have been in Victorian days as part of a well-organized kitchen garden with a climbing rose on the wall to please the gardener.

Of interest in the herb garden is a representative collection of mints. At least fifteen different varieties grow here. Laid out attractively, the mints are planted in small square plots, about 18in (46cm) square, restricted by ornamental bricks laid sideways. The effect is unusual and turns quite an ordinary herb garden into an attractive study centre.

Included are *Mentha gattefossei* with the characteristic scent and whorls of small white flowers, peppermint (*Mentha piperita*) with purple bronzed leaves, red pea mint (*Mentha rubra raripila*) with smooth leaves and purple stems, and the sweetly scented eau-de-Cologne mint (*Mentha citrata*) with heart-shaped bronze leaves which is so useful for pot-pourri. Also present is the much-loved tiny Corsican mint (*Mentha requienii*), which grows only about ½in (1cm) high and has an intense peppermint scent when walked upon. It is the ideal plant for growing between paving stones and on herb seats and is comfortingly soft to the touch.

Time should be found to admire the fine raspberries, gooseberries and blackcurrants. The quality of the produce is very high and the students learn about the work involved and then enjoy the fruits of their labour in the dining hall. When time is available cuttings are potted up for sale. Business is

Containing the mints

Mints do tend, as most gardeners will grudgingly admit, to make a take-over bid for the rest of the garden. It is a pity, because with their decorative foliage and culinary uses they are a first-class plant to grow in the herb garden.

At Threave they have solved the problem by growing different mints in small squares enclosed by ornamental bricks. These look very decorative and work well provided the bricks are submerged in the soil to prevent the underground runners spreading.

There are several other ways of containing the vigorous mint. A biscuit tin with the bottom cut out is a favourite method—and a small seed tray can be used equally effectively. Some gardeners give up the battle altogether and grow mint in separate containers such as a 12in (30cm) flower pot.

But there is no reason why you should not be ruthless and remove the unwanted roots every few weeks.

very brisk and pots are purchased by gardening visitors as soon as they are put in the sales area.

Since this is a teaching garden, different areas are being developed all the time and the best of contemporary horticultural ideas are given free rein. This is emphasized in the visitor's centre where there is a useful plan of what to see of interest in the garden on that day, where to find it and some background information.

In May and June it is the beautiful large blue poppy that attracts all eyes. The Himalayan blue poppy (*Meconopsis betonicifolia*) was discovered by a French missionary, Père Delavay, when working in China. Some years later Colonel F. M. Bailey also found a blue poppy on the Tibetan–Indian frontier. It was described as a new species and named in his honour (*Meconopsis baileyi*). When it was realized that the plant had already been discovered, the name reverted to the original *M. betonicifolia* in accordance with the rules of international botanical nomenclature. It grows particularly well here and is surely a flower that students will be keen to introduce into the National Trust gardens as a reminder of the beauty of Threave.

A novel way of containing mint at Threave.

WELSH FOLK MUSEUM (Amgueddfa Werin Cymru)

St Fagans Castle, Cardiff

Telephone: Cardiff (0222) 569441   **Owner:** National Museum of Wales

Situation: 4½m W of city centre. Junction 32, M4. **Open:** All the year, weekdays 10am–5pm, Sunday 2.30–5pm.

There is a good deal more to the Welsh Folk Museum than its herb garden but the attractive small plot could well be regarded as the centrepiece of this imaginative 100 acre (40 hectare) complex. Set in what would probably have been the kitchen garden of St Fagans Castle, an Elizabethan house with 18 acres (7.3 hectares) of formal gardens characteristic of the period, the herb garden contains a hundred or more of the medicinal, fragrant and culinary herbs in use in the late sixteenth century.

There is no record of when the garden was first designed but according to the head gardener, Mr D. B. Bowen, some elderly villagers of St Fagans recalled that prior to 1939 the entire area was planted with thyme and two women were employed during the summer months to maintain it. The National Museum of Wales took over the castle and grounds in 1947 and the present collection of herbs was started in the mid-1950s after the garden was cleared of weeds.

A parterre of box and shamrock at St Fagans.

Old style herb

Southernwood is known to the English as old man, lad's love, virgin's ruin, maiden's ruin and stabwort; to the Scottish as appleringie; to the Welsh as rabbit tobacco; and to the French as *garde robe* or *armoise*. The botanical name is *Artemisia abrotanum*. One of the strewing herbs, it was once carried in church to prevent drowsiness and in these modern times some car drivers swear that a twig or two in the vehicle helps keep them alert. There are still folk who maintain that the ashes of the burnt herb when mixed with old salad oil help the hair grow again, either on the head or on the chin. In some parts of the country, lads use it to promote beard growth. Grow it for its old associations—but a word of warning: flower arrangers will plague you for pieces of its long, arching sprays of foliage.

The garden measures 40 × 20yd (36m × 18m) and is enclosed on two sides by a yew hedge. On the third side is a fine hornbeam archway separating this garden from a magnificent parterre of box and shamrock, and on the fourth side is an embankment from which the garden may be viewed. Stone steps lead up to a terrace with a pair of superb Italian gates guarding a splendid formal arrangement of roses.

A clipped yew tree, with a comfortable seat encircling its trunk, is at the centre of the herb garden and narrow stone paving leads off to form a series of cartwheel shapes with herbs growing between the spokes.

Even though accustomed to road-signs and much other written material being in Welsh and English, it nevertheless comes as a surprise to find wormwood being described on the label as 'wermwd lwyd' and red sage as 'geidwad'. Indeed, there is much to be said for calling at the bookshop by the main entrance to purchase David Hoffman's

Welsh Herbal Medicine (Abercastle publications) and having a gentle read on that comfortable circular seat. The laws of Howel Dda, the physicians of Myddfai and the legend of the Lady of Llyn-y-fan-fach are best studied here, as is Mr Hoffman's glossary. 'Cas Gangythraul', or vervain if you are lacking in the Welsh tongue, is apparently a good herb for preventing dreams and, incidentally, is one of the magic plants of the Druids. On the same tack, 'Llysiau'r Corph'—perhaps better known as southernwood—is the main ingredient of an excellent remedy for curing 'one who talks in his sleep', while 'Briallu Mair', or cowslip, has substantial virtues for curing the bite of a mad dog.

A stroll from this small, secluded place into the wider regions serves but to underline the importance of the garden in a museum of this nature. Within the old walled garden is a mulberry grove where some trees look hardly more than half a century old, while others, gnarled and twisted though still bearing fruit, rest their far-reaching and creaking limbs on supportive frames.

Chapels, cottages, farmhouses and a number of other buildings, many furnished in period detail and with gardens to match, have been removed stone by stone from their original locations. Duck to enter the lowliest and humblest of homes; it is not difficult to imagine the consequences of not having comfrey in the garden to heal a sprain, hyssop for tightness of the chest, horehound for pneumonia and mint to conceal the smell of fly-blown meat.

Most herb gardens are for show, a salute to the past. In a sense, the well-ordered plot at St Fagans is a museum piece but few visitors will escape the feeling that any minute now a cottager of the past or a liveried servant from the great house will pass by for a plant or two for the kitchen or to put together a concoction to make cocks fight more fiercely and for longer.

GLOSSARY

ANGELICA

Name: Angelica (*Angelica archangelica*)

Family: Umbelliferae.

Appearance: Angelica is a sturdy plant requiring much space and grows to a height of approximately 6–8ft (1.8–2.4m). It has large light green leaves that are deeply indented. The flowers are big greenish-white umbels which appear in the second year of the plant's growth. Angelica dies down completely in the winter.

Cultivation: The size and shape of the plant make it an interesting architectural feature in a herb garden. It will thrive in a damp shady position and will tolerate most conditions. The seeds of this biennial have a very short germinating time but the plant will seed itself.

Harvesting and uses: The large papery leaves dry well and can be crumbled into pot-pourri mixtures. The stems are crystallized to make a delicious decoration for trifles and cakes or cooked with rhubarb as a sweetener. The hollow 'trunk' can be cut into pieces and left about the garden as sweet traps for pests.

Angelica flowers about 8 May which was originally St Michael the Archangel's day. It is known as the herb of the Holy Ghost.

BALM

Name: Balm (*Melissa officinalis*)

Family: Labiatae

Appearance: Balm has a most pleasant lemon scent and will grow to about 2ft (60cm) high. It has toothed ovate leaves of lightish green or green splashed with gold, and small cream flowers. The plant dies down completely in the winter.

Cultivation: One of the easiest of all herbs to grow, balm is easily propagated by striking cuttings, root division and by sowing seeds.

Harvesting and uses: The leaves may be used fresh to add flavour to sweet and savoury dishes and to make a soothing and relaxing tea. Dried leaves are useful for pot-pourri.

BASIL

Name: Basil (*Ocimum basilicum*)

Family: Labiatae

Appearance: Sweet basil, which grows to about 2ft (60cm) high, has large soft ovate leaves which are light green in colour. In midsummer white blossoms form on long spikes at the end of the stems. Bush basil is slighter with smaller leaves. Other varieties include one with purple leaves and another with large soft leaves resembling a small lettuce. The delicious warm scent of basil is always appreciated.

Cultivation: Basil is a half-hardy annual and will thrive best in a fairly rich soil in a sunny sheltered

192

position. It is propagated from seed sown under cover in March or April for planting out in early June. Basil grows well in pots on a sunny window-sill.

Harvesting and uses: Known as the tomato herb, basil blends well with any dish containing tomatoes and the leaves are also used to flavour savoury dishes. It is used in many Italian recipes.

BAY

Name: Bay (*Laurus no lis*)

Family: Lauraceae

Appearance: Bay is an evergreen aromatic shrub which will grow to a height of 30ft (9m) given a warm sheltered position. It has dark green shiny leaves which are oval in shape and have a leathery texture. The inconspicuous flowers are a gentle cream.

Cultivation: Since it is of Mediterranean origin, bay needs a warm sheltered position. The leaves may turn brown and wrinkled after a severe frost, but new young shoots generally grow in the summer. Cuttings may be taken but propagation is a lengthy process requiring some skill.

Harvesting and uses: The leaves may be picked at any time and will dry well. Their uses are mainly culinary. A bay leaf is often part of a bouquet garni or used to flavour milk puddings. The leaves can also be used in pot-pourri.

The leaves contain essential oil to ease rheumatic complaints. It is also a good hair conditioner.

Bay is grown in Palestine near Galilee, and the Hebrew translation means 'green and vigorous in its native soil'.

BERGAMOT

Name: Bergamot (*Monarda didyma*)

Family: Labiatae

Appearance: Highly decorative, bergamot grows to about 3ft (90cm) high with attractive red, pink or mauve flowers that last from June to September. The sturdy stems bear mid-green leaves.

Cultivation: Bergamot, a perennial, appreciates a rich moist soil and partial shade. Propagation is by striking cuttings and root division.

Harvesting and uses: The leaves and flowers may be used fresh as a refreshing tea and make a welcome addition to pot-pourri.

BORAGE

Name: Borage (*Borago officinalis*)

Family: Boraginaceae

Appearance: A sturdy plant growing to a height of about 3ft (90cm), borage has large ovate leaves which are greyish-green in colour. The stem is hollow and the whole plant is covered with hairs, rough to the touch. The light blue flowers appear in clusters of five-pointed stars.

Cultivation: An annual, borage is a vigorous self-seeder and needs very little cultivation though it prefers a sunny position and well-drained soil. The seed may be sown under cover in early spring or in the growing position, either scattered or in drills.

Harvesting and uses: Borage flowers are often used to decorate fruit and wine cups, and the leaves, when young, are useful in salads, providing an attractive cucumber flavour. There is a strong belief that borage brings cheer to the heart and banishes melancholy. Can also be candied.

CHAMOMILE

Name: Chamomile (*Anthemis nobilis* syn. *Chamaemelum nobile*)

Family: Compositae

Appearance: Chamomile has single or double creamy-white flowers resembling daisies. The plant rarely reaches more than 6in (15cm) in height. The leaves are greyish-green in colour and grow in feathery tufts. Other varieties include a low-growing, non-flowering form called 'Treneague', much used for lawns and general ground cover, and an annual (*Matricaria recutita*) grown for its healing oil.

Cultivation: The perennial chamomile likes sun and a sandy soil. The small-rooted runners can be split to increase stock but the herb will also grow well from seed.

Harvesting and uses: Fresh or dried, the flowers are used for a sedative tea and as a rinse for blonde hair.

CHERVIL

Name: Chervil (*Anthriscus cerefolium*)

Family: Umbelliferae

Appearance: Chervil is a dainty plant with lace-like finely cut leaves. It reaches a height of 12in (30cm) and has clusters of small white blossoms.

Cultivation: An annual, chervil grows well from seed sown in drills throughout the season and appreciates a warm position, freedom from weeds and a sufficiency of moisture.

Harvesting and uses: Leaves may normally be gathered within six to eight weeks of sowing. An important culinary herb, chervil has a sweet flavour that blends perfectly with fish and eggs.

CHIVES

Name: Chives (*Allium schoenoprasum*)

Family: Liliaceae

Appearance: This much-loved member of the onion family has cylindrical hollow leaves which generally grow about 8in (20cm) high. The flowers are pinky-mauve in colour and form fluffy globes. Another variety, Chinese chives (*Allium tuberosum*), has flat solid leaves.

Cultivation: A useful perennial, chives prefer a rich damp soil with plenty of humus. Every three years the clump should be dug up and divided. If the plant is required for culinary use, flowerheads should be removed as they appear. Propagation is by division of the bulbs and by sowing seed in the growing position.

Harvesting and uses: Fresh leaves give a mild

onion flavour to salads, sandwiches, cottage cheese and egg dishes. The leaves do not dry well but can be frozen.

COMFREY

Name: Comfrey (*Symphytum officinale*)

Family: Boraginaceae

Appearance: A bulky perennial, erect in habit, comfrey has a leafy stem up to 3ft (90cm) high and ovate leaves covered with rough hairs. The bell-shaped flowers vary in colour from cream to pink and purple.

Cultivation: Comfrey needs little cultivation and will grow well in a damp and shady position. It is propagated by cutting small pieces off the root at any time and planting them in shallow drills.

Harvesting and uses: Known by the country name of 'knitbone', comfrey leaves are still used as a poultice to relieve bruises or sprains and as a general tonic. It is popular as a green crop for compost and is much prized by tomato growers.

CORIANDER

Name: Coriander (*Coriandrum sativum*)

Family: Umbelliferae

Appearance: A decorative plant with pale pinkish-white flowers, coriander grows to about 2ft (60cm). Curiously, the leaves are bright green and feathery at the top but further down the stalk they become more rounded in shape.

The plant has a rather unpleasant smell when young but as the ridged seeds ripen this becomes more agreeable.

Cultivation: An annual, coriander is grown from seed sown directly into the soil or tubs and boxes on a sunny window-sill. The herb does well in a sunny spot in light, well-drained soil.

Harvesting and uses: The leaves are used fresh to add a spicy flavour to salads. The seeds can be used to add flavour to casseroles. The ripe seed is much prized by bakers and pastrycooks throughout the world to garnish bread.

Coriander may have been the manna from heaven given to the Israelites on their march through the Sinai Desert.

COSTMARY

Name: Costmary (*Balsamita major*)

Family: Compositae

Appearance: The plant has long, ovate, finely toothed leaves, which are a soft green colour, and insignificant yellowish flowers in loose clusters. The stem rises to about 3ft (90cm).

Cultivation: Costmary is a perennial and will grow in almost any conditions. It needs little cultivation except for a stake to support it during the summer. Propagate by root division.

Harvesting and uses: As its alternative name 'alecost' implies, the plant was used to flavour ale and as a stomach settler. Bible bookmarks made from the pressed leaves were very popular with the early Pilgrim settlers in America. Today the herb is grown mainly for its attractive greenery though it is also used for pot-pourri.

COTTON LAVENDER

Name: Cotton Lavender (*Santolina chamaecyparissus*)

Family: Compositae

Appearance: This is a favourite plant for use in the herb garden as an edging or to add charm with its silver-grey foliage. The leaves are small, stiff and toothed along the edges. The flowers are round gold buttons, and the plant will grow to about 2ft (60cm) in height.

Cultivation: Cotton lavender is a perennial and will grow well in a sunny situation and light well-drained soil. Propagate by striking cuttings.

Harvesting and uses: With a long history of use in knot gardens, cotton lavender is still grown as a decorative plant. The leaves can be dried successfully and used in sachets as a moth repellent.

DILL

Name: Dill (*Anethum graveolens*)

Family: Umbelliferae

Appearance: Upright in growth, dill is about 2ft (60cm) high and produces umbels of yellow flowers yielding a large crop of useful seed.

Cultivation: An annual, dill will grow well in a well-drained soil enjoying a sunny situation. The seed may be sown any time during the spring and summer.

Harvesting and uses: The seed is employed for flavouring many dishes, pickling cucumbers and as 'gripe-water' for settling babies' wind and adults' indigestion. It is good with all fish dishes. The leaves or seed may be used.

ELDER

Name: Elder (*Sambucus nigra*)

Family: Caprifoliaceae

Appearance: An elder bush is a lovely sight in early summer when it shows large flat clusters of scented creamy-white flowers and equally so in the autumn when it offers purple berries. A bush can grow to a height of 23ft (7m). The leaves are dark green, serrated and grow in groups of five to a stem. There are many varieties of this hardy deciduous shrub, one of the most popular in herb gardens being the golden elder (*Sambucus racemosa* 'Plumosa Aurea').

Cultivation: A perennial shrub, elder will grow

virtually anywhere and needs little cultivation. Golden-leaved varieties improve their colour in the sun. Elder is propagated by cuttings in the autumn.

Harvesting and uses: The flowerheads may be picked in June and used either fresh or dry to make elderflower 'champagne' and a range of healing lotions and ointments. The berries make soothing cough mixtures and country wines.

Folklore says that it was the tree on which Judas hanged himself. Another story says that the Cross at Calvary was made of elder and that since that time the tree has never grown straight or strong.

FENNEL

Name: Fennel (*Foeniculum vulgare*)

Family: Umbelliferae

Appearance: Fennel is a strikingly attractive plant that grows to a height of about 5ft (1.5m). It has thick tough stems and bright green lacy leaves. The golden-yellow flowers bloom from July to September and form flat umbels. The scent is sweet and similar to aniseed. One variety has beautiful bronze leaves with a velvet texture and makes a handsome plant in the herb garden. Florence fennel (*Foeniculum dulce*) is an annual and looks similar to fennel but the base of the plant develops to form a white bulbous sweet vegetable.

Cultivation: This perennial plant likes a fairly rich soil and some sun, but needs very little care. Fennel grows easily from seed sown outside in April. The roots are best divided in the autumn.

Harvesting and uses: The leaves can be picked fresh at any time during the growing season and used to flavour and garnish fish and to garnish egg dishes. The leaves can also be used in white sauce. The seeds make a soothing tea.

'There's fennel for you and columbine' (*Hamlet*).

GERANIUM

Name: Rose Geranium (*Pelargonium graveolens*)

Family: Geraniaceae

Appearance: Growing to nearly 3ft (90cm) high, the rose-scented geranium has aromatic soft green leaves and pale pink flowers. It is one of many highly scented members of a popular family which do well both outdoors and as house plants.

Cultivation: Scented geraniums appreciate plenty of sunshine and a well-drained soil. They need to be given cover at the first sign of frost. Propagation is by cuttings and seed.

Harvesting and uses: The scented leaves add fragrance to sponge cakes and go well with baked apples. When dried, they are a welcome addition to pot-pourri.

HYSSOP

Name: Hyssop (*Hyssopus officinalis*)

Family: Labiatae

Appearance: A highly scented plant, hyssop grows in a neat fashion reaching about 2ft (60cm) high and blossoms throughout the summer, attracting bumble-bees and butterflies and fitting well into a traditional cottage garden. In mild winters the plant is evergreen, the dark green linear leaves growing directly from the stem.

Cultivation: Hyssop is a hardy perennial and is not difficult to grow. To keep the plant flowering, remove the dead flowerheads regularly. Propagation is most commonly by root division, though seed may be sown.

Harvesting and uses: The flowers and leaves should be picked during the summer and dried. The dried mixture is used to treat coughs and colds or added to pot-pourri mixtures. Tea made from the flowers is good for chest complaints.

It has a very sweet fragrance. The flowers dry well and keep their scent.

IRIS

Name: Iris (*Iris florentina*)

Family: Iridaceae

Appearance: The plant, which can reach 3ft (90cm) high, has the long flat pointed leaves of the family and most attractive white flowers with mauve shading and a yellow beard. The root is a thick horizontal stem with many nodules and scales, called a rhizome.

Cultivation: The iris likes an open sunny position and every three years should be lifted, the rhizome divided, and replanted.

Harvesting and uses: The rhizomes provide powder of great importance in the making of perfumes and talcum powder. The root is used to make orris root powder to fix pot-pourri.

JUNIPER

Name: Juniper (*Juniperus communis*)

Family: Cupressaceae

Appearance: A hardy evergreen shrub that will grow to a height of 10ft (3m), juniper has prickly stiff leaves with berries that take three years to ripen and for the first year stay green. There are many varieties with colours ranging from a yellowish-green to an almost steel blue.

Cultivation: A juniper is quite hardy once established and gives shape to the herb garden, also providing welcome colour during the winter months. It thrives in a sunny position and will grow well in town gardens, needing little pruning—though it can be trimmed into shape. Propagate from cuttings.

Harvesting and uses: The berries should be picked in late summer when they are fully ripe and bluish-black in colour. Lay them on a tray covered with net and leave them in a warm place until dry to the touch. Use the berries in marinades, sauerkraut and spiced beef. It is said that juniper will ease rheumatic pains, help liver troubles and restore youthful vigour. Berries made into a tea act as a tonic.

A well-known shrub in the Holy Land, and used to make charcoal in the East.

LAVENDER

Name: Lavender (*Lavandula angustifolia*)

Family: Labiatae

Appearance: The lavender that Shakespeare knew and loved so much is equally popular today with its silver-grey foliage and flowers in spike formation. Plants normally grow to a height of approximately 30in (80cm) on a woody stem with narrow leaves clustered in small groups and the traditional sweetly scented flowers. There are several other varieties, notably 'Hidcote Purple' which has, as its name implies, intensely coloured flowers. Varieties with pink and white flowers are appreciated by connoisseurs.

Cultivation: Lavender, a perennial, grows well in a light well-drained soil and likes plenty of sunshine. Planted about 10in (25cm) apart it makes a good

edging round a rosebed. Cut the plant right back after it has flowered to encourage new growth. To propagate, take cuttings in August when the wood is half ripe.

Harvesting and uses: Cut the lavender spikes when they are in full flower and put them in paper bags, head first, to dry. Lavender is valued for its fragrant perfume, and English-grown lavender is the top favourite here. It also has a soothing effect on the system. As well as being used in perfume, lavender is used in bags to scent clothes.

A sprig tucked behind your ear used to be considered a headache cure. Lavender vinegar was used in Victorian days to cure the vapours.

LEMON VERBENA

Name: Lemon Verbena (*Lippia citriodora* syn. *Aloysia triphylla*)

Family: Verbenaceae

Appearance: Lemon verbena is a deciduous shrub which will reach a height of 12ft (4m) if grown in a warm, sheltered position. It has finger-like pale green leaves, slightly crinkled, and numerous small mauve and white flowers. Without doubt lemon verbena is the queen of the scented herbs and has graced English gardens for nearly two hundred years.

Cultivation: Lemon verbena deserves a little tender care. It grows well in a sheltered sunny corner, but failing this will grow well in a large container and should be brought under cover during the winter months. Propagating is done by taking cuttings during the growing season and putting them in pots filled with a good compost.

Harvesting and uses: Pull the leaves from their woody stems at any time during the summer and dry in a well-ventilated place. Simple cotton bags of dried leaves tucked beneath the pillow will promote restful sleep. A leaf adds a lemon flavour to sponge cakes and milk puddings.

LOVAGE

Name: Lovage (*Levisticum officinale*)

Family: Umbelliferae

Appearance: This traditional English garden plant grows to about 4ft (1.2m) with large, dark green leaves which die back in winter. Clusters of yellow flowers appear in the summer followed by the seeds, which have prominent winged ribs.

Cultivation: A perennial, lovage does best in a rich, loamy soil with plenty of moisture and will do well in a shady position. Propagation is by root division and seed.

Harvesting and uses: The leaves are used fresh for many dishes and will dry well. It has a celery flavour, useful for soups, and the young leaves are delicious in salads. The herb's spicy flavour is much favoured by those on a salt-free diet.

MARIGOLD

Name: Marigold or Pot Marigold (*Calendula officinalis*)

Family: Compositae

Appearance: Pot marigold has a simple charm and is so easy to grow that it runs the risk of being ignored. The old-fashioned single flowered variety has rows of flat orange and yellow petals round a central disc and can reach a height of 2ft (60cm). The flat ovate leaves are soft in texture and light green in colour.

Cultivation: A very hardy annual, marigold will grow on the poorest of soils. However, it does warm to plenty of sunshine. Seed is best sown in the growing position for the first year; it will then seed itself.

Harvesting and uses: The petals and flowerheads decorate salads and flavour cakes. They are said to possess good healing and antiseptic qualities. The colourful orange flowers dry well and add interest to pot-pourri. Also useful for pressed flower work.

MARJORAM

Name: Marjoram or Sweet Marjoram (*Origanum majorana*)

Family: Labiatae

Appearance: Majoram is a low-growing plant, spreading quickly to form circular clumps. It has ovate leaves and white or pale pink flowers which bloom from June to September. Among the varieties, pot marjoram (*Origanum onites*) has smaller leaves which are more heart shaped. A popular plant because of its gleaming leaves is golden marjoram (*Origanum aureum*).

Cultivation: Being a native of the Mediterranean, marjoram likes a warm sunny sheltered spot and also appreciates a rich loamy soil. The plant tends to sprawl and needs cutting back and trimming during the summer. Propagate by seed or root division. Sweet marjoram (*Origanum majorana*) is an annual but will sometimes withstand a mild winter. Pot marjoram (*Origanum onites*) is a perennial which tends to die back unless protected.

Harvesting and uses: The flavour and aroma is in the leaves and these can be picked fresh and used at any time for culinary or medicinal uses. They can be chopped and added to potato dishes and are most useful for pâtés. The leaves also dry well and with their intense scent are excellent for pot-pourri mixtures. Marjoram's warm fragrance was thought to soothe rheumatic pains; when dried the leaves can be included in sleep pillow mixtures.

MINT

Name: Mint of Spearmint (*Mentha spicata*)

Family: Labiatae

Appearance: Spearmint, the most common garden variety of mint, has light green pointed leaves with toothed edges. The small flowers are pinkish in colour and the plant grows to a height of about 2ft (60cm). Mints form a large family of which the following are the most popular:

Apple Mint (*Mentha suaveolens*) has ovate woolly leaves and delicate pink flowers. There is a variegated version with decorative cream and white leaves.

Bowles mint (*Mentha × villosa n.m. alopecuroides*) is the cook's choice and has thick woolly leaves which are round in shape.

Peppermint (*Mentha × piperita*) comes in two varieties. The black peppermint has a purple stem with bronze leaves. The white variety has a light green stem and leaves. Both have narrow toothed leaves.

Cultivation: Mint is a hardy perennial which takes a lot of goodness from the soil so extra compost should be added. Because the runners spread horizontally, plant in a confined area to prevent a takeover bid for the herb garden. Propagation is by planting short lengths of runners in drills or by striking cuttings.

Harvesting and uses: Mint leaves are used for a variety of purposes. In the kitchen they are used in mint sauce, but also for ice-cream, salads, and adding flavour to young spring vegetables. Medicinally peppermint leaves make a good tea to soothe digestive problems. Mint leaves are also used in the making of cosmetics, pot-pourri and fragrances. They may be cut and dried throughout the season.

NASTURTIUM

Name: Nasturtium (*Tropaeolum majus*)

Family: Tropaeolaceae

Appearance: The cheerful looking flower of the nasturtium varies in colour from acid yellow to an almost scarlet tint of orange. The height of the plant varies from a dwarf of about 8in (20cm) to a

climbing type which can reach 8ft (2.4m). The bright green leaves are circular with a wavy edge.

Cultivation: Nasturtiums are annual and ask only for poor soil and sunshine. Sow the seeds in the spring where the plants are to grow.

Harvesting and uses: The flowers and leaves are rich in vitamin C and are used to pep up salads to which the flowers also add colour. The seed is used as a substitute for capers.

PARSLEY

Name: Parsley (*Petroselinum crispum*)

Family: Umbelliferae

Appearance: By far the most popular of the varieties is the moss curled type which grows about 8in (20cm) high with bright green feathery leaves. Greenish white flowers appear in the second year. Other varieties worth growing are the plain or fern leaved parsley and Hamburg parsley, which has an edible root similar to a small parsnip.

Cultivation: Parsley is a biennial that does best in a rich soil with plenty of moisture. Extra watering may be needed in dry periods. With a reputation for slow germination, the seed should be sown either in seed trays in a greenhouse or outside in a warm friable soil. A late summer sowing is often successful.

Harvesting and uses: Parsley leaves may be picked and used fresh for decoration and for flavouring dishes throughout the year. Parsley sauce is loved by most English families. The leaves dry and freeze well. The plant contains vitamins A, B and C and valuable minerals and can be used as a general tonic.

PENNYROYAL

Name: Pennyroyal (*Mentha pulegium*)

Family: Labiatae

Appearance: A member of the mint family, pennyroyal is an important plant in the herb garden as it has a long-established reputation for discouraging ants. It is a low-growing, almost a creeping, herb and has the usual square stem of the Labiatae family with small dark green leaves in pairs. The flowers are rounded, woolly clusters of pale mauve.

Cultivation: Pennyroyal likes a shady position and grows successfully under trees. Propagation is by cutting the fast-spreading roots into sections, striking cuttings and sowing seed.

Harvesting and uses: The highly scented leaves may be gathered on their stalks at any time and should then be dried until papery to the touch. The leaves make a useful insect repellent and can be sprinkled between books to great effect.

ROSE

Name: Rose. The Apothecary's Rose (*Rosa gallica officinalis*)

Family: Rosaceae

Appearance: The Apothecary's rose makes a tidy shrub and was the one generally used by the medical men of old to make their healing syrups and conserves. This variety has semi-double crimson blooms which grow in profusion on strong upright stems and attract bees and butterflies. Of course there are many other varieties which look equally good in the herb garden but there are so many it is impossible to list them here.

Cultivation: All roses like a fairly rich soil and plenty of sun. Mulch in the spring with compost and give a liquid feed in the summer. Shrub roses need little pruning except for the essential task of removing dead flowers and cutting away weak growth. A healthy and fertile soil may help to keep roses free from mildew and blackspot. Any diseased leaves should be removed and destroyed.

Harvesting and uses: Rose flowers may be picked and enjoyed for their scent and beauty throughout the summer. The petals dry easily, and are an important ingredient of pot-pourri mixtures. A favourite garden flower in the Holy Land.

ROSEMARY

Name: Rosemary (*Rosmarinus officinalis*)

Family: Labiatae

Appearance: An evergreen, ornamental shrub, rosemary grows to about 4–6ft (1.2–1.8m) in height and has spiky green highly fragrant leaves. Although the flowers are generally blue there is a variety with pink blooms and another with white flowers.

Cultivation: A perennial shrub, rosemary appreciates a warm, sheltered spot with plenty of sun. One disadvantage is that the bush rarely survives the biting cold winds of a severe winter. Propagation is by striking cuttings.

Harvesting and uses: The leaves are used fresh or dried at any time. Do not clip the plant too hard until it is established. Rosemary, the herb of remembrance, has a wide variety of culinary, cosmetic and medicinal uses. A sprig of rosemary adds a delicious aroma to roast lamb. It is good for barbecues—a sprig thrown on the hot ashes produces a mouth-watering fragrance.

RUE

Name: Rue (*Ruta graveolens*)

Family: Rutaceae

Appearance: Rue grows to a height of about 18in (46cm). It has small blue-green irregularly cut leaves. The flowers are small, yellow and cup-shaped with prominent stamens. Among the most popular of the varieties is 'Jackman's Blue' which has true blue leaves. The plant has a strange scent which appeals to some people and repulses others.

Cultivation: Rue, an evergreen or 'ever blue' perennial, is tolerant of most conditions but has a preference for a sunny, sheltered position in a light well-drained soil. Propagation is by cuttings and, less frequently, by seed.

Harvesting and uses: Not often used today except by trained herbalists, rue is grown for its attractive foliage and historic associations with magic. It is the herb of repentance and will always be associated with rosemary because of its Shakespearian connections. Its strong smell acts as an antiseptic. It is sometimes recommended as an insecticide.

SAGE

Name: Sage (*Salvia officinalis*)

Family: Labiatae

Appearance: Sage has broad, greyish-green leaves with a rough texture and will reach a height of about 2ft (60cm). Broad-leaved sage, which is generally grown for culinary purposes, does not flower in this country. However, narrow-leaved sage, which is treated as an annual, produces bright blue blooms. Other varieties of interest are purple- and golden-leaved sages.

Cultivation: Sage is a very good natured plant and needs little attention though some careful pruning will encourage bushy growth. It tends to grow in a rather untidy fashion and should be renewed every three or four years. Propagate sage by cuttings, root division or from seed sown in April or early May.

Harvesting and uses: Sage is one of the great culinary herbs and has a very strong flavour. The leaves can be used fresh at any time of the year. They dry well and can be used in herbal medicine and for making hair rinses for brunettes. Sage mixed with oil

makes a good rub for aches and pains. The leaves make a good gargle for sore throats.

SORREL

Name: Sorrel (*Rumex scutatus*)

Family: Polygonaceae

Appearance: Known as sour grass, sorrel leaves are vivid green and shaped like arrowheads. The plants grow about 2ft (60cm) high and during the summer large spikes of red and green flowers add decoration. The common sorrel (*Rumex acetosa*) has ovate, succulent leaves and is grown as a salad herb.

Cultivation: Popular in Europe, sorrel is a perennial that will grow well in a good rich soil and in partial shade. To keep the leaves fresh and succulent remove the flowers as they appear. Sorrel is propagated by dividing established plants or by sowing seed in the spring.

Harvesting and uses: Pick the leaves as needed for salads, soups and sauces.

SOUTHERNWOOD

Name: Southernwood (*Artemisia abrotanum*)

Family: Compositae

Appearance: Southernwood grows to about 4ft (1.2m) in height and has light green feathery leaves with flowers that resemble small yellow buttons. The whole plant has a strangely sweet aroma.

Cultivation: A perennial, much loved in old-fashioned country gardens, southernwood will grow well in a light soil and a sunny position. Since growth tends to be rather straggly trim often to keep a neat shape. Propagate by striking cuttings.

Harvesting and uses: Not used much in cooking, southernwood is mainly known as an insect repellent. When dried the leaves keep insects away from wardrobes. They have a strange pungent smell reminiscent of mothballs. The charming country names, lad's love and old man refer to its reputation as an aphrodisiac and to the belief in times gone by that the ashes of the herb would promote the growth of beards and even hair on bald heads.

TANSY

Name: Tansy (*Tanacetum vulgare*)

Family: Compositae

Appearance: One of the traditional English herbs, tansy grows to a height of about 3ft (90cm) and has dark green, fern-like leaves with bright yellow flowers that appear during the summer. The plant has a slightly acrid smell but this is not noticeable unless you brush the leaves.

Cultivation: Tansy, a perennial, will grow in any situation and indeed can often be seen growing wild on the roadsides. Propagate by root division and seed.

Harvesting and uses: Tansy is seldom used now and is grown in the herb garden for decoration and its historic associations. Traditionally it was eaten in tansy cakes at Easter-time to purify the system. Its juice was included in tansy pudding to make a blood cleansing dish in the spring.

TARRAGON

Name: Tarragon (*Artemisia dracunculus*)

Family: Compositae

Appearance: Reaching a height of 2ft (60cm) tarragon has long narrow green leaves which are smooth in texture. Its branching stems grow from underground runners which spread rapidly. Clusters of greyish-green flowers may appear but they mature only in the warmest of climates. Another variety known as Russian tarragon (*Artemisia dracunculus var. inodora*) is similar but cannot compete in flavour.

Cultivation: Tarragon will grow well in a dry sunny position on light, well-drained soil. Propagation is by root division and by striking cuttings when growth is strong.

Harvesting and uses: Good cooks use the leaves fresh or dry throughout the year for a range of

dishes, though the herb is best known for its affinity with chicken. It can also be used to make tarragon vinegar.

THYME

Name: Thyme or common thyme (*Thymus vulgaris*)

Family: Labiatae

Appearance: Common thyme can reach a height of 12in (30cm) if left untrimmed. The tiny, dark green leaves are evergreen and in May and June the bush is generally a mass of sweetly scented mauve flowers. There are many different varieties of thyme, the best known being common thyme (*Thymus vulgaris*). Lemon thyme (*Thymus citriodorus*) has a rich green foliage with a delightful lemon scent, and creeping thyme (*Thymus serpyllum*) is much used for ground cover.

Cultivation: A native of the Mediterranean, thyme will thrive in dry conditions and on a poorish soil. The plant does need protection from chill winds and if given a warm sheltered corner produces luxurious green foliage right through the year. Propagation is by cuttings, layering and root division.

Harvesting and uses: Thyme should be picked fresh for use throughout the year and will always yield a sprig for the cooking pot. To dry, cut the plant back by about half and put the sprigs on trays in a warm, well-ventilated place. Thyme is a useful culinary herb; it is used as part of a bouquet garni and its rich flavour enhances most savoury dishes. It is also used in pot-pourri mixtures and as an antiseptic. The leaves are used to ease colds and sore throats.

WINTER SAVORY

Name: Winter Savory (*Satureja montana*)

Family: Labiatae

Appearance: This neat perennial reaches about 16in (40cm) in height and has woody stems and tough, dark green leaves. The small flowers are white or pink and have a subtle fragrance. Summer savory

(*Satureja hortensis*), an annual, has slightly larger leaves.

Cultivation: Like all Mediterranean plants, winter savory does well on a light, well-drained soil with plenty of sunshine. It needs to be cut back in the early spring to encourage new growth. Propagate by striking cuttings, root division and seeds.

Harvesting and uses: Known in Germany as the 'bean herb' because it blends beautifully with most bean dishes, savory produces leaves which tend to accentuate the flavour of dishes rather than add a definite taste of their own. In biblical times, it was one of the plants used for payment of tithes.

WOODRUFF

Name: Woodruff or Sweet Woodruff (*Asperula odorata* syn. *Galium odoratum*)

Family: Rubiaceae

Appearance: The highly polished bright green leaves grow in whorls around the stem of this low-growing herb and form a dramatic foil for the white star-shaped flowers which appear in early summer.

Cultivation: Woodruff is a perennial which prefers a shady position and is one of the few herbs that grow well beneath trees. It spreads quickly and should be planted out at a distance of 8in (20cm) apart. The seeds are notoriously slow to germinate so propagate by pulling apart the roots and dividing the established plant.

Harvesting and uses: The full scent of the plant is not appreciated until it has been dried. Pick the leaves in early summer and dry in a well-ventilated place until papery to the touch. Woodruff is used in sachets to give fragrance to wardrobes and is particularly popular as part of the traditional 'Maibowle' drunk in Germany on 1 May.

BIBLIOGRAPHY

Anthony, John, *The Gardens of Britain*: Derbyshire, Leicestershire, Lincolnshire, Northamptonshire and Nottinghamshire, Batsford, 1979.

Berrall, Julia S., *The Garden, An illustrated history*, Penguin Books, 1978.

Bisgrove, Richard, *The Gardens of Britain*: Berkshire, Oxfordshire, Buckinghamshire, Bedfordshire and Hertfordshire, Batsford, 1978.

Brookes, John, *The Small Garden*, Marshall Cavendish, 1977.

Brooklyn Botanic Gardens Record, *Dye Plants and Dyeing*, 1976.

Brownlow, Margaret, *Herbs and the Fragrant Garden*, Darton, Longman and Todd, 1963.

Clarkson, Rosetta E., *Golden Age of Herbs and Herbalists*, Dover Publications, 1972.

Flower, Sybilla Jane, *Stately Homes of Britain*, Webb and Bower, 1982.

Garland, Sarah, *The Herb and Spice Book,* Frances Lincoln, 1979.

Gentleman, David, *David Gentleman's Britain*, Weidenfeld and Nicolson, 1982.

Gordon, Lesley, *A Country Herbal*, Webb and Bower, 1980.

Grieve, Mrs M., *A Modern Herbal*, Jonathan Cape, 1975.

Hadfield, Miles, *Gardening in Britain*, Hamlyn, 1969.

Hadfield, Miles, *A History of British Gardening*, Hamlyn, 1969.

le Strange, Richard, *History of Herbal Plants*, Angus and Robertson, 1977.

Leeds, C. A., *Historical Guide to England*, Croxton Press, 1976.

Lyte, Charles, *The Plant Hunters*, Orbis Publishing, 1983.

Mabey, Richard and Francesca Greenoak, *Back to the Roots,* Arrow Books, 1983.

Macleod, Dawn, *Down to Earth Women*, William Blackwood, 1982.

Painter, Gilian, *The Herb Garden Displayed*, Hodder and Stoughton, 1978.

Peplow, Elizabeth, *Country Crafts, Herbs*, Hamlyn, 1979.

Peplow, Elizabeth, *The Herb Book, an A–Z of useful plants*, W. H. Allen, 1982.

Phillips, Roger, *Wild Flowers of Britain*, Pan Books, 1977.

Rohde, Eleanour Sinclair, *A Garden of Herbs*, Dover Publications, 1969.

Sanecki, Kay, *The Complete Book of Herbs*, Macdonald, London, 1974.

Sanecki, Kay, *Discovering Gardens in Britain*, Shire Publications, 1979.

Scott-James, Anne, *The Cottage Garden*, Penguin Books, 1982.

Scott-James, Anne, *Down to Earth*, Michael Joseph, 1976.

Scott-James, Anne, *The Pleasure Garden*, John Murray, 1977.

Stevenson, Violet, *A Modern Herbal*, Octopus, 1974.

Strong, Roy and Julia Trevelyan Oman, *The English Year*, Webb and Bower, 1982.

Stuart, Malcolm (editor), *The Encyclopaedia of Herbs and Herbalism*, Orbis Publishing, 1979.

Thomas, Graham, *Gardens of the National Trust*, Weidenfeld and Nicolson, 1979.

Thompson, William A. R. (general editor), *Healing Plants, A modern herbal*, Macmillan.

Verey, Rosemary, *The Scented Garden*, Michael Joseph, 1981.

Other books:

The Reader's Digest Encyclopaedia of Garden Plants and Flowers, The Reader's Digest Association Ltd, 1971.

USEFUL ADDRESSES

Gardens open to the Public in England and Wales (the 'Yellow Book') is a useful guide giving the times gardens are open, how to get there and a brief description. On sale from the National Gardens Scheme, 57 Lower Belgrave Square, London SW1.

Museums and Galleries and *Historic Houses, Castles and Gardens* are two useful publications which give brief descriptions, opening hours and information on how to get there. On sale at local bookshops or by post from ABC Historic Publications, Oldhill, London Road, Dunstable, Bedfordshire.

The Herb Society, 34 Boscobel Place, London SW1 is an organization that caters for those interested in herbs. A quarterly magazine is published and occasional lectures are held.

The Royal Horticultural Society publishes a monthly magazine and organizes the Chelsea Flower Show and other events during the year. The show garden at Wisley is open to members and guided walks are given during the year. For details apply to the Secretary, The Royal Horticultural Society, Vincent Square, London, SW1.

The Garden History Society publishes an annual journal and holds seminars and meetings all over the country. Apply to the Honorary Secretary, 12 Charlbury Road, Oxford OX2 6UT.

The British Herb Trade Association is for those associated with growing or using herbs commercially. For details apply to the chairman Geoffrey Loyd, Remenham House, Ocle Pychard, Herefordshire.

Membership of the National Trust includes free admission to many of the finest gardens in the country and your donation will help towards the upkeep of these gardens. There are also other activities such as concerts and lectures. Apply to the National Trust Membership Department, PO Box 30, Beckenham, Kent, BR3 4TL.

Culpeper Ltd., 21 Bruton Street, London, W1X 7DA has 12 shops throughout England selling herbal goods. Their plants are grown organically at Wixoe in Suffolk.

In Scotland

For details of the National Trust for Scotland apply to 5 Charlotte Square, Edinburgh, EH2 4DU.

For gardens open in aid of Scotland's Garden Scheme apply to The General Organizer, 26 Castle Terrace, Edinburgh EH1 2EL.

ACKNOWLEDGEMENTS

Thanks are due to the many owners and gardeners who invited us into their gardens and gave so willingly of their time. During the research stage and writing of the book we received much help from our friends Libby Clegg and Denis Desert and from secretaries Jill Davies and Sue Smith. We are also grateful to Nicholas Law for his part in the preparation of the book. For patient and skilled assistance in the darkroom, our thanks are due to Pickards of Leeds. For photographs, we thank Pat Shirreff-Thomas (p. 21), Denis Desert (p. 68), Clare Parrish (p. 147) and garden owners (pp. 27, 96 and 179).

Roger Mould drew the excellent plans of the gardens.

INDEX